The Key to
ATLANTIS
Vol. I

J.R. Marro

COPYRIGHT

This is a work of fiction. Any resemblance to any person, living or dead, place, or thing, including names, organizations, events, and locales is completely coincidental. This work is not intended to offend but only to entertain and although some of the content is gross by my standards, I wrote it anyway because that's what the characters demanded. A good story shouldn't be based on how much blood is spilled but how much it keeps you wanting more. With that said, let's begin.

ACKNOWLEDGEMENTS

I would like to thank Elka for the information on Gibraltar, Dr. Richard Kramer and Rebecca Morley for their answers on yucky bugs, and Dr. Jeff Wynn from the United States Geological Survey who had tons of patience and understanding when it came to stupid questions.

I would also like to include my family for helping me continue when I wanted to stop. My rock was my granddaughter, Ashlynn, who always encouraged me to never give up, and of course my daughter, Regina, who was there to read what I wrote and was honest in her opinions. I love you all very much.

J.R. Marro

DEDICATION

I would like to dedicate this novel to my dear sister, Brenda, whom I miss so much. The memories of her laughter and kindness will always lighten my life and she will live within me eternally. Thank you, Brenda, for letting me be a part of your life.

Table of Contents

PROLOGUE
Aeschylus

Library of Alexandria
Egypt, 48 B.C.

From the third story window of the turret, Aeschylus had a clear view of the street below with its various shops. To his right, exquisite fountains and lush greenery decorated the beautiful courtyard of the Library of Alexandria. In the distance, the sun was bathing the Great Sea with amber rays as it lowered in the sky, but the black smoke from the blazing fire consuming the harbor and its many ships was beginning to drown out the view. His friend and confidant, Phaidrus, had told him why and how this had happened.

It began with the Roman General, Julius Caesar, who was set on conquering the glorious city of Alexandria. Pharoah Ptolemy XIII, had hoped to stave off war with the Roman pig by giving him the severed head of his enemy and son-in-law, General Pompey. However, his plan had the opposite effect. Outraged at the brutal death of his daughter's husband, Caesar declared he would avenge Pompey's death, demanding an unreasonably high payment from the two co-rulers of Egypt, Ptolemy and his older wife/sister, Cleopatra. Wanting to overthrow her brother, Cleopatra secretly met with Caesar, and that is when their illicit affair began. It was said Cleopatra enticed the General with her beauty and words so much he changed his mind about killing Ptolemy, thereby allowing Cleopatra to remain co-ruler with her brother.

Ptolemy was infuriated, screaming he had been betrayed. Henceforth, the battle for the great city of Alexandria began. Ptolemy's army surrounded the palace led by General Achillas. Caesar and Cleopatra remained in the palace with a troop of Roman soldiers, and knowing he was outnumbered, Caesar took Ptolemy as hostage. Roman reinforcements were on the way, but Caesar knew

Achillas would not allow them to disembark, so he ordered his men to burn all the ships in the harbor. The blaze spread beyond the docks and was now threatening the Great Library itself.

Aeschylus felt a stabbing pain in his heart. This place had become more than a home, it was a place of worship, a sacred temple he cherished. On the street below, three Roman soldiers were smiling wide as the hellish fire devoured everything in its path.

The Roman dog will win, thought Aeschylus, *and the world will lose everything.*

The Royal Library of Alexandria was the most diversified place of knowledge and learning in all the world. Over five hundred thousand scrolls were in her keep, and all freely available to anyone who wished to enhance their knowledge. Schools of Medicine, Mathematics, Astronomy, and many more were here, including a large museum, several great lecture halls, exquisite gardens, a zoo, and numerous religious shrines. Over one hundred scholars reside herein carrying out duties such as researching, writing, lecturing, and translating or copying documents.

This, Julius, was not any different from other Roman excrement. He deliberately started the fire nearby, knowing full well it could destroy the Library. Every time he heard the word "Roman," a seething anger rose in Aeschylus. He recalled the first time he had learned the meaning of his name and the disgrace he was forced to hide all his life.

Very few knew of how his Greek mother, Callidora, was a victim of drunken aggression by a corrupt Roman official. Callidora died giving birth and Aeschylus was placed under the care of his invidious Grandmother, Endocia, a noxious female who knew nothing of compassion. She was the one who gave him his name which meant 'shame,' and then left him to an orphanage. Aeschylus swiped at the sweat on his brow. Stifling his anger was not easy with Roman filth so near.

If not for the kindness of the Greek scholar, Thalus, who lived in the Library, he would have remained an orphan. Thalus made him his apprentice when he was only five years old. For the next thirty-eight years, Thalus taught him all he could about life, science, kindness, everything he needed to live the life of a renowned scholar and human being. He was the best father a child could have, but as life pushes forward, Thalus left this world six months ago. The pain would remain with him forever.

A loud boom shook the turret and a fireball shot out of the cloth shop next to the Library's entrance. The Roman soldiers began cheering and laughing as if a comedy were being played out. Aeschylus could feel his hatred rising, his breathing started to race, his heart pounded. If he were to yell in anger at the soldiers from this window, he feared they would purposely set the Library on fire.

Patience, Aeschylus, he thought to himself. *They must know the cost to humanity would be unfathomable if these magnificent buildings were destroyed.*

A ferocious wind blew across the courtyard bringing in smoldering ashes. Aeschylus held his breath. Several potted plants ignited.

"No!" he cried.

The soldiers turned to him and broke into laughter, pointing at him.

"Infidels!" he screamed at them.

A soldier shot an arrow at him. Aeschylus quickly jumped to the side as the arrow whizzed past his left arm and rammed into the far wall. He peeked out the window, the soldiers saw him and burst into laughter again. He leaned his back against the wall, frantic, not knowing what to do. The Library was filled with flammable materials, if one scroll caught fire, they all would. What could he do? *What would Thalus do?*

He had recalled the directions Thalus had given him before he passed on. Down in the bowels of the Library, Thalus had shown him an old crate which he said held sacred items; three golden arks containing hallowed scrolls were in a brown sack, and also what he called a 'book,' something he had never seen before. Its papyrus was different, smoother, and pressed very flat. The cover resembled black hard leather and had a circular four-sectioned carving in its center where a strange red crystal was sitting in the upper left portion. Thalus said they were the most prized possessions of the Library, no one was to know of their existence. Then the most amazing thing happened.

Thalus had told him to place his hand over the embossment on the giant book. A small flash of light emitted, and Aeschylus immediately pulled back his hand, frightened at the occurrence. Thalus said the light signified he was now the new caretaker of the items, and he was to guard the relics with his life. Not completely understanding what had happened, Aeschylus agreed, believing it was the power of the gods, and never spoke of it again. His determination to save the items grew stronger.

To allow the Roman swine to have the holy items would be sacrilege. He grabbed the hem of his long red garment and flung it over his left arm, then hurried down the winding staircase. Fortunately, the architects of the Library were intelligent enough to install a wooden banister along the steep stairway. He stopped abruptly.

Wood, he thought. *Flammable. This will lead the fire directly to the lower room. I must hurry.*

The temperature was rising the closer he got to the courtyard. The fire was spreading. His whole body bounced with the stomps of each step. At forty-three years old, running was not an easy task, every muscle in his legs and back were burning. Would his old body allow him to conquer the Roman devils? He ran his right hand across the top of his head, feeling the lack of hair and a pool of sweat. Suddenly, his friend and student, Phaidrus, appeared running up the stairs towards him.

"Aeschylus!" he yelled. "I must speak with you!"

He was a good ten years younger and already near to being a scholar himself. But time was imperative and to stop would bring the Roman victory closer. As he passed Phaidrus, the young man grabbed his red cloak and nearly tore it off by pulling him to a stop.

"What is it, Phaidrus?" said Aeschylus, panting. "I have no time for discussion."

"I came to tell you Didymus says the Library is lost and we must evacuate."

Aeschylus felt his anger rise again. Didymus was a fool and should have never been made Head Librarian. His works were nothing but jumbled words on scrolls, some ideas even stolen from others because the man had the intellect of an insect. Yet Ptolemy XIII made the appointment and Didymus now acted as though he were Pharoah.

"I will not allow the likes of Didymus to control my actions," said Aeschylus. "You know how I feel about the idiot."

Phaidrus's words softened. "Please, Aeschylus, you are my friend. Didymus is only thinking of our safety."

"My concern is for this Library. I will salvage what I can despite the stupidity of Didymus. Now, leave me, I must go."

He pushed Phaidrus's hand away and continued down the staircase.

Phaidrus yelled, "Whatever you are doing, hurry!"

The words echoed in Aeschylus's ears. His strong fortitude kept him running. Nothing would stop him. Black smoke was becoming more evident, burning his nose. He reached the main level of the Library and stopped. Though great pillars and decorated tiles made up the giant gallery, every plant, table, and alcove filled with scrolls were ablaze. People were screaming and running, trying to find their way through the thick smoke. There was no time to waste. He sped down the stairs again, feeling the weight of the heavy smoke in his lungs. His old body was beginning to fail him. He coughed and choked, raising the hem of his garment over his mouth, hoping to filter the suffocating air.

Finally, after what seemed an eternity, he had finally reached the lowest level; a long subterranean room with a dark corridor down its middle seeming to go on forever. His legs ached at the thought of how much more he would have to run. The trek down here had nearly taken all his strength. A cloud of thick black smoke floated past him, and he squeezed the cloth around his mouth and nose.

I must continue, he thought.

He grabbed a lit torch from a wall and ran passed racks filled with scrolls sitting on thin sheets of marble, supported by shelves made of wood. Tears came to his eyes as he thought of the flames engulfing these treasures. The loss of such knowledge could never be forgiven.

Romans are the scum of the earth.

Halfway down the corridor he heard the echoes of crackling fire behind him. He turned and saw the first racks burst into flames. Without thinking, his legs bolted into full speed. His slightly overweight figure did not make it easy, and his breathing was at its end. Reaching the end of the room he stopped, bending forward to catch his breath.

His gaze went back to the flames which were now near the middle of the corridor. He had to keep moving. He hurried to the left behind the last shelves, a space filled with piles of worthless scrolls and empty wooden crates. He began throwing things aside, trying to find the chest.

There! he said to himself.

He pulled open the cover and before him lay the giant book and the large brown sack containing the sacred scrolls. Smoldering ashes began raining down upon him. The fire was no more than one hundred feet away. Aeschylus swooped up the sack and the book and rushed to the wall behind the last shelf. He pressed a protruding block and a stone door slid open.

The great Alexander was no fool...there is always a way out.

Through the racks he could see the fire consuming everything, and he whimpered again, *so much will be lost.*

He stepped into the tunnel and the stone door grinded shut.

CHAPTER 1
Max

June 15, 2028 A.D. - St. Michael's Cave, Gibraltar

"I can't believe they came this far into St. Michael's Cave," said Max, lying on his stomach and swiping at the mud on his brow threatening to slide into his eyes.

His father and sister were pointing their flashlights at the most ancient writing in the world. The cavern inside the Rock of Gibraltar was dark and gravelly. Limestone, basalt, pumice, plus a host of other ores in the forms of boulders and stones littered the ground; some heaped into piles. Rafael, their friend and guide had disappeared in the lower parts of the cave which was now a labyrinth, and darker than pitch-black. Searching and yelling for Rafael had resulted in nothing. After thirty minutes of wandering, the dirt floor had slipped out from beneath them. The three slid down a huge stalagmite, landing headfirst into a pool of light brown mud.

"The Rock was a stop off for everyone," said his dad, Jack, lying next to him. "I'll bet we're the first to see this." He made a loud sigh. "This is almost depressing."

The sadness in his father's eyes told the story. Their dad gave up a career in archeology for him and Mandy, a hard decision for someone who loves history. Instead he chose nanotechnology because there was room to advance the science, and most important, it kept him home instead of traipsing all over the world.

"Is that the Phoenician letter 'L?'" asked his fraternal twin, Mandy.

She was standing next to him in khaki shorts and a black T-shirt dripping globs of mud.

Their father outlined the carving with his finger. "Aah...so my daughter has been listening to my lectures."

"Homeschool doesn't have lectures," said Mandy, "only boring speeches."

"Either way," said Dad, rising to his feet, "you've been listening." He ran his fingers through his brown hair dropping wet mud on the ground. "I'm not sure the writing is Phoenician. It's pretty deteriorated."

Max stood up and tugged at his camo pants and Army-green T-shirt, trying to unstick them from his skin. It didn't work. At this lower level, the humidity felt like he was suffocating in a plastic bag, and thanks to their flume ride down the rock, he was a giant mud-cicle. He untied the bandanna from around his neck and wiped the sweat off his face. The cloth felt like sandpaper.

"It's volcano hot down here," said Mandy. "My clothes are solidifying. Listen, Jack, you picked this vacation spot, so you need to find a way out. I'm not dying at seventeen."

"Watch your tone, young lady. I know how old my kids are, and I never thought Rafael would get us and himself lost, so back it down a notch."

Mandy bowed her head. "Sorry. I'm just a little scared."

His dad cupped his hand on Mandy's face. "We're all a little scared, but this Rock is only so big. We'll be out of here in no time."

Mandy's eyes lit up with joy. "That's right! Okay, I'm good."

This place is a treasure trove of undiscovered caves, thought Max, *and bugs. If I tell Mandy she'll go ape.*

Mandy had inherited their mother's mild case of entomophobia, a fear of insects, thus a hatred for spelunking and jungles. Two months ago, a live Hercules Beetle escaped their neighbor's collection and decided to join their family, crawling on their kitchen floor at eleven o'clock at night. Her scream was so loud; Max swore her skin was being ripped off. She squashed it with their dad's bowling ball, bashing it over and over until the mashed critter was unidentifiable. Several expensive floor tiles had to be replaced. For her to go on this trip, his father had to suffer three weeks of headaches, trying to convince her the insects in St. Michael's Caves hid themselves because of fear. In the end, it would cost his dad two weeks in a *Breezes* Resort of her choice. The girl was not stupid.

Max illuminated the stalactite they had slid down on. It was white calcite at least eighty feet long and lying on the ground in pieces. Its base had detached from the ceiling leaving a black cavernous, unreachable hole.

"We can't climb back up," said Dad. "We'll have to find an alternate route."

Max smiled noting his own six-foot-tall physique was equal to his father in height, but not in muscle. He checked out his own lanky frame. Mandy said he looked like a pencil with a tuft of black hair on top. Many times, she had called him "Beaker," the Muppet scientist. She was always insulting. *The life of a twin sucks.* But there was no time for exercise and gyms; a result of having a 240 IQ. Science was his life; it came first. But waiting for the approval of his over sixty patents was taking too long. Dad said the Patent Office must be packed with new ideas needing approval.

Nope. They just hate me for sending so many.

"Earth to Max," said Mandy. "You with us?"

"I haven't left, moron."

"You looked like a little lost nerd crying for help."

"Shut up."

"Stay with us, dude. We need you."

Mandy kept watch on him as if he were a little kid. Even when he wasn't looking at her, he could feel her eyes on him. Keeping his concentration on any one thing was difficult, his brain was always spinning ideas and solutions, but he didn't need a nanny. It was so annoying.

She's like a mutant eagle who has nothing else to do, he thought.

His twin sister was a slender five feet tall; a fitness freak who could outrun them with ease, and more often than he liked, her punches caused him great pain. Despite her petite figure, Mandy could knock out a whale with her left hook. One time he swung his fist at her and she lost it, jumping on him. He avoided her punches with his arms until their dad pulled her off. She apologized for going nuts but swore if he ever tried to hit her again, she'd pull out all his hair. He believed her.

"You okay, son?" asked Dad.

"Yeah, just thinking about old times."

"Stay with us, Max. I know it's hard, but keep your thoughts focused."

Max nodded gazing at his dad with a smile. Their father had always told them how happy he was his two kids were facial clones of their mother who had thick black hair, big blue eyes, and pearly white skin. And although Mandy had told their dad several times he could be the brother of the "screaming hot actor, Liam Hemsworth," he considered his gray eyes and brown wavy hair unattractive. A clump of mud hit the ground near his dad's black hiking boot, and he shook his body like a dog. Glops of mud flew in all directions, but his burgundy pocket T-shirt and blue jeans remained saturated.

"Let's check out this place," said Max. He swung his flashlight around the one hundred-foot high chamber. Massive stalactites draped down like giant icicles. Their trickling water had produced gigantic stalagmites below, creating a wonderland of magnificent white dripstones. "It's amazing we weren't shish-kebobbed," he said. At the far side of the cavern was a lightless ominous tunnel. "Could that be Leonora's Cave?" He hoped the answer was no.

Over the years, people had searched for the subterranean shaft running under the Mediterranean Sea connecting Europe to Africa, but once inside, they were never heard from again.

"Don't know," said Dad, "but it's all we have to go on. It's said Leonora's Cave is about fifteen miles long, and from Africa, it emerges into St. Michael's Cave." He pointed his flashlight at the far passageway. "And that tunnel looks like an entrance. Let's take a count of our resources. Check for food, glow sticks, and water."

Max slipped off his backpack and dug into it. After about five minutes, their stock mounted up to nineteen food bars and twelve bottles of water, which the latter concerned Max. The reading on his watch said the temperature was one hundred two degrees with ninety-one percent humidity. Dehydration was now a reality.

"Glow sticks," said Dad.

"I have six," said Max.

"I have twenty," said Mandy.

"You're carrying twenty, sixteen-inch glow sticks?" said Max.

"Yes, my weirdo brother. First, I hate bugs. Second, I won't be left in the dark. Period."

Their father chuckled. "With mine, we have thirty-five. Now let's lighten our packs. Keep only the essentials."

Max had picked the biggest backpack he could find at the store. Its chassis was aluminum and the canvass had an arsenal of pockets. He needed it because they were going to explore a newly opened region of St. Michael's Caves, and the British Government had given his dad permission to take samples. It pained him to toss out thirty glass jars with screened lids and three boxes of specimen bags, but science would have to wait; their lives depended on it. He hoisted the pack onto his back.

"You're still carrying a lot of things, Max," said Dad, who was removing items from his own bag. "My concern is you won't be able to keep up."

"This has the lightest aluminum frame on the market," said Max, pulling on the shoulder straps, tightening the pack. "Besides, I'm carrying plenty of pre-treated gauze in case Mandy falls on her face."

"I kept the water treatment tablets, the hand sanitizer, the First Aid Kit, and the camera," said Mandy, tying her waist long hair into a big mud ponytail.

She totally dissed me.

It relieved Max when Mandy broke up the conversation about his backpack. He didn't want to tell his father he was carrying his laptop, his crystal *iPulse*, and his untested Subterranean Surveyor, which took up most of the room. A glint of light caught Max's eye. He walked to the wall and where it met the ground lay a ten-foot coffee-colored spear, its twelve-inch head had kept its arrow shape.

"Look at this!" he said, picking it up and bouncing it in his hand. "From the weight and tarnish, I'd say its solid brass. Check it out." He gave the spear to his dad. "Who do you think made it?"

"Not sure," answered Dad, rolling his eyes along the primitive weapon. "Brass has a long history, but I've only seen or read about wooden spears with brass heads. Wait...," he scratched the dull metal pole with his fingernail. "There's something under the oxidation. Maybe if we...."

Mandy cut him off. "Excuse me, gentlemen. I know you're fascinated with this find, but we have to get out of here, so let's solve this later."

"You're right," said Dad, holding up the spear and pretending to throw it. "This has great balance." He held it vertical and thumped its end on the hard dirt. "We need to conserve power. From here on its glow sticks. Holster your flashlights and let's move out."

He snapped two glow sticks to life and tossed one to Mandy. The yellow lights illuminated fifteen feet in front, giving off an unearthly feel.

"Follow me and stay close," said Dad. "Mandy, do you have your Flash Taser?"

Max grinned wide. It was one of his favorite inventions waiting for a patent. On the outside, the device resembled a gray thumb drive, except the unit had two red buttons, one on top and one on the bottom, and both had to be pressed together for the device to work. It was a low amperage weapon using static electricity to incapacitate a target up to nineteen feet away.

"Yep," she answered. "Right here in my pocket. Why do you ask?"

Max held up both his hands and wriggled his fingers. "Because down here the insects are the size of cars and they eat people."

Mandy punched him hard.

"That hurt!" said Max, rubbing his upper arm.

"Mess with me again, and I'll tell Senona you have the hots for her."

Max stared at his sister, *idiot*. "You wouldn't."

"Try me."

"Knock it off," said Dad. "Let's go. Be alert to what's on the floor.

We don't need sprained ankles."

They trudged down the dark passage following their dad; a layer of wet mud covered the floor. The air was getting heavier, more fetid.

"We'll be okay if Mandy doesn't go berserk," said Max.

"This place reminds me of the Son Doong Cave in Vietnam," she said. "I almost had a heart attack when that monster scorpion fell on my head. It was two years ago, and I still have nightmares from it. We have to get out of here pronto, or my death will be on your hands."

"Don't worry," said Dad. "You know I'll protect you with all I have. We can do this."

"When we get out," said Mandy, "I'm going to hunt Rafael down and beat the snot out of him."

"Mandy, don't move," said Max. "You have two big leeches on your legs."

"What?" she said, grabbing her flashlight and pointing it on the black parasites attached to her calves. She dropped the glowstick and jumped around screaming so loud, he was sure she could be heard in China. "Get them off! Get them off! They're biting me!"

Their dad grasped her arms and held her still. "Calm down," he smiled. "They're leeches, that's what they do, and we can't get them off if your moving."

"Right," she said, panting with a nervous tremble. "I'll stay still. Just hurry, please!"

"Where did they come from?" asked Dad, kneeling beside her, examining them. "Could they have been hibernating in the mud we fell in?"

"That's my guess," said Max, squatting next to him. They were six inches long and a plump three inches wide. "We can't just pull them off. They may vomit into the bite and cause a severe infection."

"What?" said Mandy. "They're going to puke inside me?" Her eyes rolled back in her head and she fainted.

His father caught her before she hit the dirt. He laid her down and lifted each eyelid. "You shouldn't have said that, Max, you know how she is. But I'm glad she's out. Let's get them off before we wake her up."

"Sorry," said Max. *Ha! And she thinks I never get her back. So…why do I feel bad?*

His father lifted the edge of one creature with his knife. "These have suckers at both ends. I suggest using the blunt end of our knives to loosen their mouths."

A thick clear slime coated the wide parasite. Holding his flashlight in his mouth, his dad pinched the top of the black leech with two fingers. He slid the dull end of his blade under its snout, carefully detaching the sucker and then held it up while working on the other end. Max did the same. The moist, gooey sound was creepy like something out of a sci-fi horror movie.

Max's leech slid off with no problems and he dangled it in the air, shining his light on the wriggling pest. "This guy is fat. I wonder what he's been feeding on."

The leech twisted its body and snapped one of its teeth-filled suckers at Max's face.

"Whoa!" shouted Max, falling back onto his rump. "Did you see that?" he said, getting to his feet while keeping the pest at an arm's distance. "It tried to attack me." He threw it on the dirt and squashed it with his black hiking boot. "That was the weirdest experience I've ever had with a leech."

"Yeah," said Dad, battling the last bloodsucker. "This one is fighting me…just about…got it!"

Mandy awoke and sat up. She looked down at her legs and screamed, "The leeches!"

"Calm down," said Dad. "We got them off when you were out cold. It's over."

She let out a deep breath and Max saw her shoulders relax.

"Thanks," she said. "Did any of them throw up?"

"No," said Max, hoping he was right. He handed her a wad of gauze. "It's pre-treated with iodine, so it'll sting bad. They're going to keep bleeding for a while because leeches secrete an anticoagulant into the bite. Do you have band-aids?"

"Yeah, the box is in the First Aid Kit," said Mandy, patting the circular wounds oozing blood. "You weren't kidding about this hurting."

Their father rose to his feet, examining the dark worm between his fingers. The segmented parasite kept snapping at him. "It's an invertebrate from the class Hirudinea," he said, "the same as Earth Worms. I've never seen or heard of a leech being this aggressive, which is leading me to believe it's a new species. Leeches have never killed a human, at least not outright. Maybe by infection, but the bite itself is nontoxic."

"You still have that thing?" said Mandy. "Kill it! Now!"

"Hey, you're talking to me, your father, not to Max. I don't take orders."

"I mean it, dad. I will tackle you down and smush that thing with a rock. There will be no science right now!"

Their dad busted out laughing. "You're so much like your mother."

"Dad…," said Max, backing up with his flashlight in hand. "I think we should leave."

Hundreds of leeches were crawling out from beneath the rocks and out of the saturated soil. The wet, sticky sounds sent chills up Max's spine. The worms were inching their way up the walls, heading for the ceiling above them. His father threw his leech against the stone wall where it burst into a splash of blood. Without warning, several large ones dropped from above and Mandy jumped away, avoiding the onslaught. One landed on Max's shoulder, and he screamed like a girl, slapping it off.

It began raining leeches.

"Run!" yelled Dad. "Pull your packs over your heads!"

As they ran out of the cavern, hundreds more were waiting on the ceiling, dropping down as they passed beneath. Max heard and felt the thumps of creatures falling on their backpacks.

They had become food for the parasites.

Mandy zipped past them with her sack on her head and holding her flashlight in her mouth. She skidded to a stop, almost falling on the ground. Six feet in front of her, the leeches were crawling on top of each other, adding to a two-foot high wall they had already built with their bodies.

"They have to be communicating with each other!" said Max. "I need a specimen!"

"Don't stop running!" shouted Dad. "Science will have to wait!"

Max watched the worms use their suckers to pull themselves up the wall and then lay flat on top of each other. "It'll kill me if I don't get a sample!"

"They'll kill you if you stop running!" said Dad.

Max stormed forward and crashed through the leech barricade, sending geysers of blood into the air. He reached for one, but the slimy creature slipped out of his hand like jelly. After stumbling to a stop, he stood on a patch of ground free of the parasites.

His father yelled, "Mandy, keep going!"

She was standing rigid with her eyes wide open in absolute fear. "I can't…"

"Snap out of it!" shouted Max. "You're almost free!"

Her condition had left her helpless to fight. The eight leeches atop her pack were slithering their way to the sides, making a beeline to her hands. He was about to help her when their dad caught up and stretched his left arm straight out doing a backward swipe, removing the parasites clean off her pack. A big one latched onto his forearm. Dad pulled her to running again. The two rushed through the breach struggling to stay on their feet, slipping and sliding, smearing the gooey bloodsuckers beneath their boots, until they hit solid rock where they stumbled to a stop.

Mandy removed her flashlight from her mouth and pushed her pack onto her back. "So much for bugs hiding. I've been traumatized for life."

"I didn't know these things existed down here," said Dad, trying to catch his breath. "I never meant for this to happen. Sorry."

"I'm not blaming you, dad," said Mandy. "It's just that I'm fighting the fight of my life and it's getting hard to keep it together."

"And you're doing great," he said.

Max did a quick check of their surroundings with his flashlight. The round chamber was fifteen feet high, fifty feet in diameter with a tunnel on the other side. His ears picked up soft gooey sounds, and he shined his light on the floor. *Crapola!* A wall-to-wall mud pool filled with wriggling leeches blocked their exit. In the distance, pounding water was unmistakable.

A waterfall! thought Max.

"I'm not going through that!" she shouted, her eyes riveted on the parasites.

Dad said, "If we run fast, they won't be able to attach. Let's go!"

He grabbed her hand and ran. With each step, their brown hiking boots sank three inches into the mass of parasites, squirting red blood in all directions.

"That's it!" said Mandy. She shook his dad's hand loose and yelled, "I'm done with leeches!"

She stomped her boots into the hoards, splashing blood all over her calves and thighs. Several parasites adhered to her legs, but she kept going. Her determination was impressive. Max was trudging with his father through the blood and viscera Mandy had created. A few had crawled under Max's jeans and he felt the hard pinch as they hooked into his calves. They reached the end of the pond and ran into the tunnel, trampling more bloodsuckers. Mandy slipped and fell, sliding on the stone floor. One leech leapt into the air and attached itself to her cheek, just missing her right eye. She yanked it off and threw it against the cave wall. His dad pulled her up, and they took off down the passageway.

"Keep going!" said Max. "The waterfall will kill them!"

"I am so out of here!" shouted Mandy, and she passed them up at the speed of light.

Max's leg muscles were on fire, and he was sure his lungs would explode. The closer they got to the thundering sounds, the leeches lessened in amount. The waterfall came into view. It was loud and furious, veiling the whole end of the tunnel. Mandy disappeared.

They heard her yell, "Run through it! It's clear on this side!"

Max sucked in a mass of air and charged through the waterfall. Mandy reined him in just before he went over a ledge and into a dark abyss. A moment later, they grabbed their father's arms and pulled him to a stop. Max unclipped his flashlight and studied their area. The waterfall was a good seventy feet high and thirty feet wide, completely blocking the exit they came out of. A shallow river flowed into the abyss. He searched the walls and roof for any parasites, but only thin stalactites brandished the ceiling that was glowing.

"There's a layer of phosphorus up there," said Dad. "Mandy, when we get out of here, remind me to hit the gym with you."

Mandy was gone. She was nowhere to be seen.

"I'm down the tunnel," they heard her yell, "away from the bugs. Join me!"

To their left lay the only exit, an eight-foot wide dark tunnel. They went in and followed it around a sharp curve, passing colorful striped metamorphic rock so beautiful, it looked like Da Vinci was down here painting. The sounds of the pounding waterfall had subsided. Mandy was her leaning on a wall checking out the two quarter-size leeches on her legs.

"These things are so disgusting," she said. "Can you get them off?"

Max felt a slight pinch on his leg. "I got three vampires on my calves, and one on my forearm. And look how happy they are?"

Their bodies were pulsating as they sucked his blood.

"That's gross," said Mandy. "Dad, I heard what you said about me and the gym. You're forty-two years old, if you exercise hard like I do you'll break things in your body."

"I got a total of four worms," said Dad, "including one on my arm, and I'm not that old yet."

"Mandy, why aren't you in a panic?" asked Max. "You should be jumping around like your feet were on fire."

"I think it's because I'm so mad at these stupid things, I want them all dead. Do you think my phobia is gone?"

"Time will tell," said Dad.

"I have lots of gauze but none with the iodine," said Max. "How are we going to clean the bites?"

"We can use hand sanitizer," hollered Mandy, "then cover them with a band aid. I have a bottle in my pack."

As they took the leeches off Mandy, she mashed each one several times with a rock. It seemed her anger was overruling her fear, and Max wondered how long it would last. Entomophobia was not something easily conquered. He and his father removed theirs, and she squished those too. Max got the five-pound container of mint green hand sanitizer from his sister's pack; she never messed when it came to germs. They cleansed their hands and cared for their bites. Their dad clutched Mandy's chin. The leech that had attached to her face left a round bite on her cheek below her right eye. The deep red swelling was a sign of infection, a result of leech vomit.

"I have to clean this," he said.

The bite was trickling blood, and Mandy winced when he smothered it with sanitizer.

"Did it puke in it?" she asked.

Max held his breath. If dad answered wrong, they would have to carry her out on a stretcher.

"The skin on your face is delicate and more susceptible to trauma," said Dad, placing a band-aid on the wound, "and this bite may leave a scar like acne. But for now, you're fine."

Max relaxed when he sensed Mandy had calmed.

"I was thinking," said Mandy. "Do you think creepy Preston has anything to do with us getting lost?"

Uh-oh, thought Max. Those were words their father never wanted to hear.

"That again?" said Dad. "How many times do I have to tell you kids Preston is my best friend? I've known him since college and Global Innovations, is the best company I've ever worked for. Max, he gives you anything you need to continue your studies and Mandy, didn't he offer to buy you a car when you graduate? I can't believe you're bringing this up again. Didn't I make it clear, no more negative comments about Preston?"

"Jack," said Mandy, "sit down on this rump-size boulder. We need to talk."

"It's dad to you," he said with a frown, "and I'm tired of you guys accusing Preston of being this evil man who's conjuring up malicious plans against me. Preston Black is a good person, so move on." He waved his hand for them to follow. "Africa is waiting. Watch your footing. There's a lot of wet moss on the ground."

To convince their father Preston was his nemesis, Max had to get substantial evidence, something they didn't have—*yet*.

He whispered to Mandy, "I'll have what we need soon."

"The proof has to be concrete or dad will never trust us again."

"It will be."

The evidence had to come from Global. The building was in the middle of Manhattan Island with a security system so advanced not even the Shadows of Doom or SHAD, the organization made up of the best black hats in the world, could break through. Deep within the dark web, a stranger from an innovative company needed a test on his buildings network. He hired the best Shadows, two men, and one woman, to hack his security. After two weeks of frustration, they had failed to breach the system. Then they disappeared. Word on the web had hinted to the Shadow leader being compensated, and soon, the three were erased from existence. All his web contacts in SHAD confirmed Preston Black was the stranger.

For as long as Max could remember, Preston was a constant in their lives. Before his mother died, he was over every other weekend, bringing lavish gifts for the family, especially for his mom, Lisa. He and Mandy saw the love he had for their mother, and the evil behind his eyes when he looked at their father. After his mom died, Preston stopped coming, saying the pain was too much to bear, and seeing them made it worse. That's when Max began his search on the web about Preston Black. To this day, they could still see the hatred in his eyes whenever he talks to their dad. He was setting up his father for something, and Max had to find out what it was. Breaking into the

Shadow of Doom's site was not an option. With only him pitted against thirty hackers working together to stop him, it was impossible. The answer was Global.

Max's thoughts converged on the network he had to break. It would not be an easy task considering there were sixty layers of encryptions.

I may not have an army behind me, but I'm one determined kid who won't stop until I find the answers.

Numbers and equations churned in his mind, filling every crevice in his brain when Mandy's words broke his concentration.

"It's been over four hours and you haven't said a single word. Were you orbiting the planet again?"

"Four hours? And I was following you guys the whole time?"

"Yep."

"Unbelievable," said Max, wondering how he did that.

"I think this is a natural tunnel," said Dad.

The dingy walls were free of chip marks from hammers, wedges, or pickaxes; hand tools used by the ancients to break stone.

"I think you're right," said Max.

Their father held his arm up for them to stop. A fifteen-foot-tall boulder was blocking their way.

"It's climbing time," said Dad. "I'll go first."

They followed him up the brown craggy stone. Mandy was sitting on top staring down the tunnel as Max sat beside her.

"Is that light way down there?" she asked.

In the far distance, there was a white glow.

"Might be more phosphorus," said Max. "But I'm not sure."

He sailed down the rock after Mandy. This part of the passage had scabrous walls littered with foreboding holes, broad enough to fit medium-size animals.

"I'll bet that light is the way out," said Mandy.

He smirked at his sister who unhooked her flashlight. Max grabbed his own and flicked it on.

Together they said, "Last one's the rotten egg!"

They dashed down the tunnel. Mandy stretched her legs leaping over small boulders as if flying through the air. She was short in height but could outrun the Bolt.

"Hey, slug butt!" she shouted from way ahead of him, "keep up or give up!"

"You suck!"

Max was pushing his lungs to the limit, squeezing every ounce of air from them and still he couldn't keep up with her. His heart was pounding in his chest like a jackhammer.

Today, I'm going to die from a heart attack.

Behind him, he heard his father's shouts telling them to stop running. A high-pitched scream echoed through the tunnel. It was Mandy, and he ran faster.

He skidded to a halt when he saw a mega-size green centipede in front of Mandy. She was on the ground crying and backing away as the insect tapped its feet on the rock floor. It was the length of a minivan. The front half of the insect rose and stood on its hind legs, widening its upper limbs ready to pounce on her. Max slipped off his backpack and swung it, hitting the bug near its head and making it fall on its side. He pulled Mandy to her feet and shoved her behind him. The monster was already up on its rear legs, the tips of its feet clicking the stone floor as it moved in a circle around them. The long antennae on its face whipped through the air while its toxic forcipules dripped white venom. Its yellow upper legs tapped its exoskeleton sounding like dry bones hitting one another. Then it lunged at Max.

He swung his pack again, but this time it jolted back. Max kept slinging his pack and missing while the creature's legs jabbed at him, trying to stab him with its clawed feet. Mandy was standing behind him, crying and shaking with hysteria when two talons hooked into Max's bag and yanked it out of his hands, tossing it to the side. Max backed up, pushing Mandy against the wall. It screeched again, ready to attack when a loud snap resonated through the cavern. The insect flung its head back and shrilled, vibrating the walls and ceiling. It turned around, and that's when Max saw his dad. The spear was sticking out of the creature's back; blue blood was spewing in all directions. Max yanked out the spear and rammed it in again, closer to the head. The insect arched its body and made an agonizing shrill, then collapsed to the ground with its legs splayed. It was dead.

Their father ran to them. "Are you all right? Did it hurt you?"

Mandy rushed into his arms, whimpering. "We're okay."

Max was putting on his backpack when he heard low clicks coming from above. "Guys… we need to leave."

Suspended from the ceiling were fifteen more green centipedes. They unleashed a barrage of ear-splitting shrieks, swinging their antennae when hundreds of large brown bats flew into the cave. Mandy went into a frenzy, screaming and flailing her arms as a slew of them fluttered around her, pummeling her with their wings and heads. Their dad swatted them away and they scattered, leaving her wide-eyed and shaking. Up above, Max saw the centipedes snatching the bats out of mid-air. They coiled their bodies around the mammals, pumped them with poison, and within moments, their victims went limp. Eight centipedes crawled away with their kill, scuttling into the craggy holes in the rock face. The remaining ones shrilled and scampered down the walls, heading their way.

"Run!" yelled Dad.

Max ran faster to the eerie sounds of hundreds of tapping feet chasing them. Mandy passed them up like a cheetah running for its life.

"Stay with us!" shouted Dad.

Not far behind them, a powerful shriek had mixed in with the shrills of the centipedes. Booms and crashes shook the pathway.

As Max ran ahead of his father he said, "Don't want to know what that is!"

They ran for what seemed forever when they found Mandy panting and bent forward with her hands on her thighs.

"I think we're far enough away," she said.

Max dropped his pack and crumpled to the ground, out of breath and out of strength. "We're a good mile away. You're trying to kill me, aren't you?"

"Not at all. I figure you'll blow yourself up one day. Hey, don't you have a thingy that can tell us how far to the end of the tunnel?"

"The Subterranean Surveyor only works in water," said Max, still heaving. "It's a sophisticated sonar unit able to map the ocean floor," he took another breath, "at a depth of over six miles. I call it the SBS for short, and it's in my pack."

"Why did you bring it?" asked Dad, leaning on the wall wheezing, "and how did you fit it in there?"

"I brought it in case we went to the beach when our so-called 'outing' was over. Its design is like a hand-held metal detector and can be taken apart for easy transport."

"How did those bugs get that big?" asked Mandy.

"I'm not sure," said Dad, "but remember, we're in an underworld that may have existed since Earth's creation. Who knows what else we'll find down here."

"Wonderful," said Mandy. "Just what I didn't need to hear."

"Hey, slug butt," said Max, "life is life. Deal with it and quit complaining."

"Shut up, Max."

Max couldn't help a smile knowing he'd won this one. Their dad led them down the main artery again where the continuous tinkles of dripping water never stopped. More hours had gone by with them smothered in the stifling humidity. Their clothes were soaking wet, their hair dripping as if they had taken showers, and Max's lungs felt like they wanted to shut down. Besides the centipedes and leeches, they had encountered six bubbling pools of mud, eight clouds of annoying gnats that Mandy screamed through, and at least fifty rats. Max wanted to take one home, but Mandy threatened him with emasculation, so he didn't. The passage seemed to be endless. It was said Leonora's Cave had pockets of poisonous gases, and he hoped they wouldn't find any.

Are we going to survive this? thought Max.

"Life is life, bro," said Mandy. "Deal with it."

She had felt his despair...*again*, he thought, disappointed.

He and Mandy called it their nexus, the name they gave to their special bonding. As far back as he could remember, they could sense each other's emotions, feel each other's feelings. Many thought it was weird but to them, it was as natural as having two eyes.

"The light at the end is getting bigger," said Mandy. "It must be the way out."

"I'm not sure that's daylight," said Dad, squinting. "There's a glaze to it."

"We have to get out of here," said Mandy, "I don't know how much more I can take."

Mandy's entomophobia was in full swing, and if there was another bout with any kind of creature she would probably pass out. What didn't help was the dank, musty smell getting heavier. Max wondered if his dad sensed the passageway had a slight downward angle.

They were descending deeper into the earth.

Max stopped walking and stared in amazement. "That's not a light. It's a giant spider web."

CHAPTER 2
Preston Black

Global Innovations, Inc.
Park Ave, New York City

"You're worthless, Roser!" shouted Preston on the phone. "You're fired!"

He bashed his fist on the glowing blue circle within the glass of his tabletop, ending the call. Roser was a drunk who got fired from the New York City Police force.

So why am I paying the loser eight hundred a day? thought Preston.

The GPS on his transparent cell phone pinged. Roser's location fueled his anger; he was in Gibraltar at a bar, the same bar he was in yesterday for six hours. Preston squeezed the clear glass phone so hard a crack spiked across the smooth face. Aggravated, he threw it across the room. It flew above his monitor and the two tufted leather chairs in front of his desk, shattering against the far wall. Darla, his well-defined secretary, came rushing in.

"Is everything all right, Mr. Black?" her voice filled with worry. Her blonde hair, shapely figure, and beautiful blue eyes were things he always enjoyed.

"Yeah, yeah," he said. "I'm fine. Get Dante."

"Yes, sir," she said, and closed the door.

His original hiree, Rafael, had successfully planted a homing device on Max so when the Williams's got lost in the caves, he would send assassins to get rid of Jack and Mandy. He needed Max alive, but the transmitter on Max had stopped working and now the Williams's were lost in the caves. It was a good possibility they were all dead, including Max.

Then contact with Rafael had stopped. He had no idea what happened, so he hired Roser to find Rafael, which was a waste of money. Through his own research, he found out Rafael had owed money to a loan shark and when he left St. Michaels Cave, the thugs were waiting. His heart fluttered to the fury inside him. He reclined back and took several slow deep breaths until his muscles loosened. Easing the stress was crucial to avoid another doctor call.

Dante will straighten out this mess, he thought.

He reached for his stylus when he noticed his reflection in the smoked-glass top. The deep wrinkles under his eyes and his receding hairline made him appear older than his age of forty-two years. He ran his finger along the edge of his forehead, feeling the waning curly brown hair. His brow scrunched in disappointment as he tapped his sagging second chin, watching it bounce. Although his six-foot, four-inch height held a weight of over five hundred pounds, his pale blue eyes against his olive skin generated a handsome appeal, attracting beautiful women. Yet none of that mattered. Money had made him respectable, and fear made him powerful.

So, what's there to worry about?

He relaxed back, noting the aluminosilicate glass making up his desktop. His violent temper demanded it be one hundred times stronger than bulletproof glass. It was the most advanced tabletop in the world, embedded with every type of high-tech gadget.

Having the best science means you set the rules.

His forty-six-inch monitor was still up, so he tapped a glowing red circle, and it tilted back, receding into the desk. Before he called Roser, he had just finished going over the paperwork for several businesses he had forced into bankruptcy, so they could be purchased at a reduced price. For those companies he had no use for, he would chain-saw them to pieces, then sell off everything, making a nice profit. Sure, thousands got laid off, families were left with nothing, but money rules the world, not sympathy or compassion.

Just ask the politicians, he chuckled to himself. *I own them all.*

His thoughts returned to Roser, and his rage fired up again. He reached for the soft blue circle of light to connect him with the moron. The craving to tell him he was going to die was strong, but he stopped, pulling back his hand. He would turn his aggravation into a useful tool. Roser would get his in the worst way, but for now, he had to take his mind off the idiot, or his heart would go into A-Fib again. He gazed around his office.

This place is my peace.

The office was fifty-by-forty feet wide. Luxuriant Bocote wood tables sat in front of five leather maroon Raúl couches. Positioned along the walls were eight Dragon Chairs by Eileen Gray and six Lotus floor lamps, similar in design to Tiffany. He pressed the button on the side of his Ulysse Nardin watch. Behind him, the shades of his eight, floor-to-ceiling windows closed. The side walls retreated downward. Live spectacular aquariums appeared. There was a low swooshing sound and except for his desk and chair, all the furniture dissolved.

He heard the soft buzzing of trillions of piconites zooming to the middle of the office. They formed a black sphere hovering four feet above the floor. Within seconds, a flash of light exploded throughout the room. Surrounding him were hundreds of exotic fish, including sharks, barracudas, vibrant octopi, and even starfish and flounders lay on the white sand floor. Schools of multicolored fish swam amidst crabs, sea urchins, and other marine life. The similes were exact, down to every scale, with moving jaws and waving fins. Stalks of kelp, lively krill, and beautiful plankton drifted in the imitation sea. There were no imperfections in the piconite creations swimming amongst the most picturesque mounds of coral he'd ever seen. He felt the slight current of the figurative water pressing against him, floating the hair on his head as if he were in the actual ocean. He inhaled a breath of air, glad these piconites could not enter a human body. A four-foot Bull Shark was heading straight for him; its undulating mouth filled with razor-sharp teeth, and he smiled as it passed his head. His scientists left nothing out. Above him on the ceiling, the sun shined on a blue rippling sea. It was like being in an underwater ocean paradise. He compared the fabrications to the real fish in the aquariums. It was impossible to tell them apart. The piconite reproductions were identical in every way.

He pressed two fingers on his left lower wrist. His pulse was normal. He'd been in this realm many times, and each time his body reacted the same way; a soothing remedy which worked better than all the pills in the world. He loved the ocean and the serenity it emanated. This imitation sea was where he could relax, gather his thoughts before he took apart the world piece by piece.

Global Innovations, he thought. *My baby.*

Stealing Max's Coverter was the best thing he had ever done for his Global. The varieties of applications were infinite. But Jack was a smart man, a deterrent, and had to be removed. He tapped his watch again, and the piconite ocean dissolved, reforming into the furniture. The aquarium doors shut, and his window shades opened. He swiveled his squeaking chair to observe the outside world from the top of Global's eighty-story building in the heart of Manhattan Island. Global's state-of-the-art safety and security measures baffled even the best. It was the perfect place for what he needed to do, and the tinted missile-proof glass ensured his survival. The top two floors belonged to him, and he made use of all the space.

New York is the best place to live, he thought. *If you're rich, you could get anything or anyone.*

The ten microphones he had planted in the Williams's condo worked perfect. He could hear all their conversations.

Stupid Jack trusts me so much he's refusing to see his children are right.

He remembered ordering the hack into Max's computer, and after seeing what the kid could do; getting everything took precedence. In one file, there were four lines of code his scientists are still unable to decipher. In another file was one page of writing describing a device able to make things invisible. He had no doubts about what Max could do, the kid was a Da Vinci, Tesla, and Einstein, all rolled into a seventeen-year-old brat. The problem was Max knew the hack came from Global. Hence, he had ordered another raid into the kid's computer and stole the proof. To keep up with Max, a third hack was ordered but this one proved disastrous. A mutating virus entered

Global's mainframe in New York, causing it to catch fire and smoke. In a split second, the virus raced through the building burning up hard drives and threatening to spread to his worldwide offices. Before they stopped it, over five hundred of the building's eight hundred computers were destroyed. Thankfully, because the core program of the system was backed up every weekend to secured servers overseas, it only took four weeks to rebuild. The cost to restore everything was eight million dollars, a small price to pay for what he had stolen from Max. All the same, the consequences of what could have been caused frightening nightmares, forcing him to wake up in a cold sweat at least three times a week. The need for Max's computer was driving him mad, and he had lost ten pounds from anxiety. He was ready to plan a burglary when the solution fell into his lap.

The moment the Williams's stepped on the plane to Gibraltar, his men were rummaging through their house, and what they found in Max's bedroom was astonishing. The kid had built a small electric engine the size of a basketball that used the surrounding air to fuel itself, and not air tanks. It used oxygen molecules to produce clean energy. *It was unbelievable!* Then there was the Coverter.

A real cloaking device! thought Preston.

The device was small enough to fit in the palm of your hand. Both items were sent to his secret Tesla Lab beneath his mansion in Colorado. There, the work had already begun on enhancing the capabilities of the Coverter. Four other minor inventions were found scattered on the floor in Max's bedroom, but the Coverter, a five-inch diameter titanium sphere, was hidden inside the mattress of his bed.

And for a good reason, it's the greatest creation of the century, and my Global will get the credit for it.

As for Jack, he too was a genius, the smartest man he'd ever met. When in school, he didn't even try to get good grades, they just came to him. They were roommates at M.I.T. where Jack breezed thru their courses in Biological Engineering, Chemistry, Physics, etc., acing every exam as if it were nothing. It angered him when he thought of how hard he struggled to just get a 'C.' Later, Jack didn't even suffer with his studies in archeology at Harvard; he mastered them too. At first, it wasn't annoying, but with time, he wanted Jack dead. Dante Kennett, someone else who detested Jack for his brains, had suggested befriending him, making him trust his buddy, Preston. If he did this, he could get all the help he needed by either blackmailing a teacher or outright stealing from Jack. The next six years of college were easy.

Then there was Lisa Avalos, the most beautiful woman he'd ever seen. She stood a delicate five feet tall with black hair down to her waist and had a figure rivaling any high-class model. Her big blue eyes and double-thick black lashes stood out against her pearly white skin. Every guy in college melted when she walked by. The many times he'd asked her out failed, even bribery didn't work because several times she had told him her feelings were for someone else. Refusing to let him know who it was, he found out the hard way. During a football game he saw Jack and Lisa kissing under the bleachers. The pain in his heart was still there and he recalled running into the parking lot, falling to his knees, and roaring until there was no more air in his lungs. He had whimpered like a baby all night, but when morning came, anger replaced heartbreak. To allow tormenting hurt to overwhelm him was a sure sign of weakness, so he swore to himself he would never feel powerless again. After years of failed briberies, Lisa paid with her life.

I gave her a fair chance, thought Preston. *No one will make a fool of me.*

Lisa got pregnant soon after she married Jack, and Preston's hatred grew each time he saw them together. Lisa was supposed to be his. Those children should have been his. Jack stole his life. After college, Jack and Lisa got married and went their own way, but Preston stayed in touch, letting them hone their skills in nanites. When Global Innovations hit the list of the Fortune 500 companies, Preston asked them to work for him.

That was four years ago. However, things now were different. His research took him into sub-atomic structures, and the unspeakable kind of genetics. Soon the world would bow at his feet because not even the most advanced nation with all its armaments could defeat his exceptional army.

CHAPTER 3
Mandy

**I have, indeed, no abhorrence of danger, except in its absolute
effect—in terror
(1840, The Fall of the House of Usher - Edgar Allan Poe)**

They stood in front of what they thought was light, but it wasn't.
Mandy was backing away.

"I've been drained of blood by vampires, attacked by psycho bats,
and chased by man-eating centipedes. I'm not dealing with spiders."

"At least the phosphorus on the ceiling makes the nests more
navigable," said Max.

"Are you insane?" said Mandy. "I'm not going through that."

"Mandy, stay here," said their dad. "Max and I will check it out."

The two approached the webs. Her breathing sped up, and she
began sweating. Waves of nausea boiled as icy chills shook her body.
Survival meant keeping a cool head, but there was no way she could
handle a lair of spiders.

I'd have a stroke, she thought.

It was hard to figure out the actual size of the chamber due to the
packed layers of silk overrunning the area. She got up on her tippy-
toes and on the other side of the cavern, the upper part of an open
tunnel became visible; a gentle breeze was fluttering torn webs. Max
was standing in front of the webs and like an idiot, he tapped the silk
with his finger. A horde of arachnids came out of nowhere, and several
leapt off the webs towards them.

"Whoa!" said Dad, stumbling back with Max.

"Very aggressive," said Max, lifting six from his olive-drab T-
shirt. "You would think they would have a fear of people living in an
isolated world with no human contact."

"At least none we know of," said Dad, brushing off his shirt and
jeans. "Let's check the web a little closer, and this time don't touch

it."

"Ouch!" said Mandy, cupping her right eye. She realized her vision was beginning to narrow and she tried forcing the eyelid open.

"Let me see that," said her dad.

He lifted one side of the band-aid and pressed around the bite.

"It still looks okay," he said, replacing the band-aid, "but the swelling may get bigger. It's normal. Are you okay?"

"I'm alive," she said, staring at the spiders, feeling her chest tighten, "but I'll die if I have to go through that."

"Stay back here," said Dad. "Control your breathing."

That's easier said than done, she thought. *It's like trying to blow air in a truck tire with your mouth. Ain't gonna' work.*

Her dad and Max approached the webs again and stopped three feet away. She could hear them talking in hushed tones, so she snuck up behind them and listened.

"I see Wolfs, Orbs, and Cross spiders," whispered Max. "None of them are poisonous. How are we going to get her through this? She'll never go."

"I don't know," said Dad, "but we have to get to that tunnel on the far side."

"Forget it, guys," said Mandy. "Not happening."

Startled, the two jumped to her voice. Max stumbled back and fell into the web. The spiders swarmed over him. Mandy panicked and let out a gut-wrenching scream, trembling as hysteria seized her.

"Don't freak out!" said Max, rising to his feet, covered in webs and spiders. "Look, they're crawling off me. They know I'm not food. These spiders are not people-killers. If we don't panic, we can make it through. You don't want to stay here with the giant centipedes, right?"

Sweating and trembling, it was impossible to hold a lung full of air for even a moment. Panic and dread were taking over. She felt thousands of legs crawling all over her, pricking her skin, jabbing her body. Fear was unraveling every nerve, and tears were ready to pour out like Niagara Falls.

"It'll be okay, baby girl," said Dad, stroking her hair. "You're hyperventilating." He took her hands and cupped them over her mouth and nose. "Force yourself to breathe slow. This will pass."

Max strolled out of the nest with the spiders in tow. Together, the two men lifted the remaining insects off Max and placed them back onto the webs where they scurried away.

"Sweetheart, this is the only option we have," said Dad, "I'll take the front making a path, and you stay in the middle. Max will have your back. We have to do this."

Mandy's world began spinning, going faster with each second. She dropped to her knees wobbling, ready to pass out.

"I'm sorry," said Dad. "If there were another way, I'd take it. But if you stay, we stay, and that means we die."

His last words opened her eyes wide and she realized her father was kneeling and holding her tight. She wrapped her arms around him, whimpering.

"I don't know if I can do this, daddy."

"I could punch you in the jaw and knock you out," said Max, "then we could carry you through." He grinned ear-to-ear. "It would be my pleasure."

Mandy stood up and got in his face. "Try it, and I'll make minced meat out of you!"

"Now there's the Mandy I know," said Max. He rested both his hands on her shoulders. "Listen, sis. You climbed a three-thousand-foot cliff. You bungee jumped off the Bloukrans Bridge that's over seven hundred feet high, and all of it done without mom and dad knowing. You were punished when they found out but, Mandy, you're the bravest person I know. The point is, these are just plain old stupid bugs. You can do this, and I have something that'll help you." He slid off his backpack and unzipped a side pocket. "At least the main parts of your face will be covered." He handed her a green diving mask.

Her hand was shaking so bad it was hard to grab. She was doing all she could to control her condition, a near hopeless task, but if she remained, they would all die because they would never leave her behind. Staying here with the Godzilla centipedes and Dracula leeches was not a choice.

"I'll be crying the whole way," she said with quivering lips. "Just the thought of them on me—"

"Hey," said Max. He cupped his hands on her face and smiled. "Forever together."

She forcibly slowed her breaths. "Forever always."

"The other tunnel is not far away," said Dad, "so we won't be in there long. Anyone have something we can use to block our ears and noses?"

Max reached into another pocket in his pack and handed a pack of tissues to their dad, who split one into several pieces and stuffed the orifices on his head. Max did the same.

"Whatever you do, Mandy," said Dad, putting tissues in her ears, "don't lose it when they're on you. The stress may draw more of them. And use the rubber strap of the mask to keep the plugs in your ears."

Here goes nothing, she thought. *Brave, Mandy, be brave.*

The mask fit snug over her eyes. She slipped off her pink kerchief covered in dry mud, shook it hard to release the crusted dirt then tied it around her head concealing her mouth.

"I'm going to keep my eyes shut," she said, "so, dad, you'll have to guide me."

"He may have to use both his hands to break apart the webs," said Max, talking through his blue neckerchief. "When he does that, I'll guide you from behind."

"I'm ready," said Mandy with a steadier tone, not wanting to let them know she was dying inside.

Her dad reached into the webs with gentle hands and tore them apart, opening a passage large enough for them to fit through. Dark brown rocks lay strewn on the earthen floor. He took her hand.

"Nice and easy," he said through the green bandanna capping his mouth.

He took a step forward and every muscle in Mandy's body froze. The several tugs on her hand didn't work.

"You have to move with me, honey. I can't be pulling you."

"Okay," she squeaked out. *I'm going to die of a heart attack at seventeen years old.*

They entered the nests. Strands of sticky webs clung to her skin. Mandy closed her eyes and squeezed her father's hand, wishing her body would go numb, but it didn't happen. It was hard not to tremble and trying to stop her knees from giving way. She focused her thoughts on Max and her dad knowing they would be killed if she failed. Tears were filling the mask. They moved forward at a steady pace when the spiders were on them. Crawling on her head, legs, and arms, she shivered to the soft touches of their padded feet. Her whole body was drenched in sweat. She wanted to scream in terror, but if she did, they would bite everyone, so she quietly whimpered.

"Mandy," Max said in a low voice, "we're almost out."

"They're in my shorts," she stuttered. "…I'm going to faint."

"Don't pass out!" said Dad. "Slow down your breathing."

"Remember the time we were on the beach in the Azores?" said Max. "We were making fun of the people passing by and drinking your favorite McDonalds Caramel Frappe. Concentrate on my words and say it with me, beach, Frappe—beach, Frappe…."

Mandy repeated the words with Max, but it didn't help. The creatures were scampering all over her exposed skin, even on the hand over her mouth. Her legs were ready to collapse when she heard her dad say, "Don't move, Mandy."

Every muscle stiffened. There was a hard tug on the front of her black T-shirt. She opened her eyes and her breath stopped in her chest. Her father was holding a gray hairy tarantula with a span at least nine inches across. Vivid yellow and orange ringlets were above its feet. Its bright flame-colored abdomen was the size of a small orange. Her whole body went berserk, shaking out of control and she couldn't stop drooling. Comforting hands began rubbing her shoulders. Max was trying to soothe her nerves.

He whispered in her ear, "We're almost out of here. Take a deep breath and try to relax."

She inhaled a long breath, forcing herself to quell the shakes. The tarantula in her dad's hand went into a frenzy, flailing its legs and wriggling with such a fierce anger, he was struggling to hold it. The smaller spiders hopped off her and sped back into the webs. Their father flicked his wrist hard and let the big spider go. It struck the compacted dirt with a pop. The insect's abdomen ruptured, spilling out its entrails.

All her spiders were gone, and she sighed in relief, exhausted from the ordeal. However, they were all over their dad from his boots to his head; darting about, searching for places to enter his body. Her father lifted one off his arm. It was a Black Widow.

"We need to get out of here now," said Max, tightening his hands on her shoulders.

Her dad swung around and ripped into the webs. There were hundreds of insects inside the nests he was tearing apart. A smaller spider, the size of a hardball, stood on the webbing in front of their father. It was up on its haunches ready to attack when a dark hairy claw broke through the webbing and snatched it away. All at once, the spiders on her dad fled, racing along the top of the silk until they were out of sight.

"What is that?" said Dad.

Eight black eyes, the diameter of coffee mugs, were fixated on them. Max pulled her next to him and wrapped his arm around her shoulder, holding her tight. His spiders were gone too. She knew he would always protect her no matter what.

"Could it be a relative of the Bird Spider?" asked Max.

"Bird Spider's burrow in the ground," said Dad, "this one's in a web. It's most likely a new species of arachnid. Maybe we can coax it out of there with a power bar then bash it with a rock."

"It took that spider at light speed," said Max. "It'll be on you before your arm goes down to hit it."

"That's it!" said Mandy. "I am done!"

She reached into her shorts pocket, pulled out the Flash Taser, and mashed the red buttons on the gray drive. Three bolts of electricity shot out from the device, hitting the center of the spider eyes. Lightning bolts lit up the webbing, setting them ablaze. The insect exploded, blasting the cavern with chunks of flesh and blue blood, which doused the flames. All the surrounding webs sprang into wild bouncing as hundreds of spiders raced towards them.

The entrails were food, and they were covered in them.

"I'm outta here!" shouted Mandy, and she bolted through the exit screaming.

She ran without stopping, the fear driving her harder. Nothing was more important than getting away from the spiders. In the distance, she heard the low rumbling of a waterfall.

A shower!

She leapt over rocks and boulders, following the sound. After stumbling to slow herself down, she turned right and entered an enormous grotto made up of what looked like white marble stone. On the far wall, a chute of water was pouring out, causing a rapid stream over the stone floor where it continued to flow beneath the opposite wall. Mandy hopped into the waterfall and stripped down to her bra and panties. Although the water was cold, it was refreshing to relieve her body of the humidity, and wonderful to get the mud out of her hair. She saw three spiders crawl out of her shorts and try to scurry away, but the rushing water drowned them. She heard voices but refused to stop her shower to look.

"This place is gorgeous," said Dad.

"Hey, sis, what makes you think there are no insects in the water?" said Max, wheezing.

"Because bugs can't handle waterfalls this strong. Go away, Max."

Her father was squatting beside the stream using a test strip to check the water. "It's safe. Don't take your time, we want to shower too."

"Why can't we rest here?" asked Max, slipping off his pack.

"When we were running, we were dropping chunks of meat off our bodies and those spiders may follow our trail. We need to keep moving."

"We are leaving!" said Mandy, redressing in a fury.

"You will wait for us, young lady," said Dad, "and you will never run off again."

"You have ten minutes," said Mandy, donning her backpack, "then I'm not responsible for how I act. Move it!"

Max walked into the waterfall fully dressed. "Ouch!" he yelled.

"What?" said Dad.

"I think I pulled a muscle," he said, rubbing his lower back. "It's Mandy's fault."

"Jerk," she said. "Hurry up."

"Your turn, dad," said Max, dripping wet.

"Mandy, turn around. I'm going to strip."

Mandy did an about-face so fast, the weight of her pack almost made her fall. "That is so not cool, dad," she said, securing the straps on her shoulders. "The thought of you half naked is sickening."

"Yikes!" yelled Dad. "You could have told me it was cold."

Mandy giggled. "When you rinse out your clothes, make sure you flip them inside out. Three spiders were in my shorts."

"You can turn around now," said Dad, stuffing his burgundy T-shirt into his jeans. "Two of them were in my pants. It's nice having phosphorus on the ceiling."

"It lasts a few more yards down the main tunnel," said Max, "then it's back to the glow sticks."

"Let's restock our empty water bottles," said Dad, "then use Mandy's water treatment tablets just in case."

Mandy rushed to the waterfall and filled her bottles. Jack and Max followed her.

"It's time to go," said Mandy, stuffing the bottles in her backpack. "Let's move out!"

Her father retook the lead.

"Hey, dad," said Max, "I meant to tell you I finished the Coverter a few days ago."

"The what?" he asked, stepping between stones.

"The thingy that makes things invisible," said Mandy.

"I thought you called it the Neutralizer?" said Dad.

"I did, but since it transforms molecules, Coverter was a better name. Mandy thought of it."

"Yep, that's right, me," she said with pride.

"Are the specs to it on your computer at home?" asked Dad.

"No," he said. "All my creations are with me on my laptop. I don't trust leaving anything on my computer since it was hacked."

"We know you don't want to hear this," said Mandy, "but we're positive Preston ordered the hack. We were ready to prove it when everything disappeared."

Their dad shook his head in disgust. "I can't believe this."

"Before you disagree, listen to our reasoning," said Mandy. "When the proof was stolen, Max rigged his desktop to send out a nasty virus if the thief came back. Well, guess what? He did, and almost all his hard drives blew up."

"Remember the week you had off last month?" said Max. "Preston lied to you when he said they had to do a systems upgrade. That was my virus."

"Why didn't you guys tell me any of this?" said Dad. "I thought you trusted me."

"We have complete trust in you," said Max, "but you believe Preston is your friend, even though he's been indicted for murder twice. All the witnesses backed out, and four of them died in a train accident. And I can't find the other two anywhere on the internet. They're gone. Your so-called buddy is an evil man, and I'll prove it when we get atop."

"Those accusations were never substantiated," said Dad, refusing to look at either of them.

"Preston knew how lethal the virus was," said Mandy, "and didn't want to hack into Max's desktop again. The only option he had was to physically steal his computer. And now, look where we are? Lost in a cave where we may never find our way out. This was all planned."

Max added, "Preston has a bulwark of firewalls and security systems in Global that I have to break, but believe me, I will do it. I'm on the verge of getting the proof you need, and then you'll see he built Global on lies, thievery, and the deaths of innocent people."

Mandy said, "Max and I became suspicious when after mom died, Preston told us he wouldn't come see us anymore because it hurt too much. He'd always said we were like the family he never had, and nothing could separate us. It didn't sit right with me and Max, so that's when we began delving into Preston Black. The drunk driver who killed mom was hit by a train. The police report said all the friends of that guy knew he had a morbid fear of trains and never walked the tracks, but that's where they found his dead body. It lands up his father died on the train tracks too, and Max's friend on the web told him the police report said his break line was cut, but Preston was never accused because he bought off the Mayor. Two city inspectors assigned to the Global building reconstruction were also hit by a train, and that police report was changed a day after it happened. That's about eight people Preston killed by trains and who knows how many more he's murdered. How can that be coincidental?"

"Where did you get this info from?" asked Dad.

"From a place known to keep secrets," said Mandy.

"Have you two been on the dark web again?" said Dad with scowling eyes and pursed lips. He was ticked. "I strictly forbade that. Why did you disobey me?"

"I know and we're sorry," said Max, "but it was the only place that had the info we needed. It's a known fact, all secrets are on the dark web. To the normal internet world, Preston is clean but on the dark web, he's a monster."

"Listen, father," said Mandy, "with Max's stuff Global could become a world power all its own. A reality that could happen with the Coverter, the miracle of the century. You didn't believe it could work until you saw our kitchen table disappear. Now be honest, Dad, what if a sociopath got a hold of it? Do you think someone who lies and murders would use it for the good of humanity?"

After years of trying to get him to listen, her father was standing there silent, taking in everything they were telling him.

"My laptop is encrypted with a code that even the best black hats won't be able to decipher," said Max. "A few tried but no one will get through. Trust me, we're safe."

Deep furrows lined their father's brow as he looked at them concerned, not saying a word. It was hard to digest. He needed time to absorb it all.

"We're sorry, dad," said Mandy, rubbing his arm. "We know this is a lot and we can talk more later. Are you okay?"

Her father took a deep breath. "Yes, I'm okay. Like you said, it's a lot to take in, but maybe it's time for a reality check."

She was saddened at the grimace on her father's face. *Time to change the subject.*

"I heard Mr. Roser got in trouble again with the cops," said Mandy. "Is that true?"

"He's a bona fide drunk," said Max.

"If I lost my wife and four kids in a fire," said Dad, "I'd be a drunk too. He's a good man who deserves respect for what he's been through."

"This muscle is killing me," said Max, bending forward and holding his lower back.

"Let me check it," said Dad.

Max raised his green T-shirt. Centered on the swale of his back were two pin size holes on a red swelling.

CHAPTER 4
Preston, Dante

Preston sat at his desk rocking his chair waiting for Dante and staring out the tall window on Park Avenue. Across the way, the solar glassed windows of skyscrapers took in his whole view. According to the Weather Channel it was ninety-eight outside; a stifling heat when mixed with New York City smog could suffocate anyone. But here in his office, the sixty-five degrees was a welcome comfort. He adjusted his black pinstriped Alexander Amosu suit jacket. His matching crew neck shirt was tailored to his corpulent neck. Long ago he'd given up wearing asphyxiating ties; his drunken dad's choice of fun.

Choke the kid until he turns blue and then let him go.

The railroad tracks took care of dear old dad. A torn gas line and the 5 a.m. train was all Preston needed. The happiest day of his life was pulling up his car in front of dad and smiling at his terrorized face when the train struck. There was a knock on the door, and his annoying chair squealed as he spun around. A thirty-two-inch monitor had risen. The display zoomed in on the man's face outside the door. Green dots and connecting lines marked the screen, studying their features. If it was someone unfamiliar, two fully loaded machine guns would drop down and hold them there until the system identified them, if not, they were taken into custody.

"Enter!" he said.

In came Dante Kennett, now his bodyguard/assassin. He was a forty-one-year-old who stood six feet, seven inches tall with pallid skin and a muscular build which had never failed to take down anyone whether it be by force, knife, or gun. He always wore a black jacket, black pants, black collared shirt, and with his pure white hair, he carried the persona of a professional hit man. His nose was long, slender and crooked, hinting to his many battles. Dense ebony eyebrows sat above sunken eyes, his oversized black pupils reminded him of a hungry shark ready to chomp down. Preston never focused on Dante's eyes for too long; they gave him the creeps. Aside from the three-inch scar on his left cheek, smile lines etched his square jaw. Most times his expression was soft and pleasant, an outgoing, courteous man who got along with everyone. But Preston knew there was more to Dante Kennett. He'd seen the look many times; a hard, desperate stare lacking any humanity. The frigid look of a cold-blooded killer.

After college, Dante had enlisted in the Navy becoming an elite Navy Seal, never failing a mission. He was serious about his work and used any means to procure the information he wanted. Preston needed his expertise, so he offered him a lucrative salary in return for handling situations requiring special attention. Rumor had it the scar on his cheek was done by a woman he was in love with and who had betrayed him. He had stabbed her fourteen times. Preston found it strange he could never get the truth out of him regarding the identity of the woman. Thus, a rift had formed in their friendship. And here in Global, Dante was getting too chummy with the steerage, even having lunch with the riffraff who were trusting him more and more each day. He was getting powerful in Global, something he couldn't allow. Preston needed someone whom everyone feared, and Dante had failed him. His time was over, but for now, he would use him up.

"You rang," said Dante, plopping into the brown tufted leather chair facing the desk.

"I don't know if the Williams's are still alive," said Preston, "and Roser's incompetent."

"Who do you want to live?" asked Dante, lighting up a cigarette.

Preston wished he could return to smoking; it was relaxing, but a strain on his heart. He had told Dante many times not to smoke in his presence, but the man refused to comply because he said it calmed him and improved his thinking. Preston's frustration wanted to punch the cigarette out of his mouth, but Dante had the ability to snap his neck in a second. Besides, the assassin's end would come soon.

"Max," said Preston, "not Jack and Mandy." He removed an

ashtray from his desk drawer and slid it across the glass to Dante. "Max still has a lot of game left. But if he aggravates me, he's dead."

"The kid is smart," said Dante, pressing back his white shoulder-length hair. "He'll figure out you killed his sister and father."

"No way," said Preston. "He still thinks his mom died from a drunk driver. Old Preston will take him in, coddle him, and give him anything he wants. I'll make him trust me and then I'll tell him the only way to get over something like this is to dive into your work. After doctors and drugs, we'll be the richest men in the world."

"What have you done with his inventions?" asked Dante, clouds of smoke were floating out with his words. "I haven't seen any on the market."

"You really have the brain of an assassin, no savvy. They're being altered and merged into eight other corporations. In this business, timing is critical. Jack's the problem. He has to go."

"And why the girl?"

"She's a distraction to her brother."

"Keep her alive in case Max doesn't cooperate. She can be your insurance."

"Hmm," said Preston, nodding his head. "You may be right; she's his twin. Okay, keep her alive, but apart from her brother. I want Max to think his father and sister are dead. If he refuses to cooperate, I'll threaten her life in front of him."

"You really are a monster," scoffed Dante.

"Of course," said Preston, smiling. "It's something I take pride in."

They both laughed aloud.

"What makes you think the Williams's are still alive?" asked Dante.

"Because Jack is relentless when it comes to solving problems. If they're lost in St. Michael's Cave, Jack will find a way out. The transmitter Rafael planted on Max died, so I have no idea where they are. The Williams's are most likely roaming Gibraltar, enjoying the sights. You, my friend, are the only one I trust to get the job done. Just make sure Max doesn't see you murder his father or it's over. Car wreck, mugging, thieves, anything that can't be traced back to Global. And bring Roser to me. I have something special planned for him. Take Brett Carson with you."

Dante shook his head. "Brett's a waste and a loser. He'll just get in the way."

"Why do you say that? He's a great asset and knows his stuff."

"He's an idiot and couldn't see a fly if it landed on his nose. I'll take Karim Stone. He's more experienced and doesn't whine like a baby."

"Fine. Just get it done."

"Don't I always?" He stood up and mashed out the cigarette. "I'll keep you informed."

***

Dante

Dante walked out of Preston's office and nodded at Darla, then glanced at the ceiling camera above the doorway. Preston's paranoia of someone trying to waste him never let up.

And he's right, thought Dante. *He's got more enemies than I can count.*

He stood with his back to Darla and faced the three-dimensional wallpaper. Piconite mock-ups of six-inch roses wandered over an almond background, going through all the colors of the rainbow every five seconds. Something Preston had special ordered for Darla, his main squeeze.

The piconites never cease to amaze me, thought Dante.

He searched for the flower he needed. It was a purple rose which never floated higher than five feet off the floor. Concealed within it was a small metal plate, the size of a tiny button. He took his security badge from his inside jacket pocket and tapped the flower. A retinal scanner dropped out of the wall. He placed his chin on the holder and a blue light skimmed his left eye. To his right, two extra-wide elevator doors retracted inward and then slid opened. After stepping in, he tapped a red button on the lighted panel and a glass plate lowered. He pressed his palm on the etched glass, and a green light appeared in the upper right-hand corner. The elevator doors shut, and the lift started downward. He leaned back on the wall and lit up another cigarette, directing his thoughts on the mission ahead.

Jack Williams. My nemesis.

When they were at Harvard together, Jack destroyed his dream of becoming an archeologist. He recalled arguing about his career choice with Remi, his biological uncle who raised him. He had told him if you find a priceless relic, you could have your millions in an instant. History was the key, artifacts were money, and archeology was the way. The black market for antiquities was a high-income business with no end in sight. At first Uncle Remi was hesitant, but then he conceded. Yet all of it came to a halt when Jack allowed him to fail. He refused to let Dante copy his work or even help him cheat on tests. Jack had always told him, "You're a smart man, you can do this yourself."

Working with Preston on all his jobs had left him with little time to study, and though he excelled in archaeo-lexicology, his ability to read ancient languages, he never got his master's degree in archeology. After the disappointment of college, he joined the Navy, something Uncle Remi wanted him to do anyway, and he had to admit it worked out for the better. He had discovered he was an excellent Black Seal; an unofficial group within the Seals who never abided by the laws of interrogation. His love of archeology never died, *and I'll never forget what Jack did.*

The day Jack gave his Valedictorian speech was imprinted in his memory. His burning hatred was so intense; he was ready to kill him in front of the whole graduation class. He reached for the gun in his pocket and was about to stand when Preston, who was sitting beside him, clutched his arm and stopped him from rising.

Preston had whispered, "One day, my friend, you and I will have our revenge. Trust me."

Dante had stormed out of the graduation ceremony in the middle of Jack's speech. While walking the streets to calm down, a homeless drunk had insulted him for not giving him money. He got into a scuffle with the man who slit open his cheek with a box cutter. Before he realized it, he had knifed him twenty times. Not telling Preston what happened was important, because sooner or later his so-called friend would use it against him.

The man has no humanity, he thought.

That day, he had begun a rumor about a woman who slashed his cheek, and Preston fell for it. He puffed on his cigarette and blew out a ring of smoke. Jack's many international contacts would make him hard to find. Severe interrogation would have to be administered to anyone connected to him. He grinned, enjoying the power this would engender, remembering all the previous missions and how he'd gotten the information he wanted at the expense of his victim.

Mission completion is crucial, he thought. *Seals never fail.*

There was a small flash of light above the floor numbers, and he frowned. He was nearing the Dungeon, a laboratory spanning three full levels below the storage facilities of the skyscraper. The animal testing done there was hidden from society for a purpose. He'd seen mutilated carcasses many times and had heard the yowls and ear-piercing squeals of pain in the hallways.

He took another puff of the cigarette, watching the floor numbers drop while the elevator glided down past the elite condos. Preston's penthouse and his private office, the one with the simulated ocean, took up the whole top floor. Below this, the seventy-ninth floor contained his automated Conference Room and his public office, where he met with corrupt officials wanting to suck the world dry. The next fifty-six levels were elaborate condominiums starting at no less than one hundred million dollars each. Preston Black never catered to anyone with less than a billion in the bank, using extreme background checks to safeguard his investments and his survival. Because no one in the business world made billions without layers of corruption.

Then there were the nineteen levels of Global Research and Development or GRD. A place so safe for humans, the military had constructed its facilities in the same manner. The GRD was the only lab registered with the United States government, and where Jack Williams used to work.

Next, the three floors, which included the main lobby on ground level, contained high-class stores and restaurants catering to the zillionaires. The prestigious lobby looked more like a tropical paradise, complete with palm trees, elaborate fountains, and life-size holograms of elephants, monkeys, exotic birds, and a host of other animals who would fly or walk with the shoppers. Gentle sounds of the creatures and enjoyable scents of the beautiful flora made it seem like a natural Rainforest and people were thrilled to be there. For three years in a row, it was acclaimed as the most beautiful place to buy anything you wanted, including futuristic cars encrusted with real diamonds. Although a cup of coffee cost one hundred fifty dollars, the restaurants were always full. Everyday hundreds came from all over the world just to visit and shop. However, before anyone entered the lobby, they had to pass behind a full-body x-ray. The shoot-out at Bloomingdale's in 2024 killing fifteen people made it necessary for the consumer's protection, and something Preston was happy to enforce. On this main level was also Global's old unused docking bays Preston was saving for expansion.

The three tiers under the main lobby were for parking. Within this level and off to the side, a hidden ramp for semi-tractor trailers led down to two more levels designated as storage facilities for the building.

Then there was the Dungeon. When they were renovating the site, he had to organize the deaths of two city inspectors who had become too curious. The public was in an uproar, but no evidence was recovered thanks to Global's innovative technology.

There was a slight bump, and Dante sighed. This elevator was the Dungeons only connection to the surface. Although the people down there were shown a staircase going up, it was a facade. If there was ever a life-threatening emergency and the elevator was unusable, Preston would let all of them die to keep the Dungeon safe. The one hundred scientists who lived there could only leave the facility with an escort, even to visit their relatives for one weekend a month. They were watched every moment of the day by a team of soldiers Preston called *Black Halo*, an elite group of ex-military mercenaries whose sole purpose was to preserve the Dungeon and its secrets.

One time, four defiant scientists fed up with Preston's cruelty decided on their next trip home, they would tell their families what was really happening. Unaware there were cameras and microphones throughout the Dungeon and inside their houses and cars, they never made it home and were never seen or heard from again. *Black Halo* burned their bodies and buried them somewhere in Africa.

The elevator doors slid open, and a blast of alcohol air burned the inside of his nose, making his eyes water. Red letters blinking above the doors read, "No Smoking." With his black Berluti shoe, he crushed out his cigarette on the beige stone floor and then stepped out of the elevator. All the ceiling lights lit up.

To conserve energy, the motion sensor lights stayed off in the hallways until someone entered. The Dungeon used vast amounts of electricity, and Preston didn't want to invite any suspicions from the government. On his left, there was a white wall, the dead-end of the hallway. Sparkling white tiled floors along with light gray walls, and rows of fluorescent lights produced a hospital-like environment. To his right, at the end of the long corridor was the key-card entry system with automatic doors, the only entrance to the facility. He strolled down the hall, dreading another strong gust of alcohol air coming from the spreading doors. As he neared the entrance, he stopped.

The smell is different, more acidic. He bent forward and sniffed the floor. *Nothing.*

He went to slip his card into the slot when something heavy pounded the floor behind him. Before he could turn to see what it was, nine *Black Halo* guards rushed through the sliding doors, slamming him against the sidewall. They surrounded someone, beating and kicking them while screaming profanities. Deafening screeches and squeals like a pig being slaughtered nearly shattered his eardrums.

What the heck? he thought, covering his ears. *This can't be right.*

Dante leaned to his right to see what it was when another guard came through the open doors and blocked his view.

"Hello, Mr. Kennett," yelled the middle-aged guard, trying to talk over the raucous.

Dante's gaze went up a seven-foot-tall caveman wearing a black uniform with gold letters embroidered above his chest pocket, "BH"—*Black Halo*. He had a protruding forehead above light blue eyes and a shiny bald head which radiated like the sun. The way his disfigured bottom lip and nose sat crooked, the bones in his face had been broken several times. What stood out was the bulbous scar running from the top left side of his head, down over his left temple, and all the way to the bottom of his ear. Whoever he had battled with was trying to open his skull. It was a quarter inch wide, dark red, and stood out against his white skin; a gruesome sight he was sure repulsed many.

I've seen this guy before, thought Dante.

The soldier shouted, "As you can see, sir, we have a situation here calling for your safety. Please," he held out his arm towards the open doors. "I will escort you to the Acquisitions Lab, but we have to hurry."

There was no reason to defy the guard's request, so he nodded and followed him through the doorway. A deep raspy voice came from behind.

"Help…please."

Dante spun his head around and saw a guard restraining a long black antennae. Another soldier fisted the largest syringe he'd ever seen. The needle was a solid quarter inch thick and four-inches long. He rammed it down hard with the force of a sledgehammer.

A loud cracking sound echoed as a blaring shriek shattered six ceiling lights.

CHAPTER 5
Jack

"The true adventurer goes forth aimless and uncalculating to meet and greet unknown fate." - O. Henry

"Strip, now," said Jack. "We have to check your clothes."

"It must have bitten me in the shower," said Max. "I killed it when I grabbed my shirt. I'm not stripping."

Mandy grabbed his T-shirt and yanked him down to her, face-to-face. "You will strip, or I will rip them off you myself."

"Max!" said Jack. "Now!"

"Fine," said Max, sneering at his sister and mumbling, "flippin' psychopath...."

"Spiderman underwear?" chuckled Mandy.

"Knock it off, one-eyed Willie," said Max, tossing his clothes to his father.

"You're such a jerk, Max."

Mandy's eye was swelled shut and he could only hope the infection wouldn't permanently affect her vision. Jack turned the clothing inside out and shook them. Nothing fell out, but he found the squashed bug in his shirt. He removed the dead spider and wrapped it in a napkin.

"I'm getting a wicked headache," said Max, putting his pants back on. "Anyone have aspirin?"

Jack touched Max's forehead; he was warm.

"I have some," said Mandy. She pulled from her shorts pocket a foil pack, ripped it open, and handed Max two yellow pills. He popped them into his mouth and swallowed.

"This thing really hurts," said Max, pressing his hand on his back.

"Mandy, give me the antihistamine cream from the First Aid Kit," said Jack, hiding his concern. He rubbed the yellow salve on the bite, worried it wouldn't be enough. Getting out just went to Defcon 1.

"Let's go. Max, give me your pack."

"I got this," said Mandy, removing her backpack. "I'll put my junk in his pack and if we have to run, I can keep up."

"I know you can," said Jack, proud of his healthy daughter.

"Yo, peeps!" shouted Max. "I found something!"

He was twenty feet down the tunnel examining the wall. There was a strange carving in the limestone; two concentric circles with double pyramid shapes inside it.

"Is that Egyptian?" asked Mandy.

Jack outlined the etching with his finger. "I don't think so." The sounds of a rock hitting the solid floor echoed. Startled, he stood up and looked down the tunnel where they had come from. "We have to go. We need more distance from those spiders."

"You got my vote," said Mandy.

Jack led them with a glowstick. He checked his watch. Twelve hours had passed since they had entered St. Michael's Cave. With the immense boulders blocking their way, it was harder and taking longer to traverse. But now, it felt like they were ascending, which was a relief. Max was holding his own, and he could only hope he could keep up.

His children were special. In the womb, they shared one placenta and were born one minute apart. When sleeping, most of the times Max would lie on his stomach and Mandy would crisscross her body over his back or vice versa, but no matter what position they were in, they had to touch. Growing up, they did everything together, never leaving the others side. Bike riding, ball playing, and games with other children in the neighborhood couldn't break them apart, insisting on being on the same team or they wouldn't play. And sometimes when they were eating, they were unaware of their parallel movements with their arms and chewing their food. Although they were inseparable, they had their differences. Mandy had an uncanny ability to reason out solutions, looking at things from a simpler point of view and was more street smart, whereas Max was all science. With a mind equal to Einstein, Newton, and Tesla, his life centered on physics. After Lisa died, they were what kept him alive, and he couldn't imagine life without them.

"Do you think that carving was pre-Phoenician?" asked Max.

"Not sure. The Phoenicians were the first to create an alphabet, but perhaps an unknown race of people had once lived in these caves. So far from what we've seen, the food in these caverns are rats, bats, and insects; dietary staples still used in many civilizations down to this day."

"I don't know if you feel it," said Mandy, shivering, "but the temperature has dropped at least forty degrees. Did we enter a Twilight Zone?"

"Halt," said Jack, raising his hand. He unclipped his flashlight and beamed it down the passageway. A dark long rounded tunnel seemed to go on forever. It was fifty feet in diameter and contained patches of glistening black stone.

"We're in a lava tube!" said Max, slapping Mandy on the shoulder. "This is great!"

"Ouch!" said Mandy. "What are you so excited about, moron? We're talking about a volcano."

"There are lots of lava tubes from extinct volcanoes," said Max. "They're formed when the walls cool faster than the lava. This one is pretty old. Do you see the horizontal ridges along both sides of the tube?" He moved his finger along a two-inch bulge running along the channel wall. "The ancient river of lava was as tall as you, about five feet high. Just because a lava tube exists, doesn't mean there's an active volcano at the end."

"This black stone is beautiful," said Mandy, running her hand over the glittering rock. "It looks and feels like glass."

"It's called obsidian," said Jack, "and be careful, it can slice your skin without you feeling it."

"I'm tired," said Max, "can we rest for a little? I think we're far enough away from the spiders."

"Let's take five," said Jack. "Mandy, do you have more aspirin?"

She gave Max another pack and lip-synched to Jack, *only one packet left.*

Max gulped down the pills, then slumped to the ground, resting sideways on the wall, not wanting to put any pressure on his back. He was in pain.

"Max, let me recheck the bite."

The swelling on Max's back had gotten bigger, and more red. The spider could have been a new species, a real killer with potent venom. They had to get out of there.

"Listen," said Jack, "I'm going up ahead to check it out. You two stay here. Just yell if you need me, I won't be far."

Jack turned to leave when Max said, "Dad, wait! Look!"

He pointed at the wall across from where he and Mandy sat. Near the bottom was another of the strange carving. Jack squatted low, inspecting the etching. His kids crawled to him.

"The circles with the pyramids again," said Max.

"This has to be a marker," said Jack. "I'm going to check for more. I'll be right back."

The twins sat against the wall. Mandy put her arm around Max, and he rested his head on her shoulder, closing his eyes. Jack sped away. If they were markers, someone had put them there. He was moving down the tunnel as fast as he could, checking every square inch of the walls when he stopped, staring at an unbelievable sight. Without another thought, he raced back to his kids.

"You've got to see this," he said, pulling Max to his feet. "Come."

A few minutes later, their flashlights were beaming on a shelf carved into a wall of shiny obsidian. Resting on it was a black book at least two feet in height. Centered on its cover was a large round carving separated into four sections; three were empty, but the top left niche had a bright red glassy ornament sitting over it, unset within its area. Next to the book, was a four-foot-long dried leather sack crammed with something. On the wall beside the alcove was an unlit torch sitting in a black metal sconce. Max sat on the ground, and Mandy placed his pack beside him.

"Anyone got a match?" asked Jack, lifting the torch.

Max reached into the front pocket of his pack and pulled out a box of waterproof matches. When Jack lit the torch, the whole area glowed in an eerie yellow light.

"I didn't want to touch anything until you guys saw this," said Jack. "Mandy, get the cam…."

She was already snapping away. Jack returned the torch to its holder. Above the artifacts, the angled chisel marks in the stone were precise, almost artistic, and led down to the flat shelf. He doubted whoever stashed these items would booby-trap them, because— *anyone finding this old lava tube underneath the Mediterranean Sea is a million-to-one. They were meant to be hidden forever.*

"We'll leave these things here and come back for them later," said Jack. "Max needs a doctor."

"No way!" demanded Max. "This is an incredible find, and we're not leaving it. Let's take it with us."

"Max is right," said Mandy, "we need to take the stuff."

"At least open the bag," said Max, "and tell us what's inside."

"If I open it, I may damage whatever is in there just by exposing it to the air."

"It's cool down here, and the humidity is almost nonexistent," said Max. "Whoever put those things here knew this place would preserve them."

Although the archeologist inside Jack's head was screaming not to do it, his curiosity got the best of him. He unlooped the leather tie of the sack and shined his flashlight inside.

"There are three arks," he said, "the kind that carry scrolls. I'm looking at ends that have golf ball size diamonds sitting on slabs of pure emerald. Two have pink diamonds and the third one has a rare blue diamond." He took a moment to calm himself. The find was incredible. "Carved into the emerald there are four small gold engravings of the Larnax, the symbol of ancient Greece."

"The Library of Alexandria?" asked Max.

"Maybe. I know this may be the greatest discovery of all time, but I need to get you both to safety, and I'm sure this is the way out. How else could someone have brought these things down here? This tunnel has to lead to freedom."

"Dad's right," said Mandy, feeling Max's forehead. "We have to leave now."

"But we haaave… to, thissss migh…," said Max, slurring his words.

There was no time to waste.

"We're leaving!" said Jack. "Mandy, put the book in Max's pack and carry it. Do you think you can carry the scrolls too? The sack is about fifty pounds. I'll take the torch and Max."

"Not a problem."

Mandy jumped to her feet and scooped up the black book. The red glassy wedge sitting on the cover slid off the book and hit the rock floor. A ping echoed along with a loud groaning. The passage rumbled. Flitters of dust and dirt rained down.

"Was that an earthquake?" asked Mandy, picking up the fragment.

"More like a tremor," said Jack, adjusting the pack on his shoulders. "They're common in this area." Jack took the glassy item from Mandy and stuffed it in his jeans pocket. "Let's go." Max's blue eyes were bloodshot. "Come on, bud," he said, lifting his son. He was almost dead weight.

Mandy slipped on Max's pack, then clamped her arms around the scroll sack. "Got them," she said. "Let's go."

Max's legs were dragging, and Jack feared the worst. The poison was working hard to end his life. Aside from the awful dread of losing his son, the tunnel seemed to get smaller, inching down. They had walked at least an eighth of a mile when they entered a large chamber.

A dead end!

"There's no way out of here!" sobbed Mandy, falling to her knees and dropping the leather sack on the rock floor. "Max…."

Jack sat him on the ground. Mandy crawled to her brother and cuddled him in her arms as tears streamed down her cheeks. Jack moved around the cavern, running the light of the torch over the walls.

"Someone brought those things in here from somewhere," said

Jack, "and I doubt if it was through Gibraltar. This has to be the way out."

"Fffeet," said Max, garbling his words.

Jack got on his knees and saw the hieroglyph. It was the same symbol; the two circles with the pyramids. But this one was different—*an added spear pointing up.* He leapt to his feet and followed the angle of the mark with his finger. *There!* Up above on the ceiling, was an inconspicuous triangle, its edges filled with packed dirt. He mashed it with the side of his fist. With a heavy boom and a giant puff of smoke, a door retracted, sliding to the side with a crunching sound. The brightness of daylight almost blinded him.

"Max!" screamed Mandy.

Max's head had slumped forward. He was unconscious. Jack yanked his son off the ground, flung him over his shoulder, and fled through the exit. Mandy was right behind him with Max's pack and the scrolls. They were in a cave at the edge of a sea where waves were pushing in. Sloshing their way through the water they made it to the outside beach. One hundred feet away, a man and a woman were sitting in their Jeep. Mandy ran towards them.

"Help us, please!" she shouted. "My brother is dying!"

CHAPTER 6
Preston

Global Innovations
Park Ave, New York

Preston was relaxing at his desk when he pulled from his pocket a section of an amulet he had stolen six months ago from the Cairo Museum in Egypt. It was wedge-shaped, one-inch thick with an arched side measuring over five inches wide.

Red Beryl, thought Preston. *One of the rarest and most expensive gemstones.* It warmed his heart to hold the beautiful piece, running his fingers over the crystal and feeling its smoothness.

Inside the red stone, thin lines of an orange-gold ore formed a beautiful filigree design. How the metal got inside the gem was a mystery his scientists couldn't figure out. And to top it off, the ornament was sitting flat within a bed of orange-gold metal that looked brand new.

Orichalcum, he thought to himself. *The most indomitable metal I've ever come across.*

The day he found it was the day his life changed. He and Dante Kennett, whose formal education included archaeology, were searching for antiquities for his mansion in Colorado. In the Cairo Museum the curator, Mr. Ahmose, was eager to please him considering his measly five-million-dollar donation if they allowed him a few relics. They had set up a special room displaying hundreds of artifacts for his choosing, yet timeworn statues and ragged mummies held nothing for him. He was ready to cancel the agreement when Mr. Ahmose insisted he accompany him to a secluded area set aside for only privileged guests.

"A special room overflowing with history lay below us," said Ahmose, "and I am sure there you will find something pleasing to your taste."

Preston agreed, and the two men followed their host to the elevator. Ahmose pushed his card into a slot, and a retinal scanner slid out of the wall. The curator put his chin on the cup and a thin blue light skimmed across his right pupil. 'Access Granted' in green appeared on the LED display. Dante was studying Ahmose's every move.

The man's a pirate, he remembered chuckling to himself.

The elevator had begun its trek downward.

"Perhaps you would care for some tea," said Ahmose. "I can have it brought to you."

"I have a meeting in forty-five minutes," he said. He recalled his knees were aching from all the walking. "I would like this done."

"Yes, my liege," said Ahmose. The elevator pinged. "We are here."

Calling it a room was an understatement, it was the size of a vast distribution center with a three hundred-foot ceiling. Hulking statues that once stood outside pagan temples lined the cement block walls. Priceless carvings, pottery, and every kind of venerable artifact stacked the floor-to-ceiling shelves. The air was crisp and smelled of old dirt.

"Please, my lord," said Ahmose, holding out his arm, "this way."

Preston nodded and followed Ahmose down a long aisle. Lining both sides was pottery with different designs, most standing over six feet tall, and all embedded with hieroglyphics only scholars could decipher.

"These items are our most favored," said Ahmose, "and I have been instructed to allow you anything you please."

Preston walked beside Ahmose as he chatted on about the artifacts, but nothing interested him. When they had reached the end of the aisle, Preston was going to rescind his offer when he saw Dante walk away to his right. He hurried behind him because this man's passion was archeology. In a dark corner behind several tall vases was a marble pedestal draped in black velvet cloth. Dante removed the fabric revealing a glass enclosure. Inside, sitting on royal blue velvet, was a colossal triangular red gemstone with gleaming orange-gold metal edging its sides. Above it, rows of hieroglyphics filled a six-by-twelve-inch wide strip of papyrus.

"What is it?" said Preston.

Ahmose rushed over to them. "This is nothing," he said, recovering the case. "It is an old relic of no value."

Dante lip-synced to Preston. *Bulletproof glass.*

"I see," said Preston. "Then let us move on, Mr. Ahmose."

Preston chose six, seven-foot-tall, variegated vases from the Fourth Dynasty. That night at 3 a.m., Dante and his elite team broke into the museum. They took the red gem, the papyrus, and from beneath the blue velvet cloth, they also stole a small notebook. The glass enclosure was redressed as if nothing happened.

Four months have passed, and no thievery has been reported by the museum, thought Preston. *Idiots.*

When they had returned home, Dante dove into the research. The translation of the papyrus with the hieroglyphics opened with,

"Complete the Amulet, and you will attain the infinite power of ATLANTIS."

Upon hearing the word 'Atlantis,' Preston had laughed so hard his stomach hurt. However, Dante wasn't laughing, his stern face told him it was time to listen. It's been three days since Preston read the story; a magnificent record of history and one he enjoyed. He tapped the pale orange circle on his desk, and a forty-inch wide screen rose in front of him. It displayed Dante's translation of the papyrus and the small book.

After the introductory line, it disclosed Egypt's four physical elements; *Earth*, *Air*, *Water*, and *Fire*. A discussion with Dante concluded the red piece was part of an amulet which had been split into four sections, and each segment represented one of the four elements of Earth. The papyrus explained how the book and the amulet section came into Egyptian possession. It was during the rule of His Majesty Thutmose III of the eighteenth dynasty.

It stated, "Two gods came flying to them like birds in the heavens, monstrous beings with the strength of three thousand oxen. Although their hair was white, their faces were young and their bodies full of vigor. Both stood over ten feet in height, tremendous men who terrified all those bowing before them. Thutmose and his priests were quaking with fear, some releasing themselves. They declared they were from the glorious city of legend, Atlantis, and gave Thutmose what they called a book with a four-sectioned carving on its cover. A brilliant red gem, which they called *Earth*, was seated in the upper left quadrant. Their thunderous voices shook the temple walls, barring them from speaking of the gifts to others, lest death beget them all. No one was to know of its existence, not even other gods who might inquire.

"Their firm instructions were that each year the High Priest was to place his hand flat on the book over the carving. A flash of light would note his acceptance; then he was to leave the room or die from a flesh-eating malady. Frightened and trembling with his face on the floor, His Highness Thutmose swore with his life to carry out their every command. After the supreme beings left in the winds of a great storm, Thutmose ordered an underground tunnel be built. It sloped downward and lead northwest from the Temple of the Sphinx. At its end was a brilliant room layered with gold and precious stones, and there the vestiges were placed on a golden pedestal. Its location was only known to Pharaoh and the High Priest, deemed forbidden knowledge it was punishable by a swift beheading."

That was the last entry on the papyrus, but the small notebook continued with the history.

It began, "For centuries the book with the *Earth* section lay protected in the tomb. Adding to its concealment, they built the great pyramid of Khufu over the sacred chamber, and only the loyal priests of the Celestial Order knew its location. When Alexander of Greece arrived in Egypt; the people had welcomed him, willing to obey. The wicked Persian satraps had surrendered their iniquitous rule, making Alexander conqueror of Egypt.

"Alexander requested to see the book from the famed City of

Atlantis. His request shocked the High Priest Ngozi. Their new ruler said he desired to only examine the relics, and not remove them from Egypt, for he knew of their sanctity. Ngozi pleaded saying they were commanded not to speak of them lest be cursed of death. Alexander said the same gods ordered him to conquer Egypt and protect the sacred items. Ngozi was unsure of Alexander's truthfulness, but he dared not question him, he was a mighty conqueror and would torture all to find the precious relics. With despair in his heart, Ngozi agreed and told him he would have the artifacts within eleven days. One thousand soldiers were ordered to accompany them.

"Ngozi returned to find Alexander had changed the name of his beloved city from Rhakotis to Alexandria, in honor of himself. What could he do? He was now their ruler. Alexander was told the objects had been sheltered in a room beneath a Pharaoh's pyramid in the land of Giza. Ngozi slumped to his knees and begged Alexander not to remove the holy gifts from Egypt, saying he was willing to exchange his life as it meant salvation for all. Alexander, the outstanding ruler he was, reassured him this was not his intention. He approached Ngozi and helped him to his feet, consoling him with kind words as if he were a friend. Recognizing his honesty and sincerity, Ngozi relaxed, then humbly offered the relics.

"Alexander snatched the book away and laid it on a table. Using a magnifying glass, he pored over the cover and the red crystal. He opened the book and saw the flat sheets of papyrus empty of writing. Alexander told Ngozi he knew the story of the vast empire of Atlantis and how these were the only remnants proving its existence. Ngozi was in awe of his knowledge and prostrated himself before him. He must have spoken to the gods. How else could a mere man know so much?

"The superior ruler then inquired about the other components belonging to the incomplete amulet. Ngozi had told him he did not know their whereabouts; the Atlantean gods had kept the knowledge from them. Alexander nodded and ordered the book and its amulet piece be returned to their resting place. Then the magnificent ruler, in all his glory, left his beautiful city of Alexandria, never to return. Rumor had said after Alexander held the items, he recognized the value of history and recorded the truthful story of his own life, revealing his good and evil. Three scrolls written by his own hand.

"Five years after Alexander had left Egypt, High Priest Ngozi had a visitor from afar, a man who had traveled thousands of miles. He had an odd-shaped flat face, puffy cheeks with thin slanted eyes, and a broad nose. His clothes were of animal pelt, lined with ivory-colored lumps of fur. Ngozi had reasoned he came from a place lacking heat. He called himself, Ashis, and gave the meaning of his name as 'blessings.' Ngozi invited him to sit. He asked Ashis where he was from and what brought him to the Land of the Sun, the holy land of Egypt.

"Ashis had told him he was from Chomolungma, the mountain called the 'Goddess Mother of the World.' His village lies at the base of the hallowed mountain which rises above the heavens. He pulled from his leather vest pocket, a frayed gray cloth and began unwrapping it, saying he believed it was something belonging to Egypt. When Ashis held up the shard, Ngozi gasped and leapt from his seat, stumbling back and knocking over his chair. The jewel was glimmering red and set within an orange-gold metal. Its similarity to their revered fragment was alarming. The servant-priests straightened his chair, and Ngozi eased back into his seat; his body trembling at the sight of the relic. Ashis crumpled to his knees and bowed his head, begging for mercy while holding the piece in his outstretched hands. Upon seeing Ashis's humility, Ngozi had calmed and nodded, but he dared not touch the relic. He ordered the priests to help Ashis and demanded food and drink. Ngozi then asked Ashis to tell him the story of how he obtained the artifact.

"Ashis said his village was destitute. The winter had been severe, and many of the livestock needed for food had died. Contained in their history was the story of ancient gods who came from the sky and hid a powerful token in a cave high up in the sacred mountain, thus the climb up Chomolungma was punishable by death. But their village was deteriorating, people were dying, and there was no hope of survival. In secret, six of their best warriors formed a plan to secure the item, fearing everyone would perish if they did nothing. In the darkness of night, they set up the mountain to find the legendary Batas Cave.

"After three weeks, only one man had returned. Bishal was crazed and delirious; madness had overtaken him. They searched his clothes and found a gray fabric with strange writing on it. Wrapped within was this large red gemstone sitting inside a bed of orange-gold metal. It terrified the village elders and they ordered its return to the mountain cave. Not one volunteered since the strongest and bravest had fallen. Soon after, a bizarre sickness spread throughout the village of three hundred people, causing the deaths of ninety-three. The oldest son of the village elder who had just returned from a six-year journey recognized the language on the cloth. It was something he had learned on his travels, saying it was from a land called Egypt, and the jewel should be returned there. Ashis admitted, he is that son and would like to give Ngozi the treasure and the material with the writing.

"At first, Ngozi was reluctant to accept the gem for fear the curse would spread to Egypt, so he excused himself and conferred with the other priests. They contended if he refused, the gods may return and punish them for failing to protect another divine relic. They reasoned if they had gifted Egypt with the book and the *Earth* shard, then another section of the amulet could only add to their glory before the gods. These were welcoming words to Ngozi, and he accepted the holy item, sending Ashis on his way with food and gifts of gold.

"Ngozi read the hieroglyphics on the cloth, the word *Air* struck him, and he deduced it is the second element of the book. To protect the relic, he burned the fabric, and then ordered the *Air* section entombed with the book."

The man was another idiot, thought Preston. *It's incredible mankind survived.* He continued reading.

"Two years before Alexander died when he was in India, a Nepali assassin snuck into his tent at night. Alexander captured the man, and after extreme torture, the assassin revealed his knowledge of the amulet piece. Though dying, the man cursed the Egyptians for keeping the divine relic, saying the gods had punished his people, allowing them to be conquered and turned into slaves. He was to execute the ruler of Egypt and reclaim the sacred jewel so it could be returned to its resting place in the mountain cave. Alexander believes he is speaking of the *Earth* component, the one he had held in his hands. He put a sword through the man's heart.

"Realizing the items had been compromised, Alexander sent two thousand soldiers to Egypt, ordering the priests to remove the book and its attachment from beneath the pyramid. The soldiers were unaware of the *Air* fragment; therefore, the priests only gave them the book and the *Earth* piece. Alexander ordered the three scrolls containing his life story and the holy relics, be placed in an old chest in the basement of the Library of Alexandria under piles of wooden crates; hidden away from curious eyes. Only the Chief Librarian knew of their existence, and he was sworn to silence.

"After Alexander left our world, Ptolemy I Soter I, one of his generals, took control of Egypt. Ngozi only trusted Alexander, so before Ptolemy arrived, he had ordered the *Air* piece moved to a room below the divine Sphinx, to be forever guarded by the Celestial Order.

"For thousands of years the *Air* section was safe, the walls of the Sphinx had proved strong until October 1992, when an earthquake shook the ground. The stone walls crumbled. Disguised as workers, it took three desperate days of searching before the priests located the holy relic. When they found it still intact, they placed it in an earthquake-resistant building, hence, the Cairo Museum. In contrast, the book and the *Earth* piece along with the scrolls of Alexander, vanished from the Library of Alexandria, and to this day, no one knows their location."

The last paragraph of the writing said the key to Atlantis would be revealed to those who connect the four elements of Earth on the cover of the book. Then there was another warning, a curse overcoming all who encountered the amulet and *blah, blah, blah*, thought Preston.

Superstitions are ridiculous. They're not based on fact.

At first, Preston blew off the whole Atlantis theory, but when they tested the metal, it registered as 'unknown.' Dante insisted it had to be pure orichalcum because the only place it's mentioned is in the story of Atlantis.

Preston stared at the *Air* piece in his hand. He held it up to his face for the fiftieth time, studying the red crystal, hoping to discern something from the thin floating lines of the encapsulated gold ore. He flipped it over and rubbed the solid base of orichalcum. It was smooth as glass with no imperfections. Tests with lasers, fire, bombs, gamma rays and even radiation revealed the metal undisturbed and impenetrable. A pleasant feeling rose within him as he realized he possessed the only metal on Earth able to resist anything any government threw at it. Not even his beloved vibranium could do that.

He reminisced when he was at his mansion in Colorado and lounging in front of the fireplace with Dante, reasoning on Plato's story of Atlantis. It began with Egyptian priests. Therefore, it would only make sense the Egyptians would have the proof. And they did. The Cairo Museum had placed the glass enclosure in the dark corner, so it would blend with all the other artifacts, but to a trained eye like Dante's, it didn't work. If Atlantis had an infinite energy source like the legend suggested, Preston had to have it. There were many stories and unproven theories of the lost city, but this shard was the first real proof it existed, and he would share it with no one.

Atlantis had become his obsession. To find it, he had to use every option available, including scholars and scientists from all over the world. And considering the secrecy of the project, they were given an ultimatum; either accept his offer, or they and their families would die. The choice was theirs.

CHAPTER 7

Dante

The soldier with Dante mashed the red button and the sliding doors shut with a hiss. All was silent once more.

"This way, sir," said the guard, his German accent clear. He pressed the mic in his ear. "Take the specimen to Lab 4."

Dante had seen the results of the grisly experimentations on animals, but something was different. The thing in the hallway had a huge antenna like an insect—*and it talked.*

"How are you doing today, sir?" asked the soldier.

"Fine," said Dante, clearing his throat. He regarded the massive structure beside him. If he had to take him down, it would be painful. "And what do they call you?"

"Armin, sir. In German, it means 'soldier.'"

"An appropriate name," said Dante, not letting on he spoke fluent German.

Without moving his head, he shifted his eyes to Armin. Muscles filled his long black sleeves, and his chest was bulging out like an unmovable mass. He carried two guns in transparent holsters, which were another Global specialty; transparent flexible aluminum. On his left shoulder was a SIG-P226 in a harness and a Desert Eagle 50 AE was in a belt holster. Both were semi-automatics, and both dead accurate. Sewn into the right thigh of his uniform was a transparent sheath holding a twelve-inch M-9 Bayonet combat knife. And all were put on display as a warning to others.

But if his eyes were not tricking him, and they never did, Armin was a walking factory of weapons. A few bulges in his many velcroed pockets were not all muscle. They were stiff while he walked, not flexing the way they should. This Armin required a thorough background check, and his good friend, Karim Stone, had Interpol connections. There was one sure thing about him—*this guy was built to kill.*

Then he remembered where he'd seen Armin before. A month ago, Preston had shown him a video of an incident where Armin disemboweled three lab assistants. They had defied Preston in front of their peers, refusing to work on his projects, threatening to inform the government. Preston thought it hilarious when Armin gutted them and drank a cup of blood from each carcass. To stifle any more uprisings, Preston forced all his scientists to watch the video. Dante found out later Armin was eager to accept the task, saying he had drank human blood before. He recalled arguing with Preston telling him to kill a person was one thing, but drinking their blood? That was another whole level of twisted crazy. Preston didn't appreciate his questioning and told Dante to update his thinking; he was failing in his purpose. Before Preston stormed out of the room, he told Dante to be careful. From that day forward, their relationship had changed, becoming more strained and distant. Preston still trusted him to get the job done, but something was missing...*the camaraderie isn't there.* Since then, he'd been left out of many social engagements he formally accompanied Preston to. Not that this bothered him, he hated being around rich asinine snobs. Then a disturbing question arose in his mind.

Is he trying to replace me with Armin? The soldier is more in line with Preston's psychotic nature.

"Are you all right, Mr. Kennett?" asked Armin.

"Just thinking about the mission," he answered.

"I understand, sir."

That's got to be it, thought Dante. His anger swelled to the point like a volcano ready to erupt, and he had to slow his breathing to not alert the sociopath next to him. He wanted to snap Preston's neck. *Easy, Dante. Find out what Preston is doing down here because you may need it later. Then there's Atlantis, the greatest discovery of all time. Play your cards right, and it'll be yours.* Deceit was now the play.

"What happened back there?" asked Dante.

"One of our scientists went Judas, and we had to restrain him. As you saw he didn't agree."

"Yes," said Dante, nodding in agreement. *Since when do scientists have antennae?* "They're weird people," he continued. "They overthink everything. How do you like working for Mr. Black?"

"It has been satisfying, sir," he answered, adjusting the knife on his thigh.

"Good," said Dante, noting the killer's sly reference to the blade; Armin was on alert too. "You seem to know your weapons."

"Yes, sir," said Armin. "I have had extensive training in all areas of combat. Mr. Black has told me I will work alongside him which, I presume," he cleared his throat with a loud cough, "will be with you."

That's my confirmation! thought Dante, keeping his cool. "It will be a pleasure working with you, Armin. Your expertise will be an asset to my team. Right now, I need to concentrate on the mission. Mr. Black likes precision."

"Yes, of course, sir."

They stopped talking. It infuriated him his once close friend loved barbarism so much he wanted him out of the way. He had never failed Preston and now he felt cheated, insulted, and worst of all, betrayed. All the torture, assassinations, and kidnappings were for a selfish man who was nothing more than a savage. He tugged at the sleeves of his jacket, collecting himself. Time was on his side, and if he kept his cool—*everything will be mine.*

A small man came walking out a door and tripped, stumbling into Dante who caught him. Armin grabbed the man's arm and was ready to throw him against the wall when Dante gripped his shoulder, stopping him.

"I have this, soldier," said Dante. "You can go."

Armin's face scrunched into a ball of red anger. He pushed the man away, making him almost fall. His black combat boots pounded the shiny floor as he stormed down the corridor with clenched fists.

The man spoke with a nasal voice; his head bowed low. "I'm sorry, sir."

Dexter Jones was a portly twenty-one-year-old kid no taller than five feet, three inches. Next to Max Williams, he was the smartest person he'd ever met. Dex was a real brainer right down to the unkempt black hair, paper-white skin, and the frequent mindless stare. Droopy brown eyes were behind thick black-rimmed glasses, which often slid down his thin pointy nose. His most prominent feature was his mouth, where thin lips sat atop his buck-teeth, and with his slacked jaw, he resembled a rabbit. Beneath his white lab coat, blotches of dried food stains from his favorite BLT sandwiches covered his rumpled blue shirt and black tie. He smiled at Dex's plaid suspenders swooping over his corpulent stomach and locking onto wrinkled green pants. Preston wasted no time in gobbling up the innocence of this new scientist. By the age of nineteen, Dex had doctorates in biology, physics, and engineering. Preston snatched him up before he had time to think, offering him fame and fortune when, in reality, it was slavery and imprisonment.

The recent bruise on Dex's left cheek was fading. The *Black Halo* guards were ruthless with the scientists, and although Dex was not a coordinated man, he insisted it was his clumsiness and not a punch. But Dante wasn't buying it. The brutality of *Black Halo* was well known in the Dungeon, and many scientists had just vanished.

Dex doesn't belong here, thought Dante. *He's just a kid.*

"It's me, Dante, your best friend."

He saw the young man's shoulders visibly relax, his face lightened up with a smile.

"Hi, Dante," said Dex, slurping his words through misaligned teeth and pushing his glasses back up his nose. "I didn't see you, I'm sorry."

"I know," said Dante, making sure he kept a safe distance away from the spatters of spit. "Your mind is always somewhere else. How's work?" Dex's facial expression turn blank. Once again, his mind had gone into oblivion. "Calling, Dr. Jones?" he said, waving his hand in front of Dex's face, "you there?"

"Sorry," said Dex. "I finished my latest project, and I'm starting another exciting one."

"That's good to hear," said Dante. He placed his hand on Dex's shoulder. "Listen, maybe we can have lunch again with the other guys. Is this good with you?"

"That would be great. We always enjoy your company."

"Good. I'll let you know when. Take care, Dex."

"Thank you, sir."

Dante watched Dex walk down the corridor.

Now to find out who this Armin is, and what Preston is doing in the labs because whatever that thing was, it wasn't human.

CHAPTER 8
Max

Seven weeks later…

"Just one more tweak," said Max, "and Nessie will be perfect."

The news was on the television in the background.

"Dad doesn't want any more tweaks," said Mandy, sitting with her legs crossed on his unmade bed.

"Yeah, well, you know how well I listen to dad when it comes to my stuff."

"You're nuts. How do you think you'll be able to see? You won't be wearing a helmet. The wind will be in your face."

"I only amped her up to forty miles per hour, which is cake. And she can take off like a jet."

"Did you fix her table?"

"Yep, and it could now hold a hundred fifty pounds."

"My butt still hurts from hitting the floor after the table gave way. You're such a jerk sometimes."

"I needed to see if it would hold your one hundred eight pounds. Want to try it again? I'm sure it'll be all right now."

"No way."

"Okay." Max rolled back his manual wheelchair and examined his all-black electric masterpiece. "It's done," he said with pride. "Nessie now has everything I need."

"Why did you pick the name Nessie?" she asked. "It sounds like the Loch Ness monster."

"And she'll remain undiscovered too. This one is mine."

Max tossed the screwdriver onto the bed and rolled himself beside Nessie. Her left arm went vertical as her seat slid forward.

"Help me get into her," he said.

Mandy stood up and slipped both her arms under Max's shoulders, clasping her hands behind his back. He wrapped his arms around her, then used his strength to pull himself up and out of the wheelchair. She swung his body over and plopped him down in Nessie's well-padded seat. Mandy straightened his legs and feet while Nessie's chair glided back to its normal position. Max gazed down his legs. His gaunt bony knees were noticeable even through the black sweatpants. What happened was still clear in his mind.

The spider was a new species, and its venom had attacked the nerves and muscles associated with his lower extremities. Two more hours and it would have killed his heart. In the hospital, his father had told him they couldn't restore the use of his legs and feet, but everything from the hips up was normal. The pain in his chest returned. It felt like only an hour ago when he had freaked out on the hospital bed, screaming and crying. There's nothing like waking up and being told you'll never be able to walk again. After fifteen minutes of pure hysteria, his dad and Mandy calmed him, promising they would do everything to help make it better. That day his father bought him two wheelchairs, one manual, and the other an ordinary electric wheelchair, which the latter turned out to be the best medicine. Nessie let him be a scientist again, making his life way more fun and manageable.

Today, Mandy looked decent wearing white Capris and a blue-flowered blouse. A big difference from the bland white T-shirt and faded jean shorts. He gazed down his own body. Sweatpants were the easiest to put on with no one's help, and his black ones matched his white Justice League 5 T-shirt.

Mandy stretched her arms high above her head, speaking as she yawned. "This is the best place we've ever lived in, but it'll be nice when we can go home."

They were on *Isla de Lobos*, the "Island of Wolves," which was part of the Canary Islands owned by Spain. It was so named because back in the 1500s the Mediterranean Monk Seals were called Sea Wolves.

They were in *Castillo Solana*, an ocean-front castle constructed in the early 1800s with gray stone walls covered in layers of green ivy.

Max recalled how excited he got when seeing the two turrets with their copper conical spires; it was like peering into the past. The small mansion had twelve bedrooms, two kitchens, and two grand living rooms for exquisite parties.

The Google search of the castle sent him and Mandy on a hunt for the four underground tunnels dug out many years ago as an escape from the Inquisitors. Spectacular armoires with magnificent carvings of flowers and angels concealed all the passages. Because of the steps leading down to the tunnels, his father and Mandy built wooden ramps over the stone staircases for Nessie. Max's room contained a cherry wood armoire dating back to 1823, eleven years before Queen Isabella II of Spain had halted the Spanish Inquisition. A recessed button on the back and near the bottom of the cabinet released it, allowing it to be rolled away, thus revealing a passage leading to an old shed on the far edge of the property. His dad and Mandy had also removed the debris from the floors of all the passageways for Nessie. As added security, at every entrance to the tunnels, their father had attached enormous sliding bolt locks to the furniture and the stone walls of the caves. Once they were set, Max doubted Superman could pull out the huge closet.

Castillo Solana had two modern elevators making it handicap accessible. All the bedrooms were on the second floor along with Max's, which was a thirty-by-thirty open room with terra cotta tile. It was a perfect windowless shelter from the salt air, and because it was at the end of the long hallway, he had his quiet. *Castillo Solana* was a home given to their friend, the United Nations Ambassador of Spain, Jacián Renaldo; a gift from His Highness, King Ricardo II, his cousin and confidant.

The castle sat on the shores of the Atlantic Ocean, and at least three times a week in the middle of the night, he and Mandy would go to the beach and test the SBS, his Subterranean Surveyor. Nessie's tires would inflate to triple their size making it easier to roll on the soft white sand. If the seas were flat, Mandy would take a canoe and go into the water, then dip the flat coil of the SBS at least three feet into the warm sea. His laptop would show a complete chemical analysis of the surrounding area, along with an intricate 3-D picture of the ocean floor. Although developed to work over six miles down into the sea, he had to wait for testing at that depth. The farthest their dad would allow Mandy was fifty feet from the beach where the water was no deeper than thirty feet; an aggravating rule which he refused to bend. His father always accompanied them, guarding the area with his *Niclex Night Vision* goggles, the best on the market. Max had his pair of *Niclex* specs housed in one of Nessie's side pockets. *Castillo Solana* was beautiful, but he missed his freedom, the right to go when and where he wanted. To fight depression, he would take one day at a time and appreciate the fact he was still alive.

He smiled at the lighted thirty-gallon fish tank next to his work desk. His bed was behind him with one side against the wall, and when he would awake at night from one of the many reoccurring nightmares, he had a perfect view of the freshwater fish. If he watched the fish long enough, sometimes he'd go back to sleep.

But most of the time I get up and build something, he thought.

Ambassador Renaldo had two work tables designed just for him. The main one was twenty feet wide and u-shaped. He could pull into the center of the desk and still have ample room for two rolling office chairs for Mandy and his dad. This desk had all sorts of tools and lab equipment including three boxes of archival gloves, one centrifuge, three oscilloscopes, three computers hooked into six, forty-two-inch quad-monitors, an assortment of microscopes, and more. The other table was in the far-right corner and was the same width, but rectangular shaped with a depth of four feet, and this is where the arks and the big book lay. Both had scratch-proof light gray veneers and hosted numerous surge protectors.

On the left side of the room, six sizable walnut dressers took up most of the wall. Mandy called them cabinets because she said furniture was for clothes, and not "science junk." Although he didn't need help in finding things, she had insisted he label each cabinet and drawer so the two could get things for him. On the floor and leaning on the TV cart was his backpack, the same one he had carried in the caves.

Above the table in the far corner, a row of track lights shined down on the artifacts, and he stared at the strange book. He recalled the book's cover was solid and hard like stone but had a leathery feel. A small orange-gold star-shaped jewel centered on a seven-inch diameter carving, separated into four quadrants. The red crystal they found with the book had a brilliant orange-gold alloy shielding its bottom and ran halfway up its half-inch side, yet its weight was next to nothing. After putting the book on the table, they snapped the ornament into place and the whole castle rumbled. Their father promptly removed it and set it aside, telling them it was just another tremor, but Max knew it was more than that. For it to happen twice, once in the cave and once on land, could not be a coincidence. Mandy's voice broke his concentration.

"He is so hot," she said, her blue eyes glued to the television.

The English-speaking Headline News was on from Spain, and a young anchorman, Roberto Benitez, sat behind a shiny black granite table. His light gray eyes were in stark contrast to his milky skin layered in makeup so heavy, Max was sure they used a cement trowel to put it on. He looked like the actor, Antonio Banderas, except his jaw was square with fuller lips. His straight black hair was brushed back while a black suit and gray paisley tie enhanced his air of professionalism.

"Scientists are still unaware of what caused the world's oil fields to drop fifty percent a year ago," said Roberto, his voice strong and smooth, "and adding to this calamity, six hundred oil rigs worldwide have had catastrophic system failures. The ninety-two nations making up the Energy Reformation Council or ERC, has said the problems are stemming from unreachable places deep within the Earth's crust, but how this could affect the systems on the oil rigs is unknown. Ten months ago, sixty new oil rigs began construction, and as of yesterday, ten of those rigs are up and working. This is an incredible achievement…."

A station hand wearing headphones walked into view and handed him a sheet of paper.

"This just in," he said. "One of the new Australian offshore oil rigs has exploded. Many casualties have been reported but so far, no deaths. Sabotage is feared."

Another sheet was given to him.

"We have more breaking news. Three functioning oil rigs in Antarctica have stopped production. Reports of catastrophic equipment failures have flooded the airways. A restart of these rigs is unknown."

They handed him another sheet.

"My goodness," he said with angst, "what is going on here? Three more offshore drilling rigs in the Pacific have failed, explosions have been reported, and it is feared many are dead. Due to the recent events, all oil production on the new rigs has been halted. Security has been tightened, and the military has been called in to protect the remaining oil rigs. Reports say the Beherrschen Brotherhood, the organization laying claim to the destruction of the Taj Mahal and the Eiffel Tower, may be responsible for the attacks, but at this moment, no one has come forward." Roberto's gray eyes met the camera. "Why would anyone want the world to go back to the stone age?"

CHAPTER 9
Dante

"You were right," said Dante on his phone, standing outside an ocean cave where the high tide was about to enter. "The hospital records confirm the Williams's are still alive. They were picked up here on this beach at the base of Monte Hacho in Ceuta, Spain. Do you want the details?"

"No," said Preston. "Just the facts."

Plausible deniability, thought Dante. "The hospital report was missing a lot of information, but I found out Ambassador Jacián Renaldo, one of Jack's close friends, sent two of the best physicians from Spain to care for Max, but we don't know what happened to him. By order of the Spanish Ambassador, all the hospital records were deleted. I'll visit the Ambassador tonight. He's the key."

"Excellent!" said Preston, his loud voice vibrating the phone. "I have to take a call, don't hang up. I'll be right back."

Preston had only one exemplary tool in his blood-filled pockets, anyone working in secret for him were off the grid, dead to the government. The ten-man team were positioned around the perimeter of the cave, ensuring the area stay clear of intruders. The mic in his ear crackled.

"All clear, sir," said his second in command.

He gave the thumbs up sign to Karim Stone, his second in command and long-time friend who was at the entrance of the cave, overseeing the men. Dressed in a beige camouflage uniform he stood at six feet, five inches tall. Hazel eyes, buzzed black hair, and wrinkle-free brown skin belied his age of thirty-five. Eating healthy and exercise was his life, and he let nothing worry him because his motto was, "Just fix it." When Karim was nineteen years old, his parents were murdered in a gone-bad house robbery. He was depressed for months, and then one day he realized all his tears would never remove the pain. The officials never found the person who put the bullets in the heads of the three men. When the case was closed, he joined the Navy and became a Black Seal. Dante never forgot the four missions where Karim had saved his life. There was no one else he trusted to have his back.

Standing beside Karim was, Rick Dirkman, a psychopath Preston hired against his wishes. His clean-shaven head was glistening in the sun like a polished orb. He was a solid six feet, four inches tall with a hefty muscular build, and steel gray eyes. Aside from the pot holes on his face, he had four disfiguring scars. One split his left eyebrow, while another maimed the right half of his upper lip. His right nostril was deformed, a slit possibly sewn with a big needle, and his left earlobe hung in shreds. Dirkman was beyond crazy, and his vicious temper had led to many confrontations within the team. All-in-all Dante had broken his nose three times, dislocated his left shoulder twice, and fractured his jaw in two places just to make him stop antagonizing the other men.

Preston cleared his throat on the phone. "I'm back. Tell me more."

"I'm standing where they exited," said Dante. "This sea cave has an open door in the back. I'm sending a four-man team inside."

"A door?"

"Yeah, a solid rock door slid to the side," said Dante, watching the men enter the carved-out doorway with rifles aimed.

The stone door grinded shut. Dante waved his arm for Karim to check it out.

"Hold on, Preston," said Dante. "Karim, what happened?" he yelled.

Karim was checking the edging of the doorway. "I don't know, sir," he said, his voice echoing in the small chamber. "They must have tripped a mechanism."

"This is getting more interesting with each moment," said Preston. "I'll do a little investigating, and let you know what I find."

"Call me when you find something," said Dante, ending the connection.

It satisfied him to know he was the only person who could put Preston away for fifty lifetimes. And he would not allow him to be in some minimum-security prison where he could buy his way out. The depraved man had to pay with his life, and Dexter Jones was the answer. Everything was going as planned. He made an alternate email for Dex to contact him; *ET* seemed appropriate for a high-tech nerd. Dante moaned at the sight of Dirkman approaching.

Dirkman's insatiable appetite to torture and mutilate would make anyone sick. He was a Jack the Ripper type, another idiot who enjoyed disemboweling. Yet he left no clues behind, just like the Ripper, whom Dirkman idolized. For now, his grisly desire was pacified by the couple who had found the Williams's on the beach. Preston hired him saying he was an asset to the team, but Dante disagreed. Dirkman's desire to torture was so intense, his jeopardizing any mission was inevitable.

Darla was right, he thought, *Preston hired Dirkman to kill me.*

Darla was Preston's secretary and his 'in' to finding out Preston's intentions. She was sweet, kind, and hated Preston but kept working for him because the money was great. So, he began secretly dating Darla who, without a second thought, dumped Brett Carson, leaving him heartbroken—*or so it seems. He'd do anything for money, even sell her out.*

Two nights ago, she confirmed what he had suspected. Preston didn't want him around because he didn't enjoy the 'unique' entertainment, and felt he was losing his hardened core. Hence, there was no place for him in Global anymore.

"What's up, boss?" said Dirkman, standing beside him.

"It's 'sir' to you, and don't forget it," said Dante.

Dirkman jerked his body to attention and saluted him. "Yes, sir!" he shouted, then lowered his hand and snickered.

Dante was about to elbow Dirkman's nose again when Karim came from behind.

"We're done here, sir," said Karim. "What are your orders?"

"We need a plan for the Ambassador's home," said Dante, still wanting to bash Dirkman in the face.

He tried to relax, but Dirkman's smirk was too much to bear, so he rammed his fist into Dirkman's gut. The soldier's face swelled red, and he grunted, cringing in pain as he wrapped his arms around his torso and bent forward. Dante kicked his shoulder, knocking him onto his back. He pressed his shoe on Dirkman's neck making him gasp for air.

"You disrespect me again and you'll wish you were dead," said Dante, flicking the ashes from his cigarette on the soldier's bald head. "Get it?"

Dirkman was turning blue as he squeaked out the words, "Yes, sir."

Dante released him, and Dirkman rolled onto his side, choking and coughing as he struggled to stand up. Dante was ready to kick him again when from inside the cave, a glint of light caught his eye. On the far wall, the sun's rays had made a beeline for the lower section near the floor. He squinted his eyes to see what it was.

"Is there something on that wall?" asked Dante.

Karim was staring into the cavern. "What would metal be doing on a sea cave wall?"

Dante tossed the cigarette in the sand and entered the cave. Karim and two soldiers followed. Crushed shells, coral stones, and heaps of wet seaweed littered the floor of the small antre. It stank of dead clams. There was no stopping his archeological side, so without regard for his eighty-thousand-dollar suit, he laid flat on his stomach on a pile of noxious smelling kelp.

It's writing!

Dante's heart skipped a beat. The embedded script contained tiny specks shining like gold.

"It looks like ancient Greek," said Dante, running his finger over the carved stone, "but I can't be sure." He rose to his feet. "Cover it up and cut it out of the wall. I don't want it damaged."

"Yes, sir," said Karim, fingering two soldiers who ran off.

Dante turned around, staring out the small cave where the waves of seawater were inching closer. The inscription on the wall was far enough down to keep it hidden for centuries. His blood pressure was rising, and it was difficult to contain his passion for archeology. But keeping a cool head was essential in maintaining the respect of his men. Without warning, the memory of her returned. She was his secret Preston would never know.

"Do you know what it says?" asked Karim.

Dante regathered his thoughts. "Not yet. I'll examine it at the hotel. Canvass the area, check for more writing. Search everywhere, walls, rocks, ceiling, and ground. We don't have much time."

"Yes, sir," said Karim. He walked to the entrance and gave the order to four men.

Dante slipped out his cell phone, laid down again on the smelly kelp, and photographed the writing. Two soldiers entered carrying two diamond-tipped Reciprocating Saws. Dante stood up and stepped aside to let them begin while he checked the clarity of his photos. The other men were searching with their flashlights, but the sunlight was fading, and the cave was getting dark. The solid block took ten minutes to remove.

Dante whirled his hand in the air. "Move out!" he shouted.

The five soldiers followed him to the two black Cadillac Escalades parked on the sand. As Dirkman entered the truck, he smirked at him before slamming the door. Dante's phone pinged, a text had come in from Darla.

Within the next forty-eight hours. Be careful, baby.

CHAPTER 10
Max

"Who would want the world to die?" asked Max.

"I don't know," said Mandy. She rubbed her eyes hard then turned off the television. "This stuff is making my head hurt. Let's talk about something else."

"This is not going away. This is a real problem."

"I know," she said gazing down at him, "but it's one more thing we have to worry about." She sat on the edge of the bed. "I don't want to deal with this right now. It's too much."

Max hesitated. "Yeah, I get it."

Global was hunting them. The surrounding puffiness of her blue eyes revealed she was weary of their suppressive life and struggling with a shortage of sleep from nightmares.

Maybe we need a change of pace, thought Max.

The arks were laying on the table in the far corner of the room. Standing upright beside them, was a seven-foot-tall roll of transparent archival paper. Each scroll had been wrapped in the clear plastic as a protection from the elements.

What a job that was, thought Max, thinking back to the painstaking procedure.

It took three days to build a clean room and four days to encase the three scrolls. The book they'd found lying in the open tunnel was in a clear vacuum archival bag complete with a red release valve and resting alongside the scrolls.

"Dad should be back by now," she said.

"You know, dad," he said. "Send him out for a few things, and he comes back with the whole store."

"Do you think Preston is closing in?"

"No. His last email to Dante suggested he knows we're still alive, but he doesn't know where we are. I'm sure the Canary Islands is not on his hunting list. We're fortunate Ambassador Renaldo loves history and has kept this castle secret from the public. He doesn't want it turned into a museum, he wants to keep it. It's his pride and joy."

He remembered the first time he'd met the Ambassador and his family. It was two years ago after an earthquake shook Seville, Spain they attended a ceremony to move the bones of Christopher Columbus to a more secure location. Mandy had started talking to a young girl, and they became friends. Senona introduced her family, and the friendship began. The pleasant personalities of the two fathers made them instant bros. Since then, his dad has helped the Ambassador on many occasions, introducing him to federal officials able to work with the Spanish government on certain matters. Max's cell phone rang. He pulled it out of his black sweatpants pocket and held it to his ear.

"Hello," he said.

"Good day, Max. This is Jacián. How are you?"

"We're doing fine, Mr. Ambassador," said Max, enjoying the man's Spanish accent. His voice reminded him of the old actor, Ricardo Montalban, from the classic movie, *Star Trek: The Wrath of Khan*. Max touched 'speaker' on his iPhone so Mandy could listen in. "Were you able to get the items I asked for?"

"Yes, and that is the reason for calling you. They will be delivered to you tomorrow. I noticed whenever I ask how you are, you always answer in the plural. I guess it is a twin's perspective, is it not?"

"Yes, sir, it is," said Max, picturing the Ambassador sitting at his desk in the embassy, his shoulders back and his neck straight while speaking to him on the phone. His black hair and bronzed skin coupled with hazel eyes gave him an aristocratic charm. He was a barrel-chested man with thick arms, a true Spaniard who stood well over six feet tall. "It was kind of you to personally deliver our samples to the lab in Madrid. Your labeling them 'Top Secret' was ingenious. Has anyone questioned you about taking the samples when you left?"

"No, they would not question an official, and it was my pleasure to help you."

"Thank you so much, Ambassador. How's Senona? I hope she's

doing well."

"When you had us over for dinner a few weeks ago, I noticed it was a challenge for you to keep your eyes off her. She is beautiful and…," he paused, "…very young."

Mandy started throwing kisses at Max. He rolled his eyes.

"I meant no disrespect, sir. I know your daughter is sixteen years old and I would pursue her without your permission—no, wait, I'm not asking for your permission—hold it, your permission is not…," Max stopped. He was stumbling over his words like a total moron. "Sir, what I mean to say is—"

"I know what you are trying to say, Max," laughed the Ambassador. "It is good to hear the young man is still within the intellect. When she is ready in a few years, ask me, if you are still interested."

"Thank you, sir," said Max, embarrassed by his performance.

Mandy was holding her stomach; her face was apple red from laughing.

"Just out of curiosity, sir," he said, keeping an eye on his sister, "have there been any more inquiries about our location?"

Mandy quit the laughter and sat straight, her eyes wide with worry.

"Nothing has come to my attention. Like I told your father, no one will find you there. You are safe. Are you enjoying your time on the island?"

"Yes. Your home on the ocean is breathtaking, and we can't thank you enough for your kindness."

"Since your father has helped me many times, it is the least I can do. Well, I must go. Give my regards to your family. Goodbye, Max."

"Goodbye, sir, and thank you again." Max tapped the end icon.

"You sounded like a blubbering idiot," giggled Mandy.

"Can it," said Max, not enjoying the humiliation. "I can't help it if she's hot. She has the most beautiful gray eyes I've ever seen, and not to mention her bod—"

Max stopped talking. The venom had left him barren, unable to have children. And even if all the parts worked, who would want to marry a cripple? He turned away disgusted. "I don't want to talk about this anymore."

Mandy came from behind and wrapped her arms around his neck.

"I'm sorry, Max," she said, talking into his ear. "I didn't mean...."

"Forget it," he said, tapping her hand. "I'm going to find a cure, and you're going to help me."

"You got that right," she said, standing straight. "We'll kick this thing together. Now, can we work on the book? I love the fact we discovered the handwritten diary of Alexander the Great. With a mother like that, it's easy to believe he was a self-absorbed, spoiled brat who whined when he didn't get his way. Can you believe he admitted to him and his mother killing his father?"

Max eyed the scrolls sitting on the far table. Although anxious about the book, they had studied the scrolls first since they were more fragile. Six years ago, a rare parchment containing the actual handwriting of Alexander was found in an old marketplace in Greece, an ancient poem he'd wrote about his deceased friend, Hephaestion. The script was a perfect match to the scrolls, and after testing, their age put them at the time of Alexander the Great.

"Philip II was very abusive," added Max. "But I'm tired of the scrolls too. Get the book."

"I'm home!" shouted a voice.

Thumping footsteps were coming down the hallway. His six-foot-tall father stood in the doorway dressed in blue plaid shorts, a food-stained slate-blue T-shirt, and worn out flip-flops. He looked like a beach bum with a hobo beard and wild wavy brown hair highlighted by the sun. There was no trace of the old Jack from seven weeks ago.

"What are you guys up to?" asked Dad.

"Did you get my ice cream?" asked Max. Cookies and Cream was his favorite.

"Yes, and I got a McDonalds Frappé for you, Mandy, and both are in the fridge."

"Thanks!" said Mandy, and she dashed out of the room.

"Bring me a bowl of ice cream!" shouted Max. He turned to his father. "Any dirt on Preston?"

"No, it's a dead end, but I finally connected with Skimmer, and if we have to run, he'll help us. How's the hack into Global?"

"They altered their firewall again," said Max, "but I'll break through. Ambassador Renaldo said all the things I ordered will be here tomorrow. How are we doing money-wise?"

"Good," said Dad, sitting on the bed. "The Ambassador has given us enough to survive on for a long time. I just wish I had more on Preston. Mandy is feeling the effects of being confined, and I can't think of anything to help her."

"She'll be all right," said Max. "We were about to work on the book when you came home."

The study of the book would be more difficult than the scrolls. The paper had the yellowish appearance of old papyrus and was flexible like cloth, yet it took a straightedge razor and their father's full strength to slice off a minute piece from the bottom corner of the last page. In Madrid, the lab's Accelerated Mass Spectrometer didn't detect any elements on our periodic table. Max leaned back in his seat knowing the world would have to wait to learn of these discoveries; their lives depended on it. He couldn't wait to test the orange-gold metal of the amulet piece.

Mandy came in sipping her Frappe drink. "I say finding out what the book says will answer a lot of questions for us." She handed Max his bowl of ice cream, and he began scoffing it down.

"Let's get started," said Mandy.

She set down her drink and slipped on a pair of white archival gloves. At the far table, there was a hiss when she pressed the release valve on the archival sac, and then slid the book out.

"It's amazing this ginormous book only weighs a pound," said Mandy, setting it down in front of Max.

It was two feet high, nineteen inches wide, and two inches thick with a black hard cover he swore was an undiscovered ore. Swirling lines of an orange-gold metal were interweaved within the solid cover, producing beautiful delicate patterns, and upon seeing it in daylight it took their breath away. Because of their being chased by freaks, they had decided to keep the book and the amulet piece apart. Jacián knew a trusted jeweler on the island where the segment was set into a large gold belt buckle, which their dad kept hidden beneath his shirt. Although its size was over five inches wide, it only weighed an ounce. It was the most awesome belt buckle Max had ever seen.

His father put on a pair of white gloves, then took the magnifying glass from the desk drawer and slowly ran it over the book's cover.

"Could the Greeks have written this book?" asked Mandy.

"No," said Max, adjusting the white gloves on his fingers. "This is beyond their science."

Their dad stood straight. "There're no signs of aging, no scratches, no pits, and no drying. It's not leather or plastic. This may be a hoax."

"Father," said Mandy, "remember how hard it was to cut off a sliver of the paper? And that science machine didn't detect any known elements. If this is a hoax and the book was put in that awful cave, why did they leave behind the writings of Alexander the Great? Sometimes science gets in the way of reason, and that's where man loses his logic. Just because you don't know what it is, or how it's made, doesn't mean an ancient culture didn't create this. Why does modern man always think no one is smarter than him? Remember the Siberian Tiger? Scientists swore they didn't exist because they said tigers couldn't live in snow, and what about our oceans? For years, they taught the bottom of the oceans were void of life; now they know they're full of life they never knew existed. You need to get past the 'it can't be' mindset and concentrate on the reality in front of you."

Max was speechless. Mandy's reasoning was outstanding.

"Those were excellent arguments," said Dad, smiling. "I'll make sure to keep an open mind."

Mandy raised her chin with pride. "You're welcome, Dr. Williams." She frowned at Max. "See? I'm not as dumb as you think. Now let's get to work. Open the book."

Max smiled and shook his head. *Wow.* He couldn't help being impressed. She was on an average education level except for math where D's ruled, but her common sense was way better than his. He'd never tell her that because she would forever rub it in.

Her gift is something I'll never have, he reasoned, *too many numbers running through my brain.*

"Earth to Max?" said Mandy.

"Yeah, yeah," he said, wanting to shut her up.

He was careful in lifting the cover when his father grabbed his hand, stopping him from opening it wide. He used the magnifying glass again, examining the inside cover, and then turned it on its side inspecting the binding.

"This is unbelievable," said Dad, pulling a chair beside Max and sitting. He handed him the magnifier. "I've never seen this before. I have no idea what the cover is made of, and there's no glue or binding of any type. Check it out."

Max took the magnifier and started at the top edge of the inside cover, looking for anything that would tell him it was some kind of paper or perhaps plastic. When he got to the binding, he stopped. "The pages are fused."

"Okay, they're glued," said Mandy. "So what."

"No, not glued, fused," said Max, "as in melded. Regular paper would burn due to the heat that's needed, but these pages have been melted together. This hasn't been invented yet."

Max's mind began working the process, trying to determine how they created the fusion, but without knowing the chemical analysis of the paper, he kept hitting roadblocks.

"It seems the mystery of this book is deepening," said Mandy. "Go for it, Max."

Max nodded and turned the first page. The yellowish paper was blank of any writing. Max skimmed over it with the magnifier.

"Well?" asked Dad.

"It's loaded with unrecognizable fibers just like the sliver, but nothing else."

"Move on," said Mandy.

The next page was blank. The following one was empty too. Max kept turning pages, wanting to see something—*anything*. He gripped all the sheets and skimmed through the book. There was no writing. Nothing.

CHAPTER 11
Dante, Losari

It was 4 a.m. under a moonless sky. The air was a warm seventy degrees, and the wind was at four miles per hour.

Perfect, thought Dante.

The Ambassador's ninety room mansion resembled something out of medieval times with scrolled carvings surrounding the grand arched doorway and the tall stained-glass windows. Dark ivy-covered most of the gray stone walls and the four visible turrets. A paved driveway looped in front of the thirty-two steps leading to the massive double doors where giant lion heads held round knockers the size of car tires. There were thirty security guards around the residence stationed at strategic points.

Did he know we were coming? thought Dante. *Doubt it. But he does know we're hunting for the Williams's, so the extra protection is just him being cautious.*

There were nine guards on the ground with dogs, eight in the house, three on each balcony of the two occupied bedrooms, and ten patrolling the perimeter of the roof. With security cameras on the trees and the building, they're mission would be harder, but they could handle it.

Global had prepped Dante and his ten-man team with the newest technology. Their black airtight uniforms included enough oxygen for ten hours. The bulletproof tinted face mask was also a digital display linked to ten of Global's private satellites. Distance, temperature, wind—everything was there. The Neural Cognition System or NCS worked with cranial sensors embedded in their helmets, giving them complete control of their digitized face masks. All they had to do was think of what they wanted to see, and it appeared on their display. And everything was full-color High-Def, unlike night vision goggles with tints of green or yellow, they saw everything as if it were daylight.

Dante had pulled up a complete blueprint of the mansion on his screen, tracking heat signatures inside and outside the home. His team were the green dots; the moving red ones were all the guards and dogs. The Ambassador and his family were blue.

Crouched down behind a bush, he shifted his position, feeling his black uniform adjust. Dante recalled the first-time Preston took him to his Tesla Lab beneath his lavish mansion in Colorado. There the scientists had collected spider silk proteins from the milk of goats and combined them with carbon nanotubes, creating an impenetrable cloth responding to pressure, heat, and touch. The exact science never interested Dante, just the needed results. Their Silk Tube Suits or ST suits were soft and lightweight and could stop armor-piercing rounds; stiffening to the impact and dispersing the energy in a split second, with no harm to the wearer. Everything they wore including their helmets, boots, and gloves, were made from Silk Tubes, except for their face masks which were bulletproof plastic. But given time, Tesla would change that too. With everything weighing at only five pounds, maneuverability was comfortable and easy.

They carried state-of-the-art black *PX38* rifles complete with integrated noise suppressors able to spit out four thousand rounds a minute. The 'smart bullets' would dissolve inside flesh in under two minutes, thus making them untraceable. It also incorporated grenades, canister launchers, and a light sitting atop its long-pitted barrel. When Karim had seen the weapon with its thick skeletal butt for the first time, he was sure it could take down a rocket in space. He and Karim also carried two Glock 94 pistols, a standard gun used by police and many citizens, but nothing compared to what Dante felt in the Velcroed pocket on his thigh.

His black Terro gun carried rocket bullets. When a hand wrapped around the dark grip of the weapon, its stainless-steel barrel would extend from four inches to twelve inches. Its one hundred fifty programmable tungsten bullets were no bigger than a .22 round, but packed a punch like a .600 Magnum, exploding like a mini-bomb within its target. At the barrels end was a tiny red light, a sensor able to read your targets physical stats like heartbeat or brain waves, and then display it in a hologram which rose from the small silver plate above the grip. From there you can make any adjustments necessary to pinpoint your kill. It could shoot around corners, up tall buildings, or into a room of crowded people where it would search and kill its target. With a speed of forty-eight hundred feet per second, the rocket ammo could blow through any bulletproof shield. The cost to develop the weapon was astronomical. Therefore, only two Terros existed, and both were kept hidden in the Dungeon where only he and Preston had access.

And you, Dirkman, he shifted his sight to the soldier on his mask, *your name is on one bullet.*

One of Global's best inventions was the Upstar device, a small black portable EMP pistol with its two inch, close-ended barrel. It could neutralize all silicon chips up to a mile away, except for their devices which were impervious. And then there were the black Ipon disks about the size of a hockey puck. When placed on a dead or live victim, a single tap to the small green dot activated a cloud of Carnivorous Piconites or CP's. In under two minutes, all flesh, bones, and blood were gone. When done, the piconites would dissolve into an odorless gas. Global left nothing to chance.

Though Preston loved money, he refused to sell many of Global's outstanding creations, claiming they were for his Oviepa, an elaborate complex being built at the bottom of the Atlantic Ocean.

A place not easily reached with normal weapons, thought Dante. *Whatever he's planning, it's going to cost the world big time.*

Having absolute power was always on Preston's mind, his life reflected that. The man hated rules and regulations thereby finding loopholes to get what he wanted. If there was anyone who was certifiable, it was him, and his taking over the world was not out of his reach. *Not with Global behind him.* His earpiece crackled. The screen showed two men ready with Upstars were positioned outside at opposite corners of the mansion.

"Phase One," said Dante. "Go."

He watched his screen light up as the Upstars took out everything electrical, including all the guards' headsets and walkie-talkies.

"Phase two. Go."

Dante heard the deep thuds of the silenced weapons and watched nine red dots on the ground stopped moving. The guards and dogs were taken out.

"Phase three. Go."

Dante and his team stood up and ran towards the house. He watched on his screen as his men placed Ipon disks on the dead guards and dogs; their heat signatures were fading. They entered the house and took out the eight guards and again, used the Ipons. As they ran up the stairs, he could hear the low fizzing sounds of the Ipons working their magic. Four of the team split off and headed for the roof. Dante checked his screen. The ten red dots on the roof disappeared.

"I love this job," said Dirkman, trotting behind him.

"Cut the chatter!" ordered Dante. "Phase four. Go."

The men on the roof repelled down in front of each bedroom and took out the six guards. Now all that remained was the sleeping Ambassador, his wife, and their sixteen-year-old daughter, Senona.

"I get to have fun with the girl, right?" asked Dirkman.

"Stay focused," he commanded. Dante's hatred was growing stronger with each moment. *Getting rid of Preston's watchdog will be a pleasure.* "Get the girl and meet me in the Ambassador's bedroom." Dirkman nodded and ran the other way.

Dante pulled up a chair and sat next to the Renaldo's bed. It was obvious the furniture was created by the renowned Gina with artisan scroll work fit for a king.

He has good taste, thought Dante.

His team surrounded the bed, aiming their guns at the husband and wife. Dante saw a blinking green light on the corner of his face mask, the Sikorsky Black Hawk helicopter was on the roof and waiting for them. He nudged Jacián's face with the barrel of his *PX38*, and the man jumped to sitting up. His wife, Elena, screamed in horror. Dante punched her face, and she fell unconscious onto her husband.

"Good evening, Ambassador," said Dante. "Are you comfy?"

"Who are you and what do you want?" demanded Jacián, holding his wife in his arms.

Dante lifted his face mask and turned on the blue flowered porcelain lamp beside the bed. "Listen, Jacián, we can do this easy or hard, but I will only ask you once. If you don't tell me what I want to know, your wife will die, and then if you still refuse, Senona will die."

At the foot of the bed, Dirkman held Senona with a knife to her throat. The teenager had short black hair and big gray eyes, a waif of a girl whom he was sure couldn't have weighed over ninety pounds. She was crying and trembling.

"She is harmless," said Jacián. "Release her and deal with me."

Dante doubted if this man had ever yelled at anyone. He was calm and relaxed, despite having the lives of his wife and daughter threatened.

"You are a noble man, sir," said Dante, "but I need answers. Again, I will only ask you once. Where are Jack, Mandy, and Max Williams?"

The blood drained from Jacián's face.

"I'm not a patient man," said Dante, "You got fifteen seconds."

Jacián's breathing sped up; he trembled. With watery eyes, he focused on his whimpering daughter.

All good signs, thought Dante.

"Canary Islands," said Jacián with a solemn voice. "They are on the Canary Islands in the Castillo Solana." He bowed his head in shame. "Now please, go."

"You're a good man," said Dante. "Is that your cell phone over there on the nightstand?"

"Yes," answered Jacián, "but why do you—"

Dante raised his hand for the Ambassador to stop speaking. Karim tossed the phone to him, and he slid his face mask back down. The screen connected to the phone, revealing all its recent calls. The initials JMM displayed the area code of the Canary Islands, and it dialed the number.

I love technology, he thought, listening to the phone ring in his headset.

A female voice answered. "Hello."

"Is this Beth Perez?" said Dante, watching the display on his mask. Mandy's voice and location were confirmed.

"No, who are you?"

"I'm sorry, I must have the wrong number, but you have a nice voice. Sorry to bother you."

"No problem. Goodbye."

He severed the connection.

"It's a go," he said, standing up. "Secure the area."

"Hey!" shouted Dirkman. "I'm taking time here!"

A flood of hatred consumed every cell in Dante's body. He yanked the Terro gun from his pocket and fired. A silver bullet shot out in a streak of red light. Dirkman's head jolted back as the slug blasted through his face mask, spraying blood in all directions. His body hit the floor with a loud thud. Splattered with blood, Senona screamed and jumped onto the bed, crawling into her father's arms.

Dante pointed the gun at each man. "Anyone else want to argue?"

No one replied.

"Good." He returned the Terro gun to his pocket. "Karim, get an Ipon on Dirkman and activate the Cleaners."

"Yes, sir."

Karim took from his sleeve pocket a small black oblong pill and set both the Ipon disk and the capsule on Dirkman's body. He pressed the green button on the Ipon and it dissolved into piconites, spreading all over Dirkman's slain corpse, devouring him. The Cleaner pill also activated, sending black clouds swarming through the room, searching out Dirkman's DNA like voracious locusts, consuming any remains.

"Who are you people?" asked Jacián.

Dante nodded at Karim, then left the room. As he headed up the stairs to the roof, he heard three gunshots.

The Renaldo's are dead.

He spoke into his headset. "Evac in ten."

"Aye, sir," came the replies.

***

Losari

Rivers of sweat were pouring down Losari's face, his pounding heart felt like it was ready to burst. Every grenade had been expended; only one magazine remained, and it was in his rifle. He raced down the tunnel keeping his *PX38* aimed and ready, the attached light led the way. Because it was his job to map the route for the cave team, the way back to the exit was easy. He shivered at the memory when they took a break. His three bald-headed friends had removed their headgear, and that's when the spiders attacked. The insects smothered them like killer bees. Their faces swelled to the hundreds of bites; their screams still echoed in his ears.

The passage was dark and littered with boulders, climbing over them was difficult, and he had to be cautious not to tear the fabric of his camo-suit. What he didn't need right now was the yellow blinking light on his face mask telling him he was running out of air. A loud plopping noise came from behind. In a panic, he swung around and fired several shots. He aimed the light. It was water dripping into a small puddle.

Easy, Losari, he thought to himself, lowering his gun. *Save the ammo.*

He took a long breath, hoping to slow his trembling and allay the gruesome fear engulfing him. It was affecting his judgment, and this was no time to lose it. Perhaps if they had worn their ST suits, they would have been protected, but because the Williams's made it out alive, camouflage fatigues with NCS helmets were all they wore.

I should have gone with my gut, he thought.

A solid red light blared on his mask. "OXYGEN DEPLETED!"

He heaved his breaths, trying to inhale the remaining air in his suit, but there was none, so he took off his helmet. Shuffling and low gurgles came from down the tunnel, and he shined the light. Thousands of spiders were crawling on the walls, ceiling, and ground, moving in waves and heading straight for him. Thrust into hysteria, he roared laying down a barrage of gunfire, and then ran, leaping over impossible boulders and sliding on wet moss struggling not to fall. Terrified and shaking, he reached the lava tube and ran for his life without looking behind. He could see the end of the tunnel, but—*wait!*

"No!" he cried out.

The door was shut. With all his might, he bashed the skeletal butt of his rifle against the hard stone over and over again, but with no results, so he turned around and flattened himself against the wall. The spiders were almost upon him. He fired into the swarm, holding down the trigger until there were no more bullets. There was a hard bite on his neck and he winced, smacking the insect. The squashed spider in his hand was a Black Widow. Another bite. He jumped around slapping his hands all over his bald head, desperate to kill anything. Then there was a deathlike silence.

The swarm stopped ten feet away, watching him. Overwhelmed with fear, he released his bowels. There was a sharp sting on his cheek, and when he opened his mouth to yell, the insect raced in. The bite on his tongue forced him to furiously choke and gag, but the insect had somehow hooked into the soft palate. A stinger rammed into the roof of his mouth and he screamed to the shocking pain radiating into his jaw and down his throat. He reached in with his fingers, gripped the bug and ripped it out, taking a chunk of meat with it. It was a small white scorpion. In anger he threw it on the ground and mashed it with his boot. His swelling tongue was beginning to block his air passage. The muscles in his face and neck started twitching. There was movement on his legs.

Through blurred vision he saw black hordes crawling up his pants. Before he could swat them, his body went rigid, his muscles solidified, and he fell to the floor convulsing. The last thing Losari saw were hairy legs crawling across his open eyes.

CHAPTER 12
Max

"An empty book?" said Max, surprised.

"We need lemon juice and a hair dryer," said Mandy.

Max turned to her.

"What?" she said. "It was in the movie, *National Treasure*. Remember when they were trying to find the invisible map on the back of the Declaration of Independence? Wasn't that stuff real?"

"Yes, it was," said Max. "How do you think we should proceed, Dad?"

"We don't know the properties of this paper, and I don't want to ruin a whole sheet trying. Let's make a three-inch rectangle. Start at the top right corner and go down four inches."

"Okay," said Max. He looked for Mandy, but she was gone. "Yo! Weirdo! Where are you?"

She came running into his bedroom holding a bowl of cut lemons and her hair dryer.

"I've been washing my face every morning with lemon juice," she said, "it's a good cleanser, and I had cut lemons in my bathroom. Be careful, don't ruin the book."

"Dad, I'll do the lemon juice," said Max. "You do the heat."

"Done," he said, and he plugged the hair dryer into a surge strip.

Max soaked several Q-tips with lemon juice and moistened the three-by-four-inch top corner of the page. Their father was running the hair dryer over the solution as he moved downward. Nothing appeared.

"This isn't working," said Max. "If it was invisible ink the heat should have revealed letters."

"Before we move on," said Mandy, sipping her drink, "let's have dinner."

"It's six o'clock," said Dad, "and I think better with a full stomach.

Let's go downstairs and talk about this." He raised his hand towards the doorway. "Max, lead the way."

As they left the room, Mandy turned to flick off the light switch when she said, "Look!"

The opened book seemed to have a slight glow. Max stared, bewildered at what he was seeing.

"Move," said Max, trying to push them out of the way. "I have to get back there."

They stepped aside allowing him to pass. The nearer he got to the book, the more he could see letters faintly glowing.

"Holy cow," said Mandy, standing to Max's left.

"It has to be the ultraviolet light on the fish tank," said Max. "It's the only light in the room that's on. Dad, close the door. Mandy, get my portable black light, cabinet three, bottom right drawer."

The paper itself wasn't aglow, just the strange lettering. Mandy handed him the black light. It was fifteen inches long with a short black handle containing a dimmer and the on/off switch. As a protection to the user, a black dome covered the light.

"Take a seat, peeps," said Max, grinning wide. "Now we're archeologists."

They sat in the chairs on both sides of him. He adjusted the intensity of the UV light to half strength and then held it over the page. The paper sizzled and smoked.

"Wait!" said Mandy, and she pulled Max's arm away.

"Chill!" said Max, yanking his hand back and replacing the light over the paper again.

"You're ruining the book!" said Mandy.

"He's not ruining it," said Dad, grinning. "It's a chemical reaction created to reveal the writing."

"Oh…," said Mandy. "Sorry."

Solid black rows of sentences came to life.

"Some letters are familiar," said Dad. "I see Phoenician, Egyptian, Greek, and Roman, but these here," he skimmed his finger above a line on the page, "I've never seen before. This is a new dialect. There has to be a key. Without it, we won't be able to decipher the writing."

"Where could the key be?" asked Mandy. "We left nothing behind in the cave. What if the key is where the book was found? Could it have been carved into the alcove? I'm letting you both know right now, I'm never ever going back to that cave."

Dad smiled. "We don't have to. You took pictures, right?"

"Yes!" she said, "and they're still in the camera. I'll get it."

Mandy ran out of the room and was back a few seconds later, handing Max the SD card. His dad moved his chair away. Max pushed Nessie's joystick sideways and all her wheels shifted to a ninety-degree angle, rolling him to his left. His father and Mandy joined him. He slid the SD card into the side of the main monitor and the screen came to life. The first picture was them and Rafael standing in front of the entrance to St. Michael's Cave in Gibraltar.

"How could he have done that to us?" said Mandy. "He was like an uncle."

The day they disappeared was the day the police found Rafael's body floating in the Mediterranean Sea with a bullet in his head. The authorities never found out who murdered him. When Max was in the hospital, Ambassador Renaldo had ordered the local police to guard him and his family. After they left the hospital and came here, their father put the family in lock-down. No outings, no stores, no nothing, not even sitting out on the balconies or porches during the day. Mandy protested saying she loved watching the sunrises and sunsets, and seeing them through a window didn't cut it, but Dad didn't give in, and while grumbling, she agreed. Their dad even changed his appearance so he could go to the store, hence, the boozer look.

"A terrible uncle," said Dad, tapping the right arrow key on the keyboard and skimming through the pictures.

Ten photos later, the lava tube displayed. The book and scrolls were resting on the obsidian shelf where they had found them. The light from the torch gave the photo a yellowish tint.

"I'm going black and white," said Max. "I think we'll get better details."

"Make a grid," said Dad. "The key can be the size of a postage stamp. Some civilizations didn't want their secrets revealed but also felt if they didn't leave hints, the gods would punish them. Let's start at the top left and zoom in. With six eyes studying each section, there's a better chance of finding something."

A chill ran up his spine, and he shivered. Max wondered if his sister and father were sensing the same thing. The glimmering black stone in the photograph projected an eerie sense of danger. Mandy slipped her arm into his and squeezed.

"I feel it too," she said.

"Definitely weird," said Dad.

After three hours of dissecting each photo, Mandy slumped back in her chair.

"This is killing me," she said. "Maybe there is no way to decipher the book."

"I doubt that," said Dad. "Someone who put so much work into this beautiful book would leave a means to translate it."

Mandy stood up and stretched her arms, making a loud yawn. "I'm going to make dinner. Garlic pasta with salad and bread. When I call you, you'd better come." She left the room.

"Maybe after a good rest we'll find it," said Dad, and he closed the book.

Max yawned, stretching his arms. "I need fresh air."

Mandy walked back in the room. "I have an idea. This may or may not work, but at least we'll have tried."

She grabbed the black light, flicked it on, and ran the light over the cover of the book. Nothing happened.

"Oh well," she said, turning off the light. "It was worth a try."

"Wait a minute," said Max, taking the light from her. "You may have something there."

"Adjust the intensity," said Dad.

Max moved the slide lever to 'maximum,' and turned it on. With the speed of a snail, he passed the light over the cover. About a quarter inch from the top, a crinkly burning sound preceded clouds of white smoke. Max kept going for another two inches.

"Stop," said Dad. "Let's see what it did."

Max blew the smoke away. A one-inch wide band became visible, and within this, orange-gold letters shined.

"It's the key!" said Mandy. "Are those metal letters the same metal as the artwork on the book?"

"That's incredible!" said Max, elated. "How did they do that? The ore—"

His father interrupted. "Max, I'm sure the translated book will have your answers."

"You're right," agreed Max. "I'll have their language deciphered by tomorrow."

"You will come down for dinner," demanded Mandy. "You need your strength, and you will not miss a meal."

"Stop telling me what to do," said Max, annoyed. "The sooner I decipher this, the sooner we'll know what's in the book."

"Mandy's right," said Dad. "This will be an all-nighter, so a good meal is in order. Mandy, do your thing, but we'll eat up here. Now, let's get this done."

CHAPTER 13
Mandy

"Dad! Mandy!" shouted Max. "Come here, hurry!"

Mandy leapt out of her bed and ran into Max's bedroom. It was 6 a.m., and she was still dressed in her white Capris and blue flowered blouse from the day before. The brain-twisting ordeal from the night had given her a headache, and she hit the sack at 3 a.m.

"Maxxus Williams," she said standing in the doorway with her hands firm on her hips, "you scare me like that again, and I'll make you cry like a sissy girl." She looked around the room. "Where's your father?"

"I'm here," said Dad, groaning as he lifted himself off the floor. "Max, don't do that again."

"You fell off the bed?" asked Mandy, holding back her laughter.

"Yes, thanks to your brother," he said, rubbing his head, "and it's not funny. I almost had a heart attack."

Mandy chuckled at the sight of her dad. His brown hair was sticking out in all directions.

"You won't believe what this book is about," said Max, smiling wide as he worked his laptop. "Take a seat. This is going to blow your minds."

Their father plopped himself in a chair next to Max, still rubbing his head. Mandy sat to the right of her brother. The excitement on his face seemed like he'd just discovered gold.

"Now," she said, "what's so important that you made your parental unit fall off the bed?"

"After Dad and I finished deciphering the language he fell asleep, so I used the black light on the back cover of the Book and look what it found. This is a flattened image of what the red amulet would look like when completed. Check out the small writing beneath the two bottom stones." He held the magnifying glass near the bottom of the scroll work.

"Whoa!" said Mandy. "Are you saying this Book is about the lost continent of Atlantis?"

"Yes, and it's written by the Atlanteans themselves," said Max, "which explains why we couldn't decipher the writing. They have a unique alphabet which contains letters from an assortment of languages because according to lore, Atlanteans were also known as the Ancients."

Mandy was trying to swallow what she'd just heard. Atlantis was a legend, a fable; nothing about it was real. It was a fabricated story passed down from person-to-person, and everyone got it wrong.

It can't be real, she thought.

Her father was resting back with his arms folded across his chest, fingering his beard. His face was scrunched in thought; his gray eyes focused on the picture. He too was trying to figure out what was going on.

"Are you sure you got it right?" asked Mandy. "It seems so…so ridiculous. Atlantis never existed."

"I can only tell you what I've read," said Max, "and I'm sure of the translation."

"Are you offline?" asked Mandy.

"Yes, máme. I disconnected the Wi-Fi on the laptop and the landlines on the computers. For now, the hack into Global has to wait. If anyone even tries to break in, my viruses will obliterate their whole system. No one's getting this."

"Before we go on," said Dad, he seemed to come out of his stupor, "have you transferred this info to a flash drive for safekeeping?"

"I did what you told me," said Max. "Everything concerning Atlantis, including the whole translation of the Book, is now on my laptop in case we have to run. Nothing is on the computers, it's all been deleted."

"I told you to put it on the laptop?"

"Yep."

"I don't remember saying that, nor getting in your bed."

"You dozed off on the desk, snoring like a drunk hippo. I told you to go to sleep and you flopped onto my bed. In all fairness, it was 5 a.m."

"I have no recollection of that."

Mandy laughed aloud. *My dad's the greatest.*

"Finding out the Book was written by Atlanteans was not the reason I shouted your names," said Max. "What got me excited is now we have the coordinates to assemble the Key to Atlantis."

"What key?" asked Dad, straightening up.

"Look at this," smiled Max.

He tapped the keyboard and a list appeared.

EARTH:	28° 44' 31.88" N	13° 49' 33.41" W
AIR:	40° 45' 47.18" N	73° 58' 11.94" W
WATER:	6° 50' 28.3" S	66° 29' 50.71" W
FIRE:	36° 46' 14.50" N	12° 03' 01.86" E

"The Key to Atlantis lies with connecting the four amulet pieces on the cover of the Book," said Max, as he typed. "It says the Book will alert you to which space each red crystal is to be placed, something about the gold star in the middle of the cut-out glowing. The locations of each amulet piece are as follows: *Fire* is on the volcanic island of Pantelleria in the Sicilian Strait. *Water* is in the Amazon Rain Forest in Brazil and—hold it," he stopped talking and continued typing. "We found the *Earth* piece in Leonora's Cave, yet it says it's here with us on the Canary Islands and…how could the *Air* piece be at the Global building in New York?"

"That makes no sense," said Jack.

"It makes perfect sense," said Mandy, hoping to impress them again with her keen mind. "It's clear the creators of this Book are light years ahead of us. I think the Book is designed to follow the locations of the pieces as they move. But what's more important, if this is right, how did Preston Black-heart get a piece of the amulet?"

"I don't know," said Max, "but I know for him to possess the power of Atlantis, he has to join the four elements of Earth on this Book. Without them, he has nothing."

"Which he will never get because we have it," said Mandy.

"This whole thing of ancient GPS is absurd," said Dad. "I'm not buying it. There's no proof."

Mandy sat forward and made eye contact with her father. "Jack, nothing we've found makes sense. We discovered Leonora's Cave under the Mediterranean Sea connecting Europe to Africa. We found the actual diary of Alexander the Great written by himself. And most important, we came upon this Book written by real Atlanteans. As Mr. Spock would say, "When you have eliminated the impossible, whatever remains, however improbable, must be the truth." He was so wise.""

"That's a Sherlock Holmes quote," said Max, "not Mr. Spock."

Their father grunted, shaking his head in disagreement.

"For now, let's agree to disagree," said Mandy. "Maybe there's an explanation further on in the Book."

"I'll accept that," said Dad. "Read on."

Max continued, "It says the Atlanteans hid the remaining three sections of the amulet all over the world. The *Earth* piece stayed with the Book, and both were guarded by a Greek named Aeschylus."

"Who's he?" asked Mandy.

"What I found hidden within the pages of the Book will answer that," said Max.

Mandy never noticed the small flat piece of papyrus resting on Max's lap. It was the size of a regular sheet of paper and wrapped in clear archival plastic. He set it on the desk in front of him.

"It looks like brand new papyrus," said Dad. "How can that be?"

"I don't know," said Max, "but whatever chemicals they used to make this Book paper, it must have preserved the papyrus."

"Can you both stop being scientists for a moment?" said Mandy. "We need to move on."

"That's asking for the impossible," chuckled Dad, "but we'll try."

"The papyrus has a date of 48 B.C.," said Max. "Aeschylus was a

Greek scholar in the Library of Alexandria. He rescued this Book and the scrolls from being destroyed in the fire caused by Julius Caesar when he tried to overtake the city of Alexandria from King Ptolemy XII. Aeschylus feared the Library would burn to the ground, so he took the most valuable possessions of the Library and escaped through a secret tunnel. His mentor had told him if the relics were threatened, he should take them to Abyla, a place where one of the Pillars of Heracles stood. He had instructed the people there to help him, and they did. Abyla is now Ceuta, Spain where Monte Hacho sits, and within this low-lying mountain is the cave we came out of."

The doorbell rang.

"I'll get it," said Mandy. "It's probably Max's junk coming early."

"Check the front window first," said Dad.

She nodded to him then jogged to her bedroom, pondering over the new information. *Could it be the real Atlantis?* Her thoughts went back to the Hollywood movies and the hundreds of books on the subject, all written as if fact. Nevertheless, here, in this giant Book, discovered beneath a gazillion tons of water in a lava cave, they had found actual text claiming to be written by Atlanteans. She turned into her room, ignoring the white furniture and the unmade bed, and headed straight for the seven-foot-high arched window.

I think we discovered the motherload.

She peeked out the sheer white curtains. From there, she had a full view of the castle's front where a Dragon Blood Tree was the center in the paved circular driveway. A brown UPS truck was parked. A loud boom shook the building, and she stumbled to keep her balance.

They blew out the front door!

Stomping boots and clicking rifles entered the house. She bolted down the hallway and into Max's room where he was sliding his laptop into Nessie's inner pocket beside his left thigh. Their father was cramming stuff into Max's backpack. She locked the door.

"We're taking the tunnel," whispered Dad. "Mandy, get the backpack."

Pounding footsteps were coming up the stairs. Mandy slipped on the pack as her dad pulled the Armoire away from the wall. Max zoomed into the tunnel, and Mandy followed. She turned and saw her father fastening the inside locks.

"Let's go," he said in a low voice, "and no talking until I say."

Mandy jogged alongside their dad down the long passage while Max drove in front of them holding a glow stick.

She glanced back. *How did they find us?*

The only people knowing their location was the Ambassador and his family. *Senona.* When the Ambassador found out about Preston, he tightened the security around their mansion, which meant Senona was most likely fine.

They must have found us some other way, maybe Global.

It was a half mile trek to the outside shed where a mini-van waited. Their father thought it a good idea to have an escape vehicle.

Just then, a barrage of machine gun fire echoed through the tunnel.

CHAPTER 14
Mandy

"Mandy, turn around," whispered Dad. He dug in the backpack. "I need a flashlight. I'm going ahead to check it out. The two of you wait five minutes, then come."

A fearful dread coursed through Mandy. If their father was caught, she didn't want to imagine what Preston would do to him to get to Max. The thought was horrifying.

"Dad, let me go," she said in a hushed tone. "I'm faster than you."

He flicked his flashlight on. "I can't put you in that kind of danger. You stay and protect Max."

"Just before I put the laptop away," said Max, "I caught a glimpse of the Madeira Islands. I think we should go there."

"Then it's the Madeira's," said Dad. "And keep your voices down."

Her father hurried off, his light faded away leaving only theirs aglow. Mandy slipped the backpack onto the back of Nessie and then studied their surroundings. Dangling roots and dried out tubers covered the earthen walls and ceiling of the old tunnel. The tinkles of dripping water, along with the smell of mold and dirt reminded her of the cave. She wanted out of there now. A soft hum came from below.

Max said in a low voice, "Step onto the foot platforms. Once you're on, they'll lift you about six inches off the floor."

Two black footplates were lowering in front of her feet.

"When did you install these?" she asked.

"About a week ago."

She stepped onto the plates and held onto Nessie's handles. "If you do over five miles an hour with me on this, I'll pull every hair out of your head."

Max let out a low minacious laugh.

"Don't mess with me, Max, I can do bad things from back here."

"Hang on and don't let go."

"Dad said to give him five minutes."

"I'm not waiting that long."

Max unsnapped the black cover on his left armrest revealing Nessie's controls. Three vertical rows of colorful buttons and toggle switches filled the ten-inch rectangular unit. How he remembered what each one did was mind-boggling. He tapped a small yellow square, and two high beams rose from the front of each armrest, lighting the way ahead of them.

"Aren't those going to drain your battery?" she asked.

"Not this kind of battery. It'll last a good fifty years without a recharge."

"What?" she said, upset he'd didn't tell her about his creation. "Why the secret?"

"It's not a secret. I don't mean to keep anything from you or dad, it's just that I forget. The idea came about a month ago, but my mind was so bogged down with getting everything right with Nessie; I forgot to tell you. Sorry."

It was typical of Max to forget the simple things, but it was no excuse to forget her. She slapped his head.

"Ouch!" said Max.

"Never do that again. I mean it."

"Fine," said Max, massaging the side of his head. "There's no time to tell you about the latest stuff, so if you see something new appear, don't hit me. Now, hang on."

Mandy gripped Nessie's handles. On his right armrest, Max pushed the black toggle switch. Nessie bucked, then shot down the tunnel at light speed. Max steered with the joystick swerving side-to-side to avoid fallen debris, forcing Mandy to hold on for dear life.

"Slow down!" she said, her face contorting from the fierce wind.

He pushed the joystick more. Mandy's knuckles whitened around the handles as Nessie sped up. Getting decapitated by a dangling root was a reality, so ducking and shifting to the sides was a matter of life or death.

He's a dead man! thought Mandy.

As they zoomed forward, a light at the end was getting brighter. A dark silhouette appeared. Max slowed down Nessie.

"It's dad," he said.

Nessie came to a stop. Mandy stepped off the plates and punched Max in the arm.

"Idiot," she said, trying to regain her senses from the wild ride.

Max was smirking as he rubbed his arm.

"The perimeter is clear," said Dad. "Let's board."

They entered the shed through an opening in the wall they had already widened for Nessie to go through. Mandy closed the tunnel door, noting the rusted wheel barrel attached to the hatchway. Their father was great with masonry; she couldn't tell the difference between the old stone and the new patch. Max was already driving Nessie up the rear ramp of the dark green Kneelvan with black tinted windows. She hopped into the front seat.

"I hope this thing does more than a hundred," said Mandy, buckling herself in. The gray leather dash board was filled with every type of high-tech.

"Max, belt yourself in," said Dad, "and use the wall hooks to brace Nessie."

"Got it," said Max.

"Oh no!" said Mandy. "We forgot the scrolls!"

There was silence.

"I can't believe we did that," said Dad. "Imagine Preston claiming he'd found the lost scrolls from the Library of Alexandria."

"But we have the Key to Atlantis," said Max, "the greatest find in all history. If the legend is true, they had an energy source that dwarfs anything we have today, and we don't want Preston to have it. Now let's get back to the Book," he said, slipping the laptop out of Nessie's inner pocket and setting it on her roll-out tray. Mandy watched his eyes twinkle as he opened it. He was in his happy place.

"Our story begins after the Great Deluge, when the young minds of men were clear and intelligent. It is regrettable many had failed this task, submitting to their own selfish desires. Nevertheless, there were those who silently challenged the King who hunted men for sport, choosing a life of solidarity to keep them separate from the vile practices of the day. These men and women gathered in subterrestrial chambers, longing to find a secure haven away from the havoc of the time, knowing if they were captured, the evil King would defile their knowledge and use it against innocents. Making up this precious group were astronomers, metallurgists, etiologists, geneticists and many more with a keen understanding of the natural sciences.

"They had decided upon a plan to take them far away from the evil one and his hordes, but as a precaution, each family left the area one at a time, boating their way up the beautiful Euphrates River, and meeting at the point where the river bends north. From there, seventy-two families trudged across the rugged terrain, until they reached the Great Sea. Despite their fear of the evil King and of bandits, their travels were incident free. The exodus took eight solar months or two hundred forty days, and demanded strong courage and a firm resolution, leaving many weak and exhausted. Upon reaching the Great Sea, a camp was built on its shore. It took a year to construct twelve large vessels with flat hulls, complete with sails and oars. Finally, without looking back, they left the land they had once called home.

"As they traveled the Great Sea, they mapped the coastlines and islands, using the sun and stars to assess their location. They came to a small narrow waterway. Their ships were heavily laden with supplies and people, and with the channel having a water depth of only eight feet, they were unsure if it was navigable. Determined not to return to the evil of men, they moved forward and were delighted the flat hulls of the vessels easily sailed through. The passage opened to a vast ocean as far as the eye can see. They called it the Atlantic, named after their glorious and compassionate leader who was soon to become their first king, Atlantin.

"After sixteen days of an east wind; they reached an island with white-topped mountains. It was here they disembarked the vessels and created small huts from the foliage lining the beach. They named the island Atlantis, and this is where our legacy begins."

Mandy interrupted, "So the Greeks didn't name the Atlantic, the Atlanteans did. And it was an island, not a continent."

"Wait a minute," said Max. "It says 'after the Great Deluge,' so this means Atlantis didn't exist nine thousand years before Plato. All geological evidence points to a worldwide deluge around four thousand years ago, which is only about two thousand years before Plato."

"I thought the deluge was millions of years ago?" said Mandy.

"What Max said is correct," said Dad. "Radiometric Dating has put the worldwide deluge around four thousand years ago."

"So why did Plato alter the timeline of Atlantis?" asked Mandy.

"He was a storyteller," said their dad. "The older something is, the more attention it gets. Just change a number, add more zeroes, and there you go; Atlantis had become a legend."

"Hmm…this guy isn't as dumb as I thought," said Mandy.

"Plato was a learned man in his time," said Max, "and well respected by everyone. But, like dad said, he was a good storyteller."

"Let's put the timeline of Atlantis beginning around four thousand years ago," said Dad. "Agreed?"

Max and Mandy both nodded yes.

"Read on, Max," said Dad.

"After almost eight hundred years of peace, our gracious King Aarix determined that I, Aldine the Fair, be given the honor to write our history of triumphs and failures. The one who unearths this Key to Atlantis will find a wealth of knowledge, understanding, and discover an incredible source of infinite energy, the Illum, a gift from the Ancient Ones. However, BEWARE, my children, if the Illum is misused, death will follow, an eternal death where life cannot be restored."

"The Illum?" asked Mandy, "as in Illuminati?"

"I don't know," said Dad, stroking his beard. "The Illuminati had their beginnings back in the 1700s, long after these people occupied Atlantis. Whatever this Illum is, it's something tangible and they feared its abuse."

"I thought the Atlanteans were the Ancient Ones," asked Mandy, "so who are the guys Aldine is talking about?"

"Don't know that either," said Dad. "Maybe he'll tell us later. Keep reading."

Max resumed, "After ten years of gathering past historical information, the Book was ready. Our honorable and wise King Aarix decreed it a masterpiece as it contained all our accomplishments, creations, and our shortcomings; things we Atlanteans should never forget because true wisdom comes from a selfless heart. Our story begins on our magnificent island, Atlantis, a land once fertile with vegetation and blessed with beautiful valleys and mountains. A land where three mountain fires—"

"Hold it," said Mandy. "What's a mountain fire?"

"A volcano," said Max.

"Ugh! I hate it when you're right," she said, feeling dumb again.

"Go on, Max," said Dad.

"…three mountain fires lying on the western edge of our island, had become a cause for concern. Although we had many gifted scholars in the sciences, no amount of knowledge can halt the inevitable. All the same, we shall speak more of this later. For now, you must learn the location of our central seat of government, the glorious City of Light."

Mandy swore Max had read the final paragraph without breathing, he was gone again. The scientist had taken over. He read aloud.

$$31°21'51.20" \text{ N} \qquad 24°24'43.85" \text{ W}$$

"Mandy, get the notebook from the glove compartment and write down the coordinates for me," said Dad. "This is unbelievable."

She handed him the written paper, and he stuffed it in his shorts pocket.

"I'm getting goosebumps," said Mandy. "We have the coordinates to the most sought after place in history."

"To its capitol, the City of Light," said Max, "and wait…it's closer to the Azores, not the Madeira Islands. I'm putting the coordinates into Google Earth on my phone."

"Hold it, Tarzan," said Mandy, "how are you getting a signal down here? We're at least thirty feet underground?"

"Never underestimate what I can do—holy crap! Look!"

He handed them his iPhone which displayed a faint outline of a submerged city to the west of the Straits of Gibraltar.

Max typed on his laptop. "The web has lots of theories about this, but Google insists ships using sonar created these lines while mapping the seafloor. They said boats can only measure a thin strip of the ocean bottom, and sometimes these lines get overlapped on the data."

"But the coordinates we have from the Book can't be a coincidence," said Mandy. "Dad, what do you think?"

"I say we check it out. Max, I hope you have your Subterranean Surveyor."

"Sure do. It's still in my backpack."

"Good," said Dad. "Let's get to the Azores and hope they didn't find us through the hack into Global. When we get out of here, I'll contact Skimmer and set up a meet."

Relief washed over Mandy. Her father reaffirmed what she was thinking; they found the Renaldo's through Global, which meant Senona and her family were safe. She would call her later to be sure.

"Uncle Skimmer is looking more like a pirate every time I see him," said Max. "The ones with a couple of teeth and a language all their own."

"And his body odor could burn down a forest," said Mandy. "He's insisted there's no need to bathe more than once a month and brush your teeth only once a week. With the scruffy beard and filthy clothes, all he needs is a parrot on his shoulder and he'd fit the role perfect."

"You know what they say about fishers," said Max. "They never die, they just smell that way."

"He was grateful we bought him a new home," said Dad.

"His last home was so old it sunk," said Mandy.

"But now he's upgraded," said Max. "The *Amalia* is the finest boat in the Azores and has all the latest tech."

Ten years ago, they had met Skimmer on a fishing excursion in the Azores. The trip lasted two weeks and they had the best time, except when Max got caught in a strong riptide and almost drowned. Skimmer saved him and their father swore he would never forget it. They kept in touch throughout the years with Skimmer spending several vacations at their home in New York. She and Max had agreed to adopt him as their uncle. Hugging them both, he strained to hold back the tears. He had no other family.

Old fishers like him are a rare breed, thought Mandy. "It's cute he named his new boat after his first love. What was she? A farm girl?"

"Yeah," said Dad, "but he never dated her because her father hated fishers, thinking they were all untrustworthy."

"Amalia's father was so wrong," said Mandy.

True fishers believed in honor and loyalty; something society had lost long ago. The last time they had seen him was when they visited the Azores eleven months ago, and their dad had bought him the new boat. His old ship the *Bria*, named after his childhood dog, had sprung a leak and within minutes, the crack opened to a crevasse. His old friend, Victor Costa had to rescue him. When Skimmer called them in New York, his sadness came through loud and clear. His *Bria* was gone. Before they knew it, they were on a flight to the Azores.

When their father showed Skimmer the three-hundred-thousand-dollar ship he wanted to purchase for him, Skimmer almost crapped a brick. He said the cost was too much and trying to figure out how to work a nuclear power plant would give him hives. Her dad reassured him he would learn and it wouldn't be too difficult, because Skimmer was a natural when it came to electronics.

The warm feeling inside her returned when she recalled their dad handing Skimmer the keys to his new home. Through tears, he said he would repay them, but her father told him payment would not be accepted, because no value could be placed on saving the life of his son. The only thing he wished for was to continue vacationing with his good friend in the Azores. Skimmer agreed then spit a wad of brown phlegm in his palm and grabbed their father's hand, shaking it vigorously. She remembered her and Max holding back their laughter as their dad turned a light shade of green. After three weeks of training, Skimmer drove off with his *Amalia*.

Mandy wondered. *Skimmer has all kinds of connections throughout the Atlantic, but can he hide us from Preston the psychopath?*

"Do you think they'll find us again?" asked Mandy.

"Preston is relentless," said Dad, "and he's not likely to give up. But we can stay ahead of him if we play it right."

Jack Williams would do anything to protect his kids, even give his life, which is what worried her. He was all they had and she couldn't picture life without him; it hurt too much. As they drove down the road, Mandy watched Castillo Solano get smaller in view. The old stone castle was beautiful. It's landscaped gardens and giant trees resembled a place where fairy tales were made, but all she had were everlasting nightmares…*and there's more to come.*

CHAPTER 15
Dante

Dante and fifteen soldiers rushed up the stairs. They reached the top of the steps and stopped. The hallway was split, they could go either right or left. The stone walls of the hallways were covered in paintings of Spanish kings and queens from yesteryear, dressed in their royal garb. At the end of the right hallway light was streaming out from beneath a shut door.

Got it! thought Dante.

They bashed their way into the room, only to find it void of people. Dante was so angered, he grabbed the *PX38* from Karim's hand and roared as he turned in a circle, shooting out all the walls.

Karim stood beside him. "Feel better?"

"Yeah," said Dante, handing him back the rifle.

Dante's eyes scanned the room. A bed, computers...*and a wheelchair...white archival gloves?* He stood next to the wheelchair and eyed the armrest. He looked at Karim. "I need to know who was in this chair."

Dante pulled from his inside jacket pocket a lipstick size tube, blue in color with a black button on one end and a clear glass dome on the other. The DermoScan or Dscan would pick up DNA from traces of leftover skin cells. Holding it vertical over an armrest he held down the button. A thin blue light emitted then widened as he ran it along the black leather padding of each armrest. The Dscan sent the results to his phone. It was a positive match to Maxxus Williams.

"So Max is in a wheelchair," said Dante.

"No wonder the hospital deleted all the records," said Karim. "They didn't want us to know the kid was disabled."

Dante kicked the wheelchair and it crashed into the wall. "Now I'm even more pissed."

"We'll get them, sir," said Karim.

"Check the place," said Dante. "There's got to be something here telling us where they went."

"What's that?" said Karim.

Next to the far wall on a table were what looked like three golden arks. Dante felt the fire of history ignite inside him. He quickly slipped on a pair of the white gloves, hurried to the table and grabbed one.

"Clear the bed," he said.

Karim threw the bed comforter and pillows onto the floor. Dante walked to the bed and gazed at the beautiful designs of gold. The Larnax of ancient Greece fueled his archeological craving even more. He carefully removed the giant blue diamond ark. The wax seal had already been broken and inside was an ancient scroll with golden rollers. His head began to spin from the excitement, and he had to remember to breathe. He carefully took out the scroll covered in clear archival plastic, then placed it on the bed and partially unrolled it. His breath caught in his chest, and he almost forgot to exhale.

"Do you know what this is?" said Dante, he heard the excitement in his own voice.

"Ancient chicken scratch," said Karim.

"It's ancient Greek," said Dante. "This scroll is from the Library of Alexandria and written by Alexander the Great himself."

He glanced at the other scrolls and then looked at Karim. "These scrolls are the diary of Alexander the Great."

"You mean, *the* Alexander the Great?" asked Karim, "the leader of ancient Greece?"

He felt himself breathing fast, almost panting, so he made a long suspire not to look weak in front of the men.

"Yeah," said Dante. "That one. I need to sit."

Karim rolled a desk chair over to the bed and Dante sat, studying the writing as he talked. "Preston is going to love this. Imagine the headlines, "Global Innovations discovers the lost scrolls of Alexandria.""

"So why would they leave this behind?" said Karim. "I'm sure they knew what they were."

"I don't know," said Dante. "My only guess is we must have surprised them." He gently rerolled the scroll replacing it back in the ark. He handed it to Karim. "I want this put with the others in the brown sack on the table in the corner. Lay the arks flat within the sack and carefully wrap the whole thing in the archival plastic, then wrap it again in the bed comforter for protection. Have four men fly this back to Global and personally put it into Preston's hands."

"Yes, sir!" he said, and he signaled four soldiers.

Dante slid off his gloves and hit redial on his phone. "We're at the location where the Williams's were supposed to be, but they're gone."

"What?" yelled Preston. "I need that kid!"

"Relax," said Dante. "I think you'll like what we found in Max's room. I believe we have the lost scrolls from the Library of Alexandria."

There was silence. He'd finally found something to shut him up.

"Say again?" asked Preston, disbelief in his voice.

"I said the lost scrolls from the Library of Alexandria—actually four scrolls written by Alexander the Great. Imagine the recognition Global will receive for finding these scrolls."

"Are you sure?" asked Preston.

"Yes," said Dante. "They're covered in archival plastic which means the Williams's knew their age. And the writing is definitely ancient Greek. But you'll have to have them authenticated before the public is informed. You don't want egg on your face."

"I'm at a loss for words," said Preston.

That's new, thought Dante. "I haven't heard from the cave team in over twenty-four hours. Finding the exact location of where these scrolls were found is important if Global wants the credit for the discovery."

"Yes, of course," said Preston. "Did the cave writing reveal anything?"

"Yes," said Dante. "It took some doing, but I finally made it out. It mentioned invaluable scrolls, which I assume are these, and an ancient book written by powerful all-knowing gods from a place abbreviated with the letters, ATLS."

"Atlantis?" said Preston.

Dante could hear Preston rising off his squeaky chair. "I'm positive the Williams's have the Book of Atlantis."

"This is outstanding," said Preston.

He'd never heard Preston this calm. The discovery had left him dumbfounded and Dante wished he could see him. The chair squeaked. Preston had sat down again; he was truly in shock.

"Remember the four elements?" said Dante. "I'll bet the book has the locations of the three remaining amulet pieces." Dante heard Preston's breathing speed up.

"I want that book!" shouted Preston, his voice vibrating the phone. There was a loud boom, Preston's fist had hit the glass desk. "I don't care who you have to kill to get it! Find…find it," his voice softened, "and bring it to me."

It was the first time Dante had heard Preston stutter his words. The man had lost all control and Dante hoped he would have a heart attack and die. Getting Preston out of the picture would leave Atlantis to him.

Dante added, "Legend says the Atlanteans had a source of endless energy similar to the sun, which is self-sustaining. You could use something like that for Oveipa."

"Please," said Preston, his voice weak, "it's imperative I have that book…find it."

Dante couldn't help but grin wide. Preston's heart was acting up. *One more sting.*

"Plato also mentioned Atlantis had a naval power with no equal, stealth flying machines that could sneak up on a man, and weapons able to level a city with one shot." *A good lie,* he thought, *and worth it.* "If this is true, then you, my friend, will have all you need to rule the world."

Preston's breathing was now erratic. Dante heard a ding sound on the other end of the line. Preston had pressed the blue button for Darla. He could hear him wheezing.

"Get the doctor," he heard Preston say.

"Are you okay?" said Dante, trying not to laugh.

"I'm fine," he answered. "Do what you have to but get me that book. They'll be a very big bonus waiting if you do."

"Done," said Dante. "I'll call in three." He ended the call.

Dante could only hope for good news from Darla about Preston. Having him die from a heart attack would fix things. He swiveled his chair and studied the bedroom. Every wall was littered with bullet holes. On the other side of the bed, Karim and two men were packing the arks. He stood up and walked around the room, opening and shutting several draws on the bureaus, which only contained junk, then stopped in front of a huge mahogany armoire against the sidewall. Intricate carvings of flowers decorated the whole piece. He lit a cigarette and clicked his lighter shut, then opened the doors of the armoire where only a green jacket and a pair of sneakers lay at the bottom. A bullet hole had gone through one of the doors and exited out the back wall of the closet leaving a black hole of nothing. As he let out a puff of smoke, he noticed the smoke was moving away from the armoire, so he put his hand inside over the bullet hole on the back wall, a small breeze cooled his palm. There was more to this castle.

"The arks are wrapped, sir," said Karim, "just as you ordered."

Four soldiers were leaving the room with the relics.

Dante crushed out his cigarette on the coral tiled floor. "Give me the IRP."

Karim handed him a small, black gun. The barrel of the Infrared Heat Pistol was three inches long with a small laser light at the end. Dante lifted a transparent screen lying flat on the side of the pistol and swiveled it towards him. He pressed the red button trigger, and the visual display turned on. Slowly, he made a one eighty around the room, detecting the heat signatures of his men, which were yellow orange figures, and then released the button. He stepped into the armoire and fit the barrel of the gun into the empty bullet hole. When he pressed the trigger, a clear visual of three bodies came on screen. One was sitting in a wheelchair and being pushed. He stared at the picture. Something was different. The bottom of the chair was displaying a purplish pink color, a strange signature for a battery.

"Do we go after them?" said Karim, standing behind him.

"Yes," said Dante.

The two stepped out of the armoire and went to the back of the closet where they tried to pull the cabinet away from the wall.

"What the heck?" said Karim, panting, "did they solder it?"

"It's probably bolted," said Dante, swiping at the sweat on his brow. "Apparently they have a plan. I have an idea."

He lifted what looked like a tiny iPod from his black jacket pocket. A small black screen along with a single white button was all the unit had. He pressed the button and the screen lit up; "System Ready" blinked in yellow. Dante checked the top of the device where a red dot confirmed the existence of a minute hole, invisible to the naked eye.

"A nanite pouch?" said Karim.

"Yeah," said Dante, making adjustments on the touch screen. "But they'll only last for about a minute. Hopefully, we'll hear enough to know where they're heading."

"Brilliant," said Karim with a smile. "Use the guys own invention against him."

Dante smiled, and then held the small opening against the bullet hole. He tapped the white button again and a low whooshing sound emitted, along with an audible speaker. They heard the faint sounds of people talking getting louder. Dante kept his eyes on the screen showing him where and how far away the sound was coming from. The three were over a quarter mile from them and although the nanites traveled very fast through air, Dante wondered if they would make it.

"Did he say Madeira?" said Karim, pitching his ear toward the pouch.

"Yeah," said Dante, watching the words on the screen begin to fade. "The nanites are fadin—dead."

Dante turned to Karim. "I want everything in this room boxed. Take all the electronics and empty the drawers. In the other rooms, pack up the closets and dressers, and check all the mattresses. When everything's out, burn this place to the ground. I want nothing but stone walls and ashes."

CHAPTER 16
Max

"Max, come and enjoy this fresh air," said Dad. "We'll hold you up to the window. The ocean is beautiful."

"Been there, done that," said Max, finishing one last web search on his laptop.

Skimmer was waiting for them in the Azores. It's been almost two weeks since they secretly boarded Victor Costa's boat, the *Isabella*. Because of their frequent stops to fish, the trip was taking longer but Max didn't mind.

It's better than running for your life from freaks, thought Max.

Skimmer had the greatest friends, deep-rooted anglers full of heart and decency, but physical cleanliness was not one of their gifts. The crew was kind, courteous, and very generous, building a ramp for Nessie so he could hide with his family below deck. However, because of their troubles, they trusted no one. They agreed not to study the Book until after a complete internet search of each crewmember. But with that finished, today they would get back to the Book.

His father and Mandy were standing in front of two open portholes. Jack Williams was a typical well-groomed man, but lately everything about him screamed "bum off the street." His white T-shirt had several tattered holes, and his frayed green Bermuda shorts were begging to be thrown out. Mandy was wearing her regular jeans and a red T-shirt. She had commented on how he needed to upgrade from black sweatpants to at least a variety of colors.

That's not happening, thought Max. *I like black.*

He gazed down at his black DC Comics T-shirt showing all the Superheroes in a burst of hues and attitudes. The Flash was his favorite. His laptop beeped. It was resting on Nessie's swing-out table in front of him. Global had found them on the Canary Islands, and he had to know how.

"What's this, our tenth cruise?" he said.

"This is not a cruise," said Mandy. "I feel like steerage on the Titanic."

"We are steerage," said Max, glancing around the small fifteen-by-twelve-foot cabin.

Aside from the empty walk-in closet, the room contained a full bed and one twin, and both donned black-and-white striped lumpy mattresses splattered with rust stains. Worn, dingy gray blankets lay folded at their bases. On Mandy's insistence, the three pillows were lying on the floor in the corner. The thought of head lice freaked her out. She slept fully clothed with a towel wrapped around her head, and every night she would wake up frantic and kicking, swearing bugs were licking her toes.

It's the rats, thought Max, *but I can't tell her that because dad made me promise not to. Sometimes he takes the fun out of things.*

There was a loud snap. In the corner of the room, he watched another crack spike up the wall to the ceiling; the rotted white fiberglass panels had given up a long time ago. Above them, mold-ridden insulation hung down from three missing ceiling slats. The *Isabella* was a timeworn seventy-foot fishing trawler from the late 1970s, designed to stay out in the open sea for months. The height of their cabin didn't make six feet. Their dad had to walk with his head down because when it scraped the dangling insulation, he'd go berserk swiping at his hair. He and Mandy always got a good laugh from that.

"Captain Victor said this is the deluxe suite," said Mandy. "I can only imagine what the other cabins look like."

There was a knock on the teak wood door.

"May I come in?" said a voice.

Max recognized their new friend. "Yes, of course, Captain."

A burly man with dark brown eyes and an unkempt black beard entered the cabin. His eyebrows seemed to merge as one above his crooked nose. Like all fishers who spend their lives out in the sea, his dark leathered skin made him appear older, hiding his actual age of fifty-three. He wore a shabby white Captains hat and a dirty short sleeve white shirt, exposing the dark curly hair on his bulging forearms. A jute rope held up his crusted gray pants, which looked as if they hadn't been washed in six months. He stood at least five feet, nine inches tall with the demeanor of a man who enjoyed your company, but if you messed with him, they'd never find your body. Mandy had covered her nose and mouth with cupped hands. The smell was so bad Max was sure his nose hairs would ignite.

"You're welcome here anytime, Captain," said Dad, shaking his hand, "and again, we can't thank you enough for what you've done."

"Any friend of Skimmer is a friend of mine," said the Captain, pronouncing each syllable with a crisp distinct voice.

His accent was West Indian though a simple web search revealed his Portuguese and Moroccan descent. Captain Victor had lived in Jamaica for thirty years before making the Canary Islands his home.

He continued, "I must apologize for not taking time to speak with you in the last two weeks. When the sea calls, I must answer. There are families to feed and I cannot fail this. But now things have calmed. I understand you are hiding but we are presently far from land. Please, join us above. It would be an honor for my crew and myself."

"Our enemy has many satellites at his disposal," said their dad, "thus remaining hidden during the day is necessary. But later tonight it will be a pleasure to enjoy the night air above with you and your crew."

"That is good news," he answered, "though I can only hope the weather cooperates. This area has wicked evening storms in the summer." He turned to Mandy. "Young missy, I have a daughter your age, Estrela, who would enjoy your company. Perhaps when your problems are cared for, we can arrange for you to meet her." He tilted his head and looked at her with curiousness. "Is there something wrong? Do you have an inflammation?"

Mandy's hands dropped to her sides. "No, sir. My…umm…face itches around salt water."

"Aah, yes," he said with a smile. "The sea can be distressing on young skin. Would you like to use a special cream I made from sea snails? It has helped many of my peers."

"Uhh…no, thank you, sir. I have cream that should work, and yes, I would love to meet your daughter. If she's anything like you, she'll make a wonderful friend."

"Thank you. A father is always proud of daughters who grow to be beautiful maidens."

"Yes, sir," said Dad. He put his arm around Mandy, pulling her close. "And we love their honesty."

Captain Victor turned to Max. "And proud of sons who can outsmart any intellect. Skimmer tells me you are the smartest man he has ever met next to your father here. Is this true?"

"Skimmer was being nice," said Max. "I'm just a normal kid who likes to play with things that run on electricity."

Captain Victor let out a bellowing laugh. "Jack, you have a good family and I will help you protect them. I must take my leave, but if you need anything please do not hesitate to ask."

"Thank you, Captain," said Dad.

"And one more thing, my chef, Duarte, will bring your dinner. His expertise is desired on many fishing vessels as he is the best. Scallops and roe are his specialities, and we will have them tonight. I hope you enjoy it."

Max saw Mandy's eyes open wide when he mentioned roe for dinner. She detested fish eggs.

"I'm sure we will," said Dad. "Thank you."

Captain Victor tipped his hat and left the cabin, shutting the door behind him. A beep from the laptop caught Max's attention. He began reading the news article on the laptop screen.

"For once, couldn't you have dealt with the odor without the theatrics?" said Dad. "Have you no shame?"

"I'm sorry," said Mandy, "but I was getting nauseous and snail cream would freak me—Max, what's wrong?

Uncontrollable tears rolled down Max's cheeks. His trembling body wouldn't let him answer. His father and Mandy rushed to his side.

"No…," said Mandy. "Not the Renaldo's, no please—" and she burst into sobs, holding her face.

His dad closed the laptop and walked to an open porthole where he hung his head and cried. Mandy rushed to his side. Max put the laptop on the bed and joined them, reaching out.

"Dad," he said.

His father wrapped his arm around him and held them tight. It seemed they had cried enough tears for a lifetime when Mandy looked at Max with swollen eyes and drenched cheeks. He cupped her face with one hand, letting her know he was feeling the same pain.

Their dad released them. "We have to move on," he said, using the back of his hand to wipe away his tears. "The Renaldo's would have wanted it that way."

"We're to blame," whimpered Mandy. "The article said it was a murder-suicide, but we know better. They were murdered because of us."

"We're not to blame for any of this," said Dad. "Preston is responsible. We almost died in the caves because of him, and I will never forgive him for Max losing his legs. He has the scrolls, but we can never, ever let him have Atlantis."

"He's right," said Max, fighting to swallow his sorrow. "When we're ready to divulge Atlantis to the world, we can tribute the find to the Renaldo's. Their names will be written in history. It's the least we can do."

"Okay," said Mandy with reddened eyes. "Now if I could just stop crying."

"No, sweetheart, this is the time to let it out," said Dad, "because we don't know what kind of danger we're heading into, and we can't let our guard down, even for a second."

Mandy flopped face down on the bed bawling. The hurt his twin was experiencing had doubled the pain in his chest. Sometimes he wished their Nexus didn't work. Max felt his father's hand on his shoulder.

Max kept his stare on Mandy. "I wish we could turn back time three years. Mom and the Renaldo's would still be alive, and I wouldn't be in this stupid wheelchair."

His dad squatted beside him. "Listen, son, whatever happens in life we have to take the good and bad, and make sure we learn from it. It's what defines us as a person. Your mother was a brilliant scientist, one of the smartest in the world. She took the piconites I created and made them super versatile. Her genius will live on in you and Mandy. Whatever happens, I will always love you and your sister. Nothing will ever change that."

Max squeezed Nessie's armrests, stressing over his father's words. "Don't talk like that. It sounds like a goodbye speech."

"It's not, but if I'm ever not around, I want the two of you to take care of each other, whether it be for one day or forever."

"What are you saying?" asked Mandy, now sitting on the edge of the bed wiping the tears soaking her face.

His father stood up and cupped his hands on both their cheeks. "I have no plans of getting caught, but I need you to swear you'll always protect each other."

"We always have each other's back," said Mandy.

"That's a given," answered Max.

"I know, but I needed to hear it," said Dad. "Right now, focusing on Atlantis will help us move on. So how about it? Are you ready?"

"Let's do it," said Mandy, sitting straight. "We have to find it before Preston does. He's not getting away with murder this time."

Senona's face flashed across Max's mind. She was one of the most amazing girls he had ever met. Even after he'd lost the use of his legs, she always included him in whatever plans she and Mandy made. She was kind, caring, and downright beautiful. He felt the trembling return, and he choked up.

"I'll miss her too, Max," said Mandy. She leaned down and kissed him on the cheek. "Forever together, bro."

"Forever always, sis," he replied. "When we find Atlantis, we can rub it in Preston's face. Now let's do this."

He lifted the laptop off the bed and put it back on Nessie's swing out table. "Mandy, did you read Plato's writings on Atlantis, his Timaeus and Critias?"

"Yes," she said. "It's obvious he dreamt up the parts about the gods, but the places where he describes the island sound real."

"The story of Atlantis has always mystified people," said Dad, "and it was easy to add droplets of fantasy as it was passed down through generations. Max, can the SBS pick up structures like buildings?"

"Yes, in 3-D and up to one hundred feet below the sand."

"Good. Let's start. Max, pull up the Book on the laptop."

"By the way," said Mandy, "is the real Book still in Max's backpack?"

His father unzipped the pack hanging on Nessie's seat back and peeked in. "Yep. Let's finish this for the Renaldo's."

Max's grief returned feeling like a knife had plunged into his chest, so he swiveled Nessie around hoping they didn't notice he was crying again. He backed up and positioned Nessie between the two of them who were sitting on the bed, then typed in the word 'Atlantis.' The screen displayed the last page they had read together. Mandy rested her hand on his shoulder.

She knows.

"This Book proves Plato was a weirdy," said Mandy. "Why did he write it in dialogue form? Why didn't he just write it like a piece of history?"

"It's a known fact Plato loved to tell tales," said Max, "and Atlantis proves it."

"Look what it says," said Mandy pointing at the screen. "Atlantis had only two Kings until the secret of longevity was discovered. Longevity? As in eternal life?"

"Maybe," said Max. "Their first King, Atlantin, died at one hundred years old in 2210 B.C.E., then Aarix took over, but it never mentions he died. Could Aarix still be alive?"

"Immortality is a dream," said Dad, "nothing more. If the story is real, then Atlantis and its people were all killed when the volcanoes erupted, and this Book is all that's left of them."

"What if they discovered a way to stop disease and aging?" said Max. "If that's the case, they may still be alive."

"I doubt that," said Dad, "but we're short on time, and this speculation is getting us nowhere, so let's move on. It says they built magnificent structures including Great Halls of Science, History, Literature, and Art. A three-hundred-foot statue of their first King Atlantin stood at the entrance to the Hall of Science."

"Hold it," said Mandy. "Dad, are you still wearing the amulet piece?"

"Yes," he said, lifting his white shirt and revealing the luxurious belt buckle. "Why are you asking?"

"Just checking."

"Are you sure you don't want me to wear it?" asked Max.

"Absolutely. I will not endanger my kids." He lowered his shirt, concealing the ornament again. "Now let's continue. If this Book is real, we should be able to find something at the coordinates, because not everything gets pulverized in earthquakes."

"Aldine says the giant statue was solid orichalcum," said Max, "and so were parts of their buildings. I'll bet it's the same ore the amulet piece is sitting in. I wish I had tested it when we had the chance."

"The Atlantis story is the only place that talks about orichalcum," said Dad. "It's not mentioned anywhere else in history."

"A lot of people think the ore was a mixture of gold and copper," said Max, "which could be, but I think there's more to this orichalcum. If it's present on or below the seafloor, the SBS will pick it up as an 'unknown.'" He typed again, and a full picture of the outlined city on the sea bottom appeared on the screen. "I can't wait to get there."

"Me too," said Dad, glancing out the porthole. "It's getting dark. Duarte will be here any minute now, and I'm starving. Mandy, mind your manners. I'm sure he worked hard to make the meal for everyone."

"Father, I'm always courteous and polite," said Mandy, "and—"

The three jumped in fright to loud booms hitting the main deck. Running people and gurgling screams came from above.

CHAPTER 17
Max

"What's going on up there?" asked Max, hearing the desperate cries of men.

"Keep your voices down," whispered Dad. "We're going to hide. Max, back yourself into the closet. Mandy, go around the room and grab our stuff. I'll roll up the mattresses, we're going to make it like no one's been here."

Gut-piercing screams vibrated the air, and the rapid fire of automatic weapons sent shivers down Max's spine. He returned Nessie's table to its hideaway and stuffed the laptop inside her inner pocket. Mandy ran around the room grabbing clothes and shoes, while their dad hustled to roll up the mattresses with the blankets inside. Max backed Nessie into the closet and Mandy slid into the space behind him. His father entered and closed the teak louver door. Slits of light were peeking through the slats as they waited in silence.

Max readied the Flash Taser set within Nessie's left armrest; Mandy already had hers out. Thumping footsteps were coming down the stairs. The pounding of doors being kicked open was getting closer. Max steadied his finger over the fire button. Their cabin door was bashed open, sending a thin crack spiking up the closet wall.

"Find the Book!" shouted a man.

Two giant figures enter the cabin. Both had to hunch over almost ninety degrees due to their height, which meant they were at least nine feet tall. One wore a long sleeve red collared shirt and spandex type black pants which enclosed his feet like shoes. A bracelet with a bright turquoise stone wrapped his right wrist. His pure white hair and smooth beige skin made him appear human, but the thing next to him—*is not human.*

It had grayish-brown skin and long greasy strands of blonde hair draping from its disfigured skull. Although hunched over, hulking muscle and bulbous joints were visible. A long row of protruding blade-like bones ran from the base of its neck, all the way down its spine. Its hands and feet were enormous and deformed with crooked toes and fingers; some twisted and bent out of shape. The atrocious odor had to be coming from the creature, and not the man.

It must be in constant pain, thought Max.

"No one here, master," said the creature, his voice strong and raspy. "Olid wrong."

"This is unacceptable!" shouted the man. He kicked the single bed and it crashed into the outer wall where it broke into pieces. After taking several heaving breaths, he turned around.

"I need the Book," he said in a calm voice. "How else can I fix you, Scaph? Gather the others and let us return to *Rakys*. Loar will be punished for this."

"But, master, Loar make Olid. If punish, prize wait."

The man glowered at Scaph who bowed his head in submission.

"Perhaps you are right," he said. "If Loar fails again, I will rip out his heart."

"As you wish, master."

"Are the carcasses ready for travel?" asked the man.

"Yes, my lord."

"You will enjoy fresh meat tonight. Come, let us return."

When Scaph turned around to follow his master out of the room, Mandy made a quiet gasp. Scaph stopped and stared at the closet. The creature's black eyes were sitting uneven on his face and bulging out. A visible half inch of slimy red flesh surrounded his white sclerae with pitch-black irises. Both eyes were leaking a gooey yellow liquid. Max presumed its eyelids were hidden. Two oval holes were where his nose should be, and his teeth were sharp fangs overlapping scarred mangled lips.

A chill ran up Max's spine. *This is a beast of nightmares.*

Scaph began wobbling towards them, his arms swinging like an ape while green saliva drooled from the corners of his mouth. The smell of dead skunk was getting stronger, and Max wanted to puke.

"Come, Scaph!" shouted his master. "We have many things to do!" He stopped his approach.

"Yes, master," he said, and he scurried out of the room.

Max heard the splashes of people jumping into the water, and then there was silence.

They're from the sea, thought Max, *and their city is called Rakys. Are these creatures the Atlanteans of legend? What are we dealing with here?* The thought of Atlanteans turning into frightening monsters was alarming, and he couldn't shake the disturbing image from his head.

The three waited in the closet in silence with no movement. After twenty minutes, their father signaled he was going out to check the boat, and they were to stay put. He was careful not to make noise opening the louver door and closing it behind him. Five minutes later, he returned.

"It's safe to come out," he said aloud. "There's no one on the boat, not even Captain Victor."

"Where did they go?" asked Mandy.

"I don't know, but we need to get atop."

Max rolled out Nessie with Mandy behind him. Through the porthole, he could see it was dark outside, and the clouds rushing by the full moon seemed to be hastening them to leave the area.

"Do you think that monster killed everyone?" asked Mandy.

"Not sure," said Dad.

"That big man told the creature he would have fresh meat tonight," she said holding her stomach, "If that thing took Captain Victor—ugh, I'm going to be sick."

"This means the Book is real," said Dad. "Max, start speed reading. Mandy, push him so he can concentrate. We're going on deck. We can't turn on the engines, nor any lights. Our eyes will adjust to the darkness. Once up top, I'll contact Skimmer. Agreed?"

Max nodded along with Mandy. They followed their father out of their cabin and turned left for the make-shift ramp, while Max slid out Nessie's desk and placed the laptop on it. The hallway was dark and smelled of dead fish like the rest of the boat. The light of the full moon was not quite making it this far into the ship, silhouetting the round buoys hanging on the walls. A blustery wind whistled through the open corridor and for the first time tonight, Max could feel the rough seas swaying the vessel.

They were approaching the stairs when the bow of the ship shot upwards. His father stumbled back and almost fell onto the laptop. Nessie's safety system engaged. Four grappling hooks shot out from her underside and into the floor, hooking into the wood beneath the fiberglass. A segmented metal harness zoomed out from behind Max and looped around his shoulders, crisscrossing over his chest and snapping in below the armrests.

Max slammed the laptop shut and held it to his chest. "Hold onto Nessie!" he shouted. "She can take it!"

His dad flipped around to the side of Nessie and wrapped his arm around Mandy, then placed his other arm across Max's chest, gripping the furthest armrest. Max's stomach was rebelling. The *Isabella* was going vertical.

"The wave will be over soon!" said Dad. "Hold on!"

"If it's not," said Max, "I'm going to blow chunks!"

There was a thump on the floor.

"A buoy fell off the wall!" said Dad, squeaking his words out.

The nose of the *Isabella* dropped, racing down the wave like a roller coaster. They screamed together, hearing beds and furniture rolling in the cabins, bashing against the walls. Soon, the ship leveled off, rolling to the undulating sea.

"Does Nessie have wings too?" asked Dad, releasing them.

"No, but she can float, and her Flash Taser's power is adjustable."

"I hope the two holes in the floor won't sink the ship," said Mandy.

"I designed Nessie to analyze her surroundings and avoid any mishaps or dangers. Dad, the ocean is rough, so I think Mandy and I should stay down here."

"I am not staying down here in this creepy darkness," said Mandy. "We're all going up."

"I'll go first," said Dad. "Wait for my signal."

He raced up the stairs and out of sight. A moment later, his face appeared at the top of the steps.

"It's not bad!" he said. "Come up!"

Mandy pushed Max again.

"Hold it," she said. "There's a buoy blocking the ramp. I'll move it."

Mandy hurried to the front of Max and before he could stop her, a blood-curdling scream ensued, and she hit the deck with a loud thud.

CHAPTER 18
Max

Max zoomed over to Mandy who was out cold on the floor. Their father came running down the stairs and took her in his arms, tapping her face. Max retrieved his night-vision goggles and stared in horror, not wanting to believe his eyes.

"Jack, I mean Dad," he said, holding out the goggles for him to take. "You have to see this."

"It's Captain Victor's head."

"There's more."

His father took the goggles and gasped.

"They're cannibals," said Max, "but they don't eat the heads. They impaled them on the walls." A wave of nauseousness overcame him, and he wrapped his arms around his stomach. "I feel sick."

"Take these," said Dad, dropping the goggles onto Max's lap, "and don't faint. I can't handle the two of you passed out."

Mandy sat up and screamed again. His dad picked her up and ran up the stairs. Max dashed up the ramp, glad to leave the gruesome scene. On deck, the winds were waning. A burst of rain came down hard, the droplets felt like needles puncturing his skin. He sped to the safety of the covered pilothouse, thankful Nessie's instruments were waterproof. Max stopped in front of the helm and opened the panel cover on Nessie's left armrest. Holding the orange button down, his seat raised high enough for him to see all the ship's controls. His father was consoling Mandy.

"Bad things happen, sweetheart, but we can't give up."

"I know," she said, whimpering. "I'll never forget Captain Victor's face."

"Neither will I. But I need you to pull yourself together. Those creatures are still out there and we have to get out of here. Are you with me?"

"Yes," she said, standing to her feet and brushing off her jeans and red shirt. "I'm sorry I lost it." Her wavy long black hair was loose and hanging down to her waist.

"Umm…there's a ship coming towards us," said Max, keeping his eyes on the radar. "It's less than a mile away and closing in."

"Another ship?" asked Dad, hurrying to the helm. "Crap."

In the distance, a wobbling bright light shown through the dark rainfall.

"Could it be Preston?" asked Mandy.

"Maybe," said their dad. "Any suggestions?"

There was silence. Their predicament left them with few options. Either face the creatures from the deep, or the hit men. Not good choices.

"Before we do anything, I need aluminum foil," said Max. "Those monsters said they detected the Book. If we cover it with metal, it might stop the detection. It's only a guess."

"Good idea," said Dad, "I'm sure there's some in the galley. What other weapons do you have on Nessie besides the Flash Taser?"

"Ugh…."

"Think about it and let me know when I get back. Mandy, do you still have your Flash Taser."

"Yeah, I got two of them."

"Isn't one enough?" asked Dad.

"After the caves, it's peace of mind." She handed him a small Taser. "I thought you said the monsters were gone?"

"They are. If they were still here, they would have shown themselves by now."

"So why do you need the Flash Taser?" she asked.

"Peace of mind. I'll be back in a second," and he left the bridge, running back down the stairs. "Think of a plan!" he shouted.

Max felt his nerves begin to fray. They were in the middle of the Atlantic with nowhere to run. There was no way Nessie could battle psychopaths with automatic guns. The only weapon Nessie carried was a pimped-out Flash Taser, and it only worked if the people were standing in front of him. He regarded his twin and wanted to cry.

Did I give them a death sentence? Was I so immersed in my misery I never thought of my family? What have I done? There was only one thing he could do to save them.

"Preston wants me, not you," said Max, "so leave me. I could never live with myself if you both die."

"And where do we go? This is a boat. They'll search every crack. Besides, we're not giving Preston anything, especially you. Give it up, dude, we stay together."

A foghorn sounded through the heavy downpour.

"Why are they alerting us to their presence?" asked Mandy.

"To arouse more fear."

Mandy took his hand and squeezed it. "I think it's working."

The thought of his father and sister being captured was messing up his mind, and he couldn't think straight. He would never allow Preston to have them, no matter what they said. A voice came from behind, startling him.

"Have you guys thought of anything?" asked Dad.

"Nothing," he said. "I'm sorry. I was only thinking of myself. I should have built a flamethrower or a—"

Just then, the radio crackled. "This be the *Amalia*. Vic, ya there?"

It's Skimmer! A rush of relief coursed through Max.

Help had arrived. Max loved everything about Skimmer. His jargon, his mannerisms, his humor, the list was endless.

"Mandy, talk to him. Max and I need to cover the Book."

Mandy picked up the mic. "This is Mandy, Uncle Skimmer. We can see you."

"Aye, lassie, I's almost to ya."

Off the starboard bow, the lights of the *Amalia* were closing in. Max remembered the day their dad bought Skimmer the ship, one of the most beautiful vessels he'd ever seen. She was a three-level, fifty-foot inboard motor fishing boat with enough antennae and satellite arrays to contact the Mars Station. The galley, beds, and bathroom were on the lower level. Above this was the pilothouse or the main flybridge containing the navigational controls for the ship, and this sat on a flat fiberglass deck which stretched from stem to stern. White metal stairs led to the upper flybridge housing a duplicate helm. What stood out the most were the two outriggers on both sides of the craft designed to keep fishing lines apart when trawling.

"How are we going to get me aboard the *Amalia*?" asked Max, securing the foil around the Book. "Nessie weighs over a hundred pounds."

"We'll think of something," said Dad, sliding the foil-wrapped Book into Max's pack behind Nessie's seat.

"What's that?" asked Mandy, her finger was pointing at an object on the sonar screen.

"Whatever it is, it's not big," said Max.

"No," said Dad, "but it's moving like a missile and heading right for us. We have to get off this ship now!" He grabbed the mic out of Mandy's hand. "Skimmer! This is Jack. Move your butt! We're in trouble!"

"I's see it!" he shouted. "Me *Amalia's* at full speed! Where's me friend, Vic?"

"I'll explain later. Just get here fast!"

"Aye! Gets ready to hitch the tubs! I's have a ramp fer Max."

The pouring rain was beating down like Angel Falls. The white hull of the *Amalia* was struggling with the rolling waves as she pulled up alongside the ship. She was twenty feet shorter than the *Isabella* with six blue fenders dangling from the gunwale for protection. His father and Mandy rushed to the starboard side of the *Isabella* and latched their ropes around the *Amalia* cleats, pulling the ships together.

"We have less than four minutes!" said Max, holding the toggle down on Nessie, lowering his seat.

Mandy leapt like a gazelle over the walls of the two ships and onto the Amalia. She helped Skimmer unfold three sheets of plywood braced with two-by-four studs held together with sturdy brass hinges. They flipped the first part of the ramp onto the *Isabella*, the middle section laid flat on the two hulls, while the third sheet rested on the

Amalia.

"Quick, Maxie, boy," said Skimmer, trying to hold the ramp steady. "I's hold it whilst ya rides over. Where's the crew? Victor?"

"They're all dead," said Dad, frowning. "I'm sorry."

Skimmer's face turned white.

"I know this is hard," said Dad, "but we have to get off this ship now. Please, Skimmer, help us."

"Aye," said Skimmer, coming out of his daze. "Come on, Maxie. Ya can do this, son."

Max was uncertain he would make it over the makeshift ramp. The waving seas were causing the wood to bounce on the two hulls, and the torrential rain would only make it slippery.

"It'll be okay, Max," said Mandy. "We got you, bro."

"I'm here," said Dad, holding down the sheet of wood on the *Isabella.* "Don't worry. Now go for it!"

Max positioned Nessie across from the unsteady ramp, leery it would stay together.

"Put her in high gear and zoom over!" said Mandy. "You can do this!"

Max held down the small red button on Nessie's control panel, decreasing the pressure of her tires.

"Good thinking," said Dad, "better traction, but you have to move now. There's no time."

Here goes nothing, thought Max, hoping he could keep her straight. Zooming face first onto the hard fiberglass floor of the ship, or worse, into the Atlantic, was terrifying. He held his breath and rammed Nessie's joystick forward. Her wheels skidded on the wet deck and then took off, bouncing hard as she hit the first sheet of wood.

"Whoa!" shouted Max as Nessie raced over the ramp.

She pounced on the deck of the *Amalia* and her automatic brakes squealed on, but she broke into a slide and was heading towards the opposite wall at full speed. He cringed, ready to crash, when Skimmer grabbed Nessie's armrest and pulled her to the left. Max's body was lifting out of the chair when his father pushed him back into the seat.

Nessie skidded to a stop.

"You okay?" asked Dad.

"Yeah," said Max, panting. "I never want to do that again."

Skimmer shouted from the main helm, "We needs to skedaddle! Hangs on!"

His father and Mandy had just finished folding the ramp when the engines of the *Amalia* roared. The vessel swerved away from the *Isabella* at full speed, her bow breaking through the waves with incredible ease.

"Whatever those creatures are," said Dad, "they want to erase all evidence they were here. Let's hope we get far enough away—"

The *Isabella* exploded with thunderous booms and billowing balls of fire.

CHAPTER 19
Max

His father and Mandy threw their bodies over him at the same time the missile demolished the *Isabella*. Max peeked through the cluster of arms and saw a giant ball of blackened smoke and fire rise high into the air. Chunks of wood and metal showered down on the *Amalia*.

"Run!" shouted Dad, grabbing Nessie's handles and dashing under the roof of the flybridge.

The ferocity of the explosion had turned the sea into tumultuous waves, knocking the *Amalia* about.

"Holds tight!" shouted Skimmer, maneuvering the ship through the rough seas.

They reached a safe distance, and the *Amalia* stopped. The mighty Atlantic had snuffed out the ocean fires and claimed what was left of the smoldering *Isabella*. As if knowing an injustice had occurred, the rain stopped, and the skies cleared. The light of the full moon glistened against the calm seas.

Skimmer was standing at the helm. He was fifty-six years old and his angular build of five feet, ten inches reeked of rotten fish with a hint of pipe tobacco. The coppery tough skin of his face housed a bristled salt and pepper beard on a squared jaw, and with no upper front teeth he looked like an old buccaneer straight out of a pirate story. Whitish eyelashes surrounded his slate-blue eyes and were topped with graying eyebrows thick enough to mop a floor. A tattered white Captains hat with frayed edges was covered with so much dirt and grime, its nautical symbols were barely visible. It had to be months since soap touched his dark blue pants. Beneath his black suspenders, splotches of blood and dried fish scales covered his once white pocket T-shirt.

I'm sure his clothes can stand on their own, thought Max.

"How did me friends die?" asked Skimmer, his eyes filling with tears.

"We don't know who or what killed them," said Dad. "Creatures from the sea boarded the ship and decapitated all of them." He put his hand on Skimmer's shoulder. "I'm sorry, my friend, I wish there was better news."

Skimmer stared at the area where the *Isabella* was obliterated. "He was a good man and me good friend. Everyone on that ship was good men. The best I's ever known. What do I's tells Vic's family?"

"Tell them the sea took their lives," said Max. "It's not a lie."

"Aye," said Skimmer, swallowing hard. "I's gotta get to the upper helm."

Max rolled out of his way and watched Skimmer climb the metal stairs. He took a seat at the secondary helm and swiveled the white chair around, facing the bow of the ship, staring straight out over the ocean as if in a trance.

"Let's take a moment to relax," said Dad. "It's been an awful night."

The two sat on a long white bench on the portside of the ship. Then Max noticed something he never thought he'd see.

The Amalia is spotless.

He had envisioned fish guts and tackle lying about with chips and scratches in the fiberglass, but instead, the deck and benches were in pristine condition, immaculate white with no stains. The old salty swore he would keep the vessel in tip-top shape—*and he did.*

"He's taking good care of his ship," said Dad.

"I wish he'd take care of himself the same way," said Mandy. "The smell is killing me."

"Behave yourself," said Dad, his expression stern. "You will not insult another man who saved our lives."

"I know," said Mandy, flustered. "I know."

Max kept his eyes on Skimmer. His head was lowered, and he had slumped forward, gripping the helm's wheel. His shuddering body told Max he was crying. After several minutes, Skimmer lifted his head and started mumbling indecipherable words.

A fisher's prayer? thought Max.

Whether his eyes were open or closed, he didn't know. Skimmer finished his whispers then pulled from his pocket a mangy rag and wiped his face. He came down the stairs and sat beside his dad without saying a word. Mandy rose from sitting and stood next to him in Nessie. Their father was eyeing her, signaling her to sit again. She didn't move.

Skimmer removed a corn cob pipe from his pants pocket. After tapping the bowl a few times on the palm of his hand, the loosened tobacco fell out, and he tossed it over the side of the ship. He replaced it with a pinch from his crusted shirt pocket. A swipe of the match on his bristled chin lit the fire, and he puffed on the pipe as the tobacco burned.

Max smiled. *Just like a pirate.*

"Me *Amalia's* on auto and runnin' at full speed to get us away from here. The radar and sonar is up. If anyone or anythin' within two miles comes near, we'll knows about it."

"Why did you come out here?" asked Dad.

"Me friends on Madeira tolds me some sea snake types landed there yesterday. Theys were askin' about ya, pushin' their weight around, being nasty. I's tolds Vic to meet on the open sea, 'cause it be more safe. He's said he would talks to ya and let me know, but when he's didn't call back, I's knew somethin' be wrong. Me *Amalia* can kick butt when she has to."

"Thank you, Skimmer, you're a good friend," said Dad, "but considering what's happened to the *Isabella*, taking us to the Azores will be enough. We don't want to put you in danger."

Skimmer took a drag from his pipe and blew out the smoke. "Whatever killed me friends may come back. No, matey, I's stay with ya's and don't be trying to change me mind. I's not have it."

"You're being pig-headed," said Dad. "Dangerous people are after us, and I can't lose another friend. Please reconsider."

"Nays," said Skimmer, shaking his head. "I's not." He stood up and approached Mandy. "So, lassie, how's are ya?" He spread out his arms. "Come and give ole Skimmer a hug!"

Dad glared at her and nudged his head. Without getting too close to Skimmer, she bent forward and gave him a light hug. Skimmer wrapped his arms around her like a bear and lifted her off the floor.

"Oh my," said Mandy, "how nice."

The green tinge on Mandy's face told Max she was ready to puke. Skimmer put her down and smiled, exposing a wide black space where four teeth should be.

"Look how cleans me are?" said Skimmer. "I's even bathed fer ya."

He may have bathed, thought Max, chuckling inside, *but he didn't wash his clothes. She's going to barf any moment.*

"Yes," said Mandy, stepping out of his grip. "Thank you, Uncle Skimmer."

"Now, Jack," said Skimmer, "I's needs the coordinates. Either ya coughs it up, or I's stop the *Amalia* and we stays here till ya do. Don't be messin' wit' me."

Max was familiar with this old fisher's stubbornness; there was no changing his mind. His father gave him the small note from his shorts pocket.

"These are the coordinates," said Dad. "You're a bull-headed mule."

"That be true," said Skimmer, "but I's not the idiot who hooks a man's hat and throws it out to sea four times, and the last one almost pierced me nose for free."

Max laughed along with Mandy. Their father grunted.

Skimmer glanced down at the slip of paper. "We be close to these coordinates. Now tells me what this be all about."

Mandy said, "We found a Book containing coordinates to the legendary city of Atlantis, and we're trying to confirm our findings."

Skimmer nodded his head then walked to the main pilothouse where he punched the coordinates into the GPS. The *Amalia* started turning. Max drove to Skimmer who was staring at the open sea. His father and Mandy joined them.

"Are you all right, Uncle Skimmer?" asked Max.

Skimmer sat on the white seat and took another drag of his pipe.

"I's told no one this truth," he said, "and ya's have to swear you'lls not repeat me words."

Skimmer's crunched brow and distraught eyes revealed a fear Max had never seen before in the man. He wasn't afraid of anything, yet what he was about to tell them was something that truly frightened him.

"We swear," said Dad.

"Twas thirty years ago," he said, blowing out smoke, "when I's was a younger lad. Me and me Uncle John were fishin' aboard his ship, the *Maria Lee*. Twas a good fishin' day and we were headin' back to port wit' a good eight hundred pounds a fish. Then the winds kicked up, the clouds rolled in, and the *Maria Lee* was toppled over by a wave, the likes I's never seen before. Over we went into the raging blue, screaming to hear each other, but nothin' got through the roars of the angry sea. I's struggled to stays afloat, gulping in the briny deep and flailing me arms to keeps me head above water. I's wokes up on a sandy beach, me body feeling like it been runs over by a tanker. The bow of the *Maria Lee* was layin' beached. Her stern was missin', she been broke in half. Concerns fer me Uncle John, I's went looking fer him."

He took another drag of his pipe and continued, "The beach had big rocks, the kinds a man could hide behind. I's saw me Uncle a ways down, lyin' flats on the sand. I's began runnin' to him when I's saws two monsters come out of the water. Theys were giants, fulla' muscle, and walk'ded like apes. I's never seen ugly faces like these, alls crooked like they were in a fish grinder. The sight of them made me legs shake, so I's gots behind a rock hoping they didn't see me."

He stopped talking and bowed his head.

"Did they hurt Uncle John?" asked Max.

"Worse than that, me boy," said Skimmer. "Me Uncle wokes up and saw them. He screamded like I's never heard a man scream before. They…they," he went silent again.

"You don't have to talk about it," said Mandy.

Skimmer's face squeezed in anguish. "They ates him alive, lassie. He was screaming while theys ripped him apart. Chawin' on his flesh like sharks on a dead carcass."

A shiver ran through Max's spine.

"I's never told anyone," said Skimmer. "I's just said me Uncle John drowned at sea. I's went over it in me head fer years, trying to convince meself I's could have done somethin', but inside me soul, I's knew there was nothin'. After, theys tore's off his head and carried it wit' them back into the sea." Skimmer's gaze went to the floor. "Do ya thinks I's was a coward?"

"You're one of the bravest men I've ever met," said Mandy. She clutched his hand. "You are not a coward. You did the right thing, and I feel safe when I'm around you."

"Thank ya, lassie," said Skimmer. "I's needed to hear that. I's fishded all over this world, but only these parts have legends of man-eatin' monsters. Whatcha' suppose that means?"

"It means they live in this area of the Atlantic," said Max.

"I can deal with psycho humans," said Mandy, "but man-eating monsters? No way. I think we should forget this whole thing and just lie low."

"This is *the* Atlantis, Mandy," said Max, "not a fictitious story. If we give up, the Renaldo's would have died for nothing. We have to pursue this."

Max sensed Mandy's fear. Hideous cannibals and a ruthless psychotic were chasing them, not to mention the cripple in a wheelchair who might get them caught. If he was to back away from the situation, his father and Mandy could find Atlantis. His heart ached from the reality. All his life he waited for a moment like this and now that it was here, he had to leave it behind. Mandy and his dad were talking to each other. He had to protect them. They were his life. There was no choice.

"I'll go with Skimmer," said Max, "and you guys find Atlantis."

His father and Mandy stopped talking.

"Dude," said Mandy, "there's no way we're going without you. We do this together, or we don't do this. Period."

"It's a noble gesture," said Dad, "but we're not separating."

"But—"

Skimmer interrupted. "Ya done good till now, son, why spoils it?"

I'll never forgive myself if anything happens to them, thought Max. *I'll have to run when I get the chance. But how? My freakin' legs won't move. I need a plan.*

"So, how do we fight these things?" said Max.

"We don't," said Dad, "we avoid them. Let's get to the coordinates, make a quick scan with the SBS and then get out of there. We'll find a place to hide on land, and there we can continue with Atlantis. What do you think?"

"Anything that gets us away from the water sounds good," said Mandy.

"I agree," said Max, wondering if he could make his escape when they reached land.

"And one more thing, Max," said Mandy.

She leaned down in front of him, gripping Nessie's armrests; her expression filled with malice. He could feel her breaths on his face.

"I know you're thinking of running, but don't try it. If you do, there will be consequences."

He turned away, not wanting to look into her eyes. *Stupid nexus.* "Go away," he demanded.

"I don't care if you're in a wheelchair, I will beat the living crap out of you. You'll have so many bruises; people will think your skin is a natural blue. Remember the movie, *Alien*? The beating will be way worse."

"Max, are you going to run?" asked Dad.

Mandy stood straight, still glaring down at him. "If he's smart—never."

"I's be listenin' to ya sister, laddie," said Skimmer. "She'd be given me a fright wit' those words."

Max scowled at her. Sometimes being a twin was precarious, downright dangerous. Mandy was ruthless at times, and when she threatened him like that, she always carried it through. The worst fight they ever got into was when they were twelve years old.

A fight implies two people, thought Max, *but I didn't stand a chance.*

It was a special midnight showing of the old movie *Alien* on the big screen. Their parents had insisted it was too scary for them but they didn't care, so they snuck out of the house and walked to the theater. When it was over it was 2 a.m. and pitch-black outside. Max recalled how he had planned to scare Mandy as a joke. He knew she would be terrified alone in the dark. She kept saying the *Alien* creature was scary, and insisted Max not try anything. Of course, he couldn't resist, the plan was already in motion, so he hid behind a tree. Mandy was frantic and ready to bawl when she couldn't find him. Max had slipped on a monster mask and jumped out in front of her roaring. She had screamed so loud he thought he would go deaf. When she had realized it was him; the beating began.

He tried to defend himself, but she was like a raving mad gorilla. The punches to his face and arms along with the kicks to his legs left bruises all over his body that hurt for days. It was summer, and they both got grounded for three weeks, which meant he had to stay in the house with King Kong. She refused to talk to him, and every time he tried to start a conversation with her, she'd punch his arm hard, leaving another bruise. It was the worst summer he'd ever had, and the most painful. And now he was in a wheelchair, defenseless. *Maybe the Flash Taser?* She would kill him.

His father squatted beside him and held his hand. "My son, the hero. Always thinking of others before himself. But this time, I need you to think of how much my heart would break if I lost you. Please, Max, promise me you won't run."

Max gazed into his dad's warm and caring gray eyes. *Could I lie to him? Should I do it to protect them?* They were his life and legs. If he was captured, Preston would use them to get to him. *What if those monsters come back?* The Flash Taser on Nessie was set at quarter power, but at full strength the creatures might be disabled or even fried. He sighed. *I can't lie to him and I may be their only protection from those creatures.*

There was no choice. He had to stay.

"I promise," he responded, "but I don't like it."

"Good," said Skimmer, "'cause we at the coordinates."

CHAPTER 20
Max

The *Amalia* was floating above the coordinates with her engines off. Max was at the helm and readying the SBS when he noticed the sun cresting the horizon. The sea lightened its colors as it approached the sun, ranging from deep blue to sapphire, and ending with a bright amber gold. Glowing hues of apricot and copper infused the billowy clouds and radiated outward like a brilliant crown. Streaks of crimson and yellow set the heavens ablaze, fanning out for miles across the cerulean sky. The sea itself was flat with an occasional fish rippling the surface. If he didn't know better, he would think the majestic sunrise was supposed to relax him.

It doesn't and can't, thought Max.

The grisly night was still fresh in his mind. The storm, the cannibals, and the missile that destroyed the *Isabella* were terrifying thoughts he wished he could forget.

"Max," said Mandy, "quit daydreaming. I want out of this place."

"Don't you like sunrises? This one is beautiful."

"I love them but right now, staying alive is more important."

"Right," he answered.

He had created the SBS with an attached slide-out pole, which could slip back within itself for travel. Being that its only purpose was to lower the SBS into the water, five-inch PVC pipe was perfect. It connected to the head of the unit, a black circular eighteen-inch metal saucer with a sensing element hidden inside. On the flat bottom of the disk beneath the sensor was a tiny round door. His dad had clamped the extended white pole to the port side hull. The saucer had to sit at least three feet in the water.

"It's at four feet," said Mandy, reading the laptop screen. "What now?"

"Watch and learn."

On Nessie's swing out desk was his laptop and what he called the *iPulse*, a reconfigured *iPad*. It took Max three weeks to alter the transparent *iPulse* to work with the SBS. The tablet was a rectangular crystal made of fused quartz and transparent silver. It was twelve-by-nine-inches with a thickness of only one-eighth-inch and weighed a mere six ounces. With his adjustments, it now held two petabytes of information. Mandy thought it wasn't enough, but when he told her one petabyte could store the DNA of the entire population of the USA and then clone them twice, she retracted her statement.

I love science, he thought, feeling the smoothness of the device and remembering how satisfied he was when he had finished creating it. His integrations worked perfect.

"Concentrate, Max," said Mandy.

"Right, I'm sorry."

He rechecked the two black sealed wires going into the PVC pipe connecting to the sensor. They were unmovable. He plugged one end of a USB cable into the *iPulse* and the other end to the laptop. Next to the boat, a volley-ball size bubble came up from the water and popped. Max smiled.

"What was that?" asked Dad.

"Just part of the process," said Max, trying to concentrate on the *iPulse*. This is the moment he'd been waiting for. The real test of his SBS. The warmth of the three bodies hovering over him were making him sweat, but they were excited too. Yellow scrolling equations filled the nineteen-inch screen of the laptop.

Not two seconds had passed when Mandy said, "Are we there yet?"

"No, and don't bug me. I'm making the adjustments now, and…we're there."

The top two-thirds of the screen displayed a bright three-dimensional High Definition color picture of the seafloor. Below this was a horizontal yellow graph with titles and scales.

"Whats we lookin' at?" asked Skimmer.

"The Canary Basin," said Max, "about four miles down."

"I only see rocks, seaweed, and fish," said Mandy.

"Patience, sis. My program is still gathering data. This type of stuff takes a little time."

"How ya doin' all this, laddie?" asked Skimmer.

Max looked straight up at Skimmer. A slimy band of dark saliva edged the stem of his corn cob pipe. The thought of it plopping on his head was making him sick.

"The mechanics are based on a small pod about the size of a pen tip filled with millions of piconites. When ejected from the SBS, the pod travels four hundred miles a minute—"

"Holds it!" said Skimmer. "Laddie, nothin' can go that fast and not be a spaceship, and ya needs tons a gas to run those things."

"Humans need gas," said Mandy, "but Max isn't human."

Max ignored her comment. "It's new science. Now, the pod makes its way to the bottom and blows open just before hitting the seafloor. The piconites spread out in a one hundred-foot-circle and then send their data wirelessly to the *iPulse*."

It was difficult for everyday people to comprehend the intricacy of his inventions. Though his father knew what he was talking about, Mandy and Skimmer had to be told in a simpler way.

"Hey, moron," said Mandy. "Wake up, we want out of here."

He wanted to slap her head, but she'd beat him up for it. "You're not scientist material."

"Explain how these itty-bitty metal things can resist the high pressure of the ocean?" asked Mandy.

"Remember the T-1000 dude in the Terminator movie? They work just like that. The alloy can adjust itself to the pressure, even liquefying, but always keeping its original function. It's simple physics, that's all."

"Holy cow, Max," said Dad, grinning, "you're changing science as we know it."

"Mom helped me with the formula but after she died, it was hard to keep working on it because it reminded me of her. I finally finished it a few months ago. Now just before the ball hits bottom, it explodes, releasing millions of telemetric piconites. It takes about two minutes for the piconites to consolidate their data into one signal and then send the findings back to the *iPulse*." He turned around, shifting his eyes between Mandy and Skimmer. "Do you two understand?"

"Aye," said Skimmer, scratching his head. "Now tells me about ya energy source."

"Max makes his own batteries," said Mandy, "the kind that don't need recharging for fifty years."

Skimmer straightened up, and Max sighed in relief knowing there would be no black gooey tobacco falling on his head.

"Well, me boy, no wonders the devil man wants ya. Yer' smarter than all the egg heads put together."

"Why am I finding this out now?" said Dad. "Why didn't you tell me about the batteries before?"

"There are a lot of things I forget to tell you guys about. It's not that I don't want to, it's just that my head gets bogged down with formulas and equations, and sometimes even I have a tough time keeping up with it. I know the battery thing was important, and I'm sorry."

"Is there anything else you haven't told me about?"

"Well...," Max hesitated, knowing what he was about to tell their dad would upset him. "I created a base formula for infinite energy, something similar to the sun that can regenerate its own power."

"What?" said Dad. "When?"

"I had written the four lines of code on my computer right before the first hack from Global. Preston has it, and I'm hoping he can't decipher it."

His father stood up and shook his head. "There's nothing you can do about that now, but I wish you would keep me informed about your creations. It means a lot to me."

"I will," said Max, "and I'm sorry."

Mandy pointed at the laptop screen. "What are the empty rows on the bottom for?"

"Data. The first line is water temperature, pressure, and currents, which are strong at that depth."

"The current is only fourteen feet an hour," said Mandy. "That's not strong."

"No," said Dad, "that's fourteen feet a second. Now imagine the tons of water moving in that current. It's strong."

"Wait a minute," said Mandy. "That picture you showed us on the *Isabella* of the outlined city, when did Google make it?"

"That one wasn't from Google," said Max. "I hacked it off the NASA site, and it's from this year. The first Google picture is from 2009, but they said the lines were overlapping datasets, so in 2012 and 2024 they fixed it." He tapped a key, and Google's new rendition of the seafloor appeared. "This is their up-to-date version and if you look close, the lines are still there."

"You hacked a government site?" asked Dad, his eyebrows were burrowed hard and stiff.

"Don't ask," said Mandy. "I know it's upsetting, but now is not the time to get into this."

"Change your tone, young lady."

"Sorry," she said, "but we need to get out of here pronto and quibbling about stuff already done is wasting time."

"Yer full of fire, lassie," said Skimmer, grinning, "but she be right, Jack. Settles it later."

If dad only knew how many times I've hacked NASA, thought Max, *he'd have kittens.*

"I's thought Atlantis was round like a plate, not square," said Skimmer.

"Wait a minute," said Mandy. "What if those lines aren't overlapping datasets, what if they're tunnels that once existed beneath the destroyed city? Obviously, the buildings are gone but every capitol has its secret tunnels, so why not Atlantis?"

There was silence.

"My daughter, the outstanding archeologist," said their Dad. "That makes sense and would explain why the lines aren't concentric. You're way smarter than you think."

"See," said Mandy, slapping Max on the arm. "I've got brains too."

"No, you don't," said Max rubbing his arm. "Your brains are made of caramel Frappes."

Mandy stared at him. "I can't argue with that."

They both laughed.

"Now what's the second line on the bottom of the graph for?" asked Dad.

"The program will search for any anomaly not belonging on the sea bottom, and this is where the dimensions will appear. The third line is for chemical analysis. These bottom two lines will take longer to come in."

"Are ya looking fer anythin' particular, son?" asked Skimmer, bending over him again.

His breath could grow mold in mid-air, thought Max.

"Yes, orichalcum. If it's present, it'll appear as an 'unknown.'"

"I's heard of that," said Skimmer. "That be the gold of Atlantis."

The laptop beeped. The second line was filling with data.

"It found something," said Max, working the tabs on the *iPulse*. The picture displayed the precise yellow lines of a hexagon. "It's man-made and fifty feet below the sea bottom."

"Maxie, ya blowin' me mind," said Skimmer. "How do ya know that thing be man-made?"

"Because only man-made objects would have precision angles like that," said Max.

The three behind him leaned in closer, almost smothering him.

"Back up, all of you," said Max, reaching up and trying to push them away. "I can't breathe."

"Is that real?" asked Mandy.

"Yes," said Max, relaxing after the near suffocation. "I think it's a broken pillar tilted at an angle."

"What's its diameter?" asked Dad.

"The measurements are in and…almost," said Max, making more adjustments. "There. The second line," he pointed.

"Seventy-five feet wide?" said Mandy. "That's huge for a column."

"Imagine its height," said Max.

Three loud beeps sounded on the laptop. The words "unknown" scrolled sideways across the bottom line. The display blinked a few times and then went black.

"What the—" said Max, tapping the *iPulse*. He typed on the laptop. "I don't know what happened. There must be some kind of interference."

"We don't know the properties of orichalcum," said Dad. "Maybe it's blocking the signals."

"Or it could be the gadgets malfunctionin'," said Skimmer. "I's not be tryin' to upset ya, boy, but the sea has secrets it don't wanna' be sharin'."

The *Amalia* shuttered. Ripples of water flowed out from beneath her.

"What was that?" asked Mandy, squeezing Max's shoulders. She was afraid again.

Skimmer ran to the bridge. "Maxie, I's turnin' on the radar and sonar," he shouted. "I's need to check the area."

"Go for it," said Max, and he shut the laptop disconnecting the USB leaving it dangling off the *iPulse*. "It's not working anyway."

Another hard tremor shook the *Amalia*. There was a loud snap. The fishing outriggers broke off from the ship and swung around, crashing into the side of the vessel. Max held the laptop to his chest with one arm, the other hand was holding down the *iPulse*.

"Jack!" yelled Skimmer, "ya best come look at this!"

The shaking got worse. Nessie's segmented seat belt sprang out, securing Max in place, while Mandy wrapped her arms around Max from behind. His father staggered over to Skimmer struggling not to fall. Skimmer reached out and took his arm, pulling him to the helm. The trembling stopped. The sea was flat again. The eyes of the two men were glued to the sonar.

"Is that what I's thinks it is?" asked Skimmer.

"It's another missile, isn't it?" yelled Mandy from behind Max. "We've got to get out of here!"

"Let's go!" said Dad. "Mandy, bring in the SBS, we're leaving!"

Skimmer turned the key. Nothing.

"We have to go!" cried Mandy, handing the SBS to Max. "Can't you jump-start it?"

Skimmer laid on the floor and slid under the helm. "This ain't a car, lassie, if the engines don't start, they be broke. Me *Amalia's* never done this."

Max watched Skimmer yank out two wires. He touched them together several times, but there was no spark. The batteries were dead.

"We have less than three minutes!" shouted Dad. "Skimmer, inflate the raft. We'll carry Max aboard and leave Nessie behind. It's our only chance."

Skimmer nodded and rushed to the bow of the *Amalia*. He lifted a hatch on the floor and pulled out a folded orange raft. After yanking the yellow cord, it began inflating, and he flung it over the side, holding onto the attached rope.

The sea started swirling like a whirlpool, roaring and spinning the *Amalia*. The rope was jerked out of Skimmer's hand and he was thrown back, sliding on the floor until he hit the helm. Their father pulled him to standing and both struggled to make it across the deck to him and Mandy.

"Grab onto Nessie!" shouted Dad.

Nessie's grappling hooks shot out and bashed through the floor anchoring themselves.

"Ya put two blasted holes in me ship!" cried Skimmer.

"Sorry!" yelled Max.

It was difficult to breathe as the spinning got worse. The loud groans and squeals from the Amalia were getting closer together; she was going to be ripped apart.

"No!" shouted Max as the *iPulse* was torn away from him. It flew into the ocean, dragging the PVC pole and the SBS.

In front of the ship, an explosion from below sent a plume of seawater into the air. A giant swell sent the bow of the Amalia soaring upwards, then thrust her backward with a massive force. The four screamed as the ship rocked and swayed to the violent sea. Max could see popping muscles and veins in the arms of the two men squeezing Nessie's armrests. With no signs of stopping, the sea had miraculously calmed as if silenced by a god. It was flatter than paper. Max looked at the others whose expressions were saying the same as him.

What just happened?

Several loud pounding thumps came from the stern of the ship, dipping the aft into the water. Before Max could turn around, a loud inhuman roar vibrated the vessel.

CHAPTER 21
Preston

Preston had just left a business meeting in London and was sitting comfortably aboard his private jet. The flight would only take a mere forty minutes over the Atlantic due to the hypersonic engines aboard his modified Concorde 6. The jet looked more like a spaceship with its sleek elongated body, an aerodynamic delta wing, and engines that could take-off and land vertically. The aircraft contained the latest in Global technology and thanks to the Coverter, it was invisible to any radar. Its undetectable fifteen air-to-surface missiles and one high-powered laser guaranteed his survival. The jet bounced a few times, and he nervously grabbed the armrests for support.

It's just turbulence, he reassured himself. *I'll be back in New York soon.*

His soft corpulent stomach was slowing its rolling waves, and he sighed. One of his labs was doing a new study on sea kelp where obesity would be a thing of the past. Imagine eating all you want and never gaining weight. His scientists promised it was just a year or two away, but patience was something he severely lacked. He smirked when he recalled the last words of Dr. Ernst Biermann in the Biomimetics Division, "Get out of my lab!" The sledgehammer to his head was more than comforting—*it was pure ecstasy.*

With his muscles now relaxed, his eyes perused the exquisite cabin. White plush cushioned sofas and chairs sat on a sea-blue rug. In front of him, a ninety-six-inch television was centered between marble pilasters. Down the main hallway, Rembrandts and Bernini's graced the walls. The galley was on the left where several chefs awaited his commands. His elegant bedroom took up the whole back half of the jet and came complete with a whirlpool tub and sauna. This jet was the most prestigious aircraft ever built and his pilots were the best. Soft music was playing in the background, so he snuggled into his burgundy recliner, making sure his head was set firmly against the cushioned back so he could link with his favorite toy, the NCS or Neural Cognition System. Thinking of what he stole from Max, a blue beam flickered on in front of his chair and it grew to a life-size 3-D revolving hologram of the kid in a wheelchair.

He was glad Max survived. The spider venom that almost took his life was from an unknown species of arachnid. If the Williams's did find a book written by the Atlanteans, it would unearth the most valued prize in all history. The studies on Atlantis revealed they had the secret to eternal life. At first, he scoffed at the idea of any human living forever, but Jack Williams would never chase legends or fairytales. And most important, it was said they had a source of endless energy, something he desperately needed for Oveipa.

The hologram changed from Max to a live transmission of the construction of his underwater city with its giant silver domes and connecting walkways. Oveipa was a Greek word meaning 'dreams,' an appropriate name he chose because it was his dream coming true. Its location was three hundred miles off the Brazilian coast, a mile and a half down and in an area unexplored and uninteresting.

A place no one would care to look.

Right now, the only access to Oveipa was from above on an isle he had purchased and named after himself, Black Island. It was a six-mile islet complete with a two-hundred-room mansion, docking facilities for his luxurious yacht, and several helicopter pads. What no one saw was the seven decrepit jail cells beneath the mansion, complete with dirt floors, snakes and spiders big enough to scare any man. The solitary confinement cell or the Hole was outside the house hidden amongst the trees. It was a basic cement box placed in the ground with an additional heater that could pump in hot air.

A secret passage behind the fireplace in the library led down to a diving facility, which stowed ROVs (Remotely Operated Vehicles), deep sea bathyspheres, and every kind of machinery needed to build Oveipa. One of the bathyspheres was designed just for him, and he cringed at the memories of being in the seat harness and lowered into the small ship. Because the bathysphere confinement was distressing, he'd only been to Oveipa four times.

One day I'll go there and never come back.

The live hologram slowly revolved. Divers and submersible cranes were finishing the last of the sixty-five silver housing domes. In its center, an immense dome housed the Power Plant and Labs. Shops, restaurants, theaters, parks, pools, and even a fully stocked hospital were almost finished. His beloved Oveipa would have everything his private army and their families would need to survive. If all goes well, it was eleven months away from completion.

I have eighteen engineers monitoring the site 24/7 from the Dungeon, and so far, they've caught everything.

Oveipa would take a small city of people to run it, and a select group to maintain it. He needed a race of beings who could breathe water and be impervious to the high pressures at over seventeen thousand feet below sea level. They had to be controllable, both mentally and physically, a slave race able to perform all the menial and life-threatening tasks.

I got the best geneticists, he thought. *Give them lots of money, a good challenge, all the equipment they want, and they're in.*

Human DNA cross-typing with insects and amphibious creatures was working, though it was excruciating for the person and many of them died. But live subjects were not a problem. There were plenty of third world countries where humans, male and female, meant nothing. With the Coverter, silent helicopters picked up useless people, including the thousands of homeless in the United States. They were taken to the Dungeon in New York where the scientists anxiously awaited their new specimens. But until the ultimate mutation was successful, robotic rovers would have to make the outside repairs on Oveipa, something that was not cost effective.

From Oveipa, by way of his satellites, he would be able to hack any system whether on land or sea, change whatever he wanted, and force the mighty nations to turn on each other, thus annihilating themselves and leaving the remaining survivors to him. If the governments decided not to bomb each other, he would do it for them. Oveipa was his kingdom, his dream, and he would be the self-appointed King.

The problem was Oveipa took vast amounts of energy to keep it running. Six building-size generators had already been completed. Nonetheless, the Coverter needed more. So, he ordered three more generators to be constructed, and these still weren't enough. There was only so much room in the Power Plant, and space was becoming an issue. Atlantis and Max were the solutions. If Atlantis failed, the kid was his second option. Getting Max was crucial.

The door to his private quarters opened, and he closed the hologram. Darla was wearing a tight red sultry dress divulging her voluptuous figure. Her wavy blonde hair lay softly on her shoulders, and her hypnotic, sexy blue eyes could light up any man. Without any doubt, she resembled Marilyn Monroe, except with longer hair. As she approached him, her Imperial Majesty No. 1 perfume scented the air.

The stupid bottle cost me over five hundred grand. Of course, the Baccarat crystal bottle came with a ten-carat diamond attached to a twenty-four-karat gold collar.

Darla was by far the most trustworthy of all the secretaries he'd had, and the most accommodating. She was slightly overweight which made her even more attractive.

"The pilot says we'll be landing in New York in fifteen minutes," she said with her cute chirpy voice; her beautiful blue eyes glinting. "Do you want a meal waiting for you at Global?"

"Make it a thirty-ounce Porterhouse, three baked potatoes, and broccoli."

"Rare with sour cream, bacon, butter, and the broccoli with olive oil, right, sir?

"Perfect," he said, ogling her. "And what's for dessert?"

She smiled and was about to answer when another hologram arose, displaying a phone number.

"Dante must have found something," he said. "Get out."

CHAPTER 22
Max

"You not belong here," said a grated voice.

Max spun Nessie around to see three creatures standing at the rear of the ship, monsters over nine feet tall. They resembled the one that had attacked them on the *Isabella*. He cringed at the grotesque red flesh surrounding their bulging eyes, and the long slender teeth overlapping their drooling mouths. The thought of being eaten alive like Skimmer's uncle made him tremble.

"Who are you?" asked Dad.

"Drexin. Give us Book."

"Why are you here?"

They bent their knees and held out their fists roaring. Gooey lines of green saliva linked both jaws. The *Amalia* vibrated like it was going to fall apart, and then they charged. Max adjusted the Flash Taser and bashed the button. A white beam shot out and hit the first monster in the chest sending it flying back into the other two, and all three were thrown to the deck. The stunned one rolled and squirmed to the electro-static bolts arcing through its body. The unaffected fallen pair swung their legs and leapt to their feet. The electric discharges faded on the first one and it growled, straining to stand.

"Full power, Max," said Mandy.

"That was full power."

Without warning, three humanoid figures flew out of the water, flipped in the air, and landed on the stern of the boat, behind the animals. There were two males and one female, and all of them couldn't have been over sixteen years old. Their pure white hair seemed to be natural. The two men were six feet in height and wearing black pants with attached feet; an orange-gold belt wrapped their long sleeve collarless shirts. One wore a blue shirt, while the other was green, and both sparkled with tiny yellow diamonds. What stood out the most was their oversized eyes. The blue man blinked, and it took longer than usual because of their bigness. On their right arms, each was wearing a silver wristlet with a turquoise oval stone in its center.

The girl was about five feet tall and wore a pink pearl necklace with a bright red pendant. Long thick white hair cascaded over her shoulders to the center of her thighs. Beneath her hair he could see a multicolored bandeau of glimmering shells covering her breasts. Her facial features were subtle and delicate, but her big violet eyes were so beautiful he had to remember to breathe. He leaned forward in Nessie, squinting his eyes.

Is she half naked?

Her long hair covered most of her front, but he could make out the sides of her body. Large twinkling scales began at her waist, covering everything necessary, then got smaller as they continued down her legs becoming specs of light on her feet. His mouth dropped open.

A mermaid?

"We will not allow you to harm these Narins," said the boy in the green shirt.

We're Narins? thought Max.

"Book ours," growled the creature. "Go, Ranyn, you live."

Those beasts are immense, said Max in his mind. *How are those kids going to fight them?*

"Scaph," said Ranyn, "you cannot win this." He held out his hand. "Leave these Narins and let us help you."

It's the same freak from the Isabella!

Scaph's two companions were looking at each other confused. Max hurried to the portside with his dad. Mandy and Skimmer were on the starboard side opposite them.

"We not come!" shouted Scaph. "You cause pain. You die!"

Scaph leapt into the air towards Ranyn who kicked him away. His body flew up the middle of the ship and bashed into the *Amalia's* helm. Electric sparks jumped across the navigational panel as the beast rolled off. He leapt to his feet and his black eyes rolled back white as he charged Ranyn with his claws out. Ranyn shifted to the side and punched the back of Scaph's head with his fist. The creature crashed through the transom and tumbled off the ship, splashing into the sea.

"Me ship!" cried Skimmer.

The two remaining Drexins were grappling with the humanoids who were averting their swings and grabs. One Drexin hit the boy dressed in blue. His body went fifty feet into the air and then hit the deck causing a crack to spike across the floor. He sprang to his feet and punched the creature in the face, knocking him down and making him delirious. The girl sent a swift kick to the other Drexin's gut. The monster went airborne over the ocean and hit the water three hundred feet away with a giant splash.

They're just as strong, thought Max, amazed at the sight.

"Aleena, get the boy!" shouted Ranyn.

Max stiffened up. *What?*

The girl was almost to him when his father jumped in front of him, blocking her approach. She stumbled to a stop, then turned to Ranyn. Max saw small bolts of pink static formed around the turquoise stone of Ranyn's silver bracelet. He lifted his palm and an electrified coral beam hit his father in the chest, flinging him against the sidewall of the pilothouse where he slid to the floor unconscious.

"Dad!" cried Mandy.

"I's got him!" said Skimmer, who rushed to his dad.

Max held his breath. The girl started running towards him again when Mandy threw herself in front of him. The woman snatched her instead and leapt into the water.

"Mandy!" screamed Max, reaching out to her as she went overboard. An ear-shattering boom vibrated the air.

"That'll be enough," said Skimmer, holding a sawed-off shotgun.

Everyone froze. His dad was lying still, not moving.

"Now explain what in blazes is happenin' here," said Skimmer, "and don't be tryin' anything. I's a good shot."

"Kiet," said Ranyn.

With his wristlet glowing yellow, the boy in blue thrust out his hand. A golden beam whisked the shotgun out of Skimmer's grasp, and he flung it far into the Atlantic. The boat tilted to portside. Thick deformed fingers had gripped the wall of the *Amalia*. Two Drexins climbed aboard the vessel. Scaph's long fangs had bitten into his bottom lip, red blood was streaming out. The delirious Drexin sat up and growled, then stood next to Scaph. Ranyn nodded to Kiet, and both raised their palms at the three Drexins. Their wristbands glowed in unison and blue beams encased the creatures. They roared and flailed as they rose into the air. With one quick fling, they hurled them out to sea where Max lost sight of them.

"We must have Max," said Ranyn. "We will not harm him."

Skimmer got in front of Max. "Ya nots be takin' me boy."

Ranyn nodded at Kiet again. A coral beam from Kiet's hand slammed Skimmer against the console, knocking him out. The two boys now stood before Max. He kept bashing his fist on the Flash Taser button, but it was dead.

"Your weapon has been disabled," said Ranyn.

Max clutched the laptop to his chest. "You'll get nothing out of me until you tell me where my sister is!"

Ranyn didn't reply as he lifted him out of Nessie and dove off the *Amalia*. The last thing Max saw was a hand coming over his eyes, and then everything went black.

CHAPTER 23
Dante

Dante told Preston on his satphone, "They're in our sights, and we've jammed their frequencies."

Through his binoculars, he saw Jack and Mandy standing on the main deck of the *Amalia*. Their friend, Skimmer, was there too. Max had to be with them, they wouldn't leave him behind. The Intel forced out of the fishers on Madeira was correct. Pointing guns at the malodorous men didn't work, so one man was blown to bits with a grenade. The others became cooperative, and when they got the info they needed, a bullet to each head took care of them. The Ipon disks assured their bodies would never be found.

"There's an eight-figure bonus if you catch them now," said Preston on the phone, "but wait, I have to tell you about the brunette I met in London."

Dante's heart nearly leapt out of his chest, and he lowered his binoculars. The millions would be enough to take care of Jenna for the rest of her life. The tormenting grief returned, and he closed his eyes. He would never forget the grisly accident that ruined a kid's life.

***

2027 A.D.

After receiving an honorable discharge from the military, the peaceful drive up to Canada on his Harley was a welcome pleasure. He arrived at the home of his friend Pierre, his wife Monique, and their four-year-old daughter, Jenna. Several cuts and bruises were still on his face from the last battle with Isis when he'd met Jenna for the first time outside her home. A blonde haired, blue eyed pretty little girl who hugged him. She said she wished she had the boo-boos instead of him. The kid was almost crying, and he couldn't understand why.

Is she a retard? What's wrong with her?

Jenna crawled onto his lap and he froze. He had never held a child. There were more important things in life than having a family and— *this doesn't feel right.* Not knowing what to do with his arms, he crossed them over his chest. She was holding an ugly doll, a lifeless piece of plastic and cloth with one smashed eye and scissored blonde hair.

"Wow," he said, pulling on the matted tufts. "What happened to her hair?"

Jenna's gaze dropped to the ground. "I was a bad girl for not getting mommy her cigarettes. I was on the potty and hurried, but she got mad, so she cut Jasmine's hair and broke her eye."

The suppressed hatred he had carried for years sprang up like a ravenous wolf ready to pounce. Jenna was wearing a dirty pink T-shirt and filthy brown shorts. He noticed smudges of dirt on her face, arms, and legs. Her blonde hair was hanging in oily ringlets, and blotches of white flakes covered her scalp.

Then he saw it.

The edge of a black and blue mark just beneath her collar. He lifted the back of her shirt, stopping his gasp before she heard it. Raised scars along with fresh cuts and bruises covered her small back. Jenna yanked her shirt down and bowed her head again.

"Did mommy do that to you?" he asked.

"Daddy too. I'm always a bad girl, but I don't mean it."

Dante remembered struggling to hold back the powerful emotions wanting him to go inside and blow their heads off. Familiar with her pain, he was careful to pick her up and set her on the ground.

"I have to talk to mommy and daddy," he said. "You stay here and play with Jasmine."

He leaned on the kitchen door jamb watching the two cutting vegetables on the counter. The knives were looking *real* good. He wondered why he considered Pierre and Monique his friends. They were druggies wasting their lives away. Jenna was born when he was in the Seals, and their letters were filled with resentment because of having a girl. They had even considered giving her up for adoption. He cleared his throat.

"You're here!" said Monique, hugging him. "How was the ride up?"

Pierre shook his hand as he patted his shoulder. "Good to have you back, buddy."

"I met Jenna outside. You always beat your kid like that?"

Monique stepped back. "What did she tell you? She lies all the time, makes up stories about us."

"Those kinds of bruises don't lie."

"She fell down the stairs," said Pierre, "and that's the truth."

Not believing a word they said, he would give it careful consideration when he was alone. They were not going to get off that easy. To clear his mind, he insisted on taking Jenna for a ride on his Harley.

A drunk driver ran a red light, and he and Jenna went flying off the bike. The accident left Jenna a quadriplegic. In the hospital, he recalled sitting on a chair beside her bed, his face bandaged from top-to-bottom, holding her hand as she cried, begging him to make the boo-boo go away.

All his assassinations had involved people, adults who got in Preston's way. Never before had he murdered a kid, but this felt like he had. Jenna would never be able to play with Jasmine again, could never walk again, could never be a child again. And it was his fault because he was the one who took her for a ride on his bike. While he was unconscious in the hospital, Pierre and Monique had given up Jenna to the state. Their excuse was due to their finances, they couldn't raise a crippled child. Their addiction to drugs and alcohol had made them selfish and cruel, so when he was released from the hospital, he corrected the situation.

They'll never find those three bodies, he thought.

The brutal memories of his childhood came back like a raging fire, consuming his thoughts and emotions. Every bone, muscle, and tendon stiffened to the overpowering hatred. He would never forget the last merciless whipping from his parents at the young age of eight years old.

***

1994 A.D.

Dante had come home late one evening from a friend's house. They were playing video games, and the time had slipped away. His parents, Jacques and Vera were plastered as usual and waiting for him. Before he could explain why he was late, the beating began. The kicks, punches and swipes with the electric cord created lesions and bruises all over his body. He cried, begging for them to stop but in their usual drunkenness, they continued until he passed out.

The next morning, Uncle Remi, his father's younger brother and a former Navy Seal, woke him up. He was still on the kitchen floor lying on his back in dried blood. The painful breathing was unbearable, and he had to force himself not to faint again. Uncle Remi was gentle as he slid the sweaty black hair off his eyes.

"Who did this to you, Dante?" asked Remi.

His broken ribs made it difficult to speak. "Mama...papa," he stuttered.

"Have they done this befor—wait, all those times were beatings and not bicycle accidents?"

Dante nodded his head. Uncle Remi's face reddened as he heaved his breaths. He carefully laid him back down, then ran into the living room and started shouting at his parents. Dante dragged his body to the doorway, sliding on the tile floor. Blood oozed from the gashes on his back and uncontrollable tears rolled down his cheeks, but he had to see what was happening, so he peeked around the corner.

Uncle Remi and his father were grappling with a gun, and his mom was screaming at them. For a second, Uncle Remi glanced at him in the doorway, then both men stumbled to their knees still fighting. The gun went off and his mother's body slammed backward onto the couch. Blood poured from the hole in her chest. His dad jumped to his feet horrified, staring at his wife, and when he turned back around,

Uncle Remi was still on his knees with the gun aimed at his father's head. He said the words he'd never forget.

"You always thought you were a tough guy, and I've got the scars to prove it. This ends here."

Dante's whole body lurched to the sound of the gun. The bullet entered his father beneath the chin and blew out the back of his head. He collapsed onto the couch next to his wife. Uncle Remi was walking toward him with the gun in hand. Dante backed away terrified, too weak to get on his feet and escape. He was trembling, panic-struck, not knowing what to do, but when his uncle knelt before him, he saw the kindness in his eyes, a compassion he had never seen before in anyone.

"I'm sorry you saw that, kid," he said. "I was stupid to believe them when they told me all those times were bicycle accidents." His lips pursed in anger, and he shook his head in disgust. "Your parents were bad people. They should have never done this to you. Listen, Dante, right now I need your help. I'm going to wipe this gun clean, and I need you to hold it tight. The police will look for fingerprints, and I need yours to be on it. When they see what they did to you, they'll know why you killed them. Trust me, you won't go to jail. You can live with me, and I'll be the best dad anyone could have. I'll make you great." He smiled and held his chin. "Everything will be okay, son."

*****

PRESENT DAY

From then on, his life was comfortable. Although Uncle Remi was harsh at times, he never hit him. He had taught him all he needed to know about survival. As a former Black Seal, he trained Dante to show no mercy, no pity, just get the job done and get out of there. But his most important lesson was, "Never lose your humanity, because that's when you lose yourself." Uncle Remi had often reminded him to keep that part tucked away in the back of his mind and heart, so he could survive as a real person, and not a psychotic nutjob who only lives to kill. He remembered the many times Uncle Remi would squeeze his shoulder and say, "You are my humanity."

Jenna needed help, and he was going to make it happen. So, after adding another identity to his portfolio, he assumed the role of her uncle and had her placed in a small-town hospital in Canada. Because of its remoteness, he had to buy all the equipment needed to care for her. Cat Scan units, MRI scanners and a host of other machines had cost him hundreds of thousands, not to mention the salaries of the people who knew how to work them. He needed more money, and Preston was his ticket. But keeping her away from him was a challenge, the man could access any satellite, including the secret military ones. As a cover, he fabricated a rumor about a romantic affair with a nurse he'd met on a plane, which explained all the hefty donations to the hospital. That was a year ago.

Am I going soft? He was an assassin, a ruthless murderer, yet he was devoting an enormous amount of time and funds to care for a five-year-old girl who wasn't related to him. *So why am I doing this?*

A flashback of his demented parents rushed through his mind. When he'd seen how Jenna was beaten and thrown out like trash, his hatred resurfaced.

Jenna is my humanity, he reasoned, calming his nerves. *She keeps me real.*

Preston finally finished the story about the slut he'd met in London.

"Sounds like you had fun," said Dante. "Get the transfer ready "because we're coming up on their bow."

"Call me when you have them." There was a click.

He looked through his binoculars again and pressed his ear mic. "Prepare to board," he said. "Secure the prisoners and scuttle the ship."

The cocks of rifles never sounded better.

"Locked and loaded, sir," said Karim.

"Cut the engines!" said Dante. "What are they?"

CHAPTER 24
Dante

The bright sun was warm against Dante's pale skin as he inhaled the unadulterated air of the Atlantic. He was sitting in a chair on the deck of the *Apocalypse*, a nine hundred-foot gray battleship rivaling any military vessel ever built. The open hatchway of the ten-story hexagon shaped superstructure was in front of him; the only visible edifice on the ship. Its broad base spread across the deck becoming flush with both sides of the craft.

Hidden below were missiles, cannons, railguns, six long-range lasers, and all could be raised within seconds. Using seawater for propulsion, it was silent, dependable, and thanks to Max's Coverter, invisible. Even satellites couldn't find it. Its wedged shaped double-bow made it the fastest ship in existence, reaching speeds of over ninety knots. The *Apocalypse* was EMP proof, created to start a world war. And five more were almost finished. Dante wished he could use it to send a missile to Preston. But except for Karim, the remaining soldiers were loyal to Preston. Getting rid of the men would be easy, but neither he nor Karim knew how to work the boat, so all had to stay as is.

He puffed on his cigarette, and his muscles relaxed. Aside from having the Book and Max's wheelchair, the best part of the mission was coming up. Jack Williams was lying flat on the deck in front of him, groaning. He had been out for near twenty minutes, and nothing they did would revive him. His mussed up wavy hair, two-inch beard, and worn green Bermuda shorts answered why his contacts couldn't find him. He looked like a vagrant and not like the pristine Jack that worked at Global.

On a table beside him, the unwrapped Book and its amulet piece were lying atop a stainless-steel briefcase. When he had called Preston to inform him he had the Book, the man switched him over to the

Tesla Lab where the scientists almost drove him insane. They had a lot of questions and demanded he send them pictures. It was a deliberate attempt to annoy him.

All the more reason to waste him, he thought.

Jack moaned.

Dante kicked his leg. "Wake up, cupcake. We need to talk."

Jack blinked a few times. "Where am I?"

"You're aboard the *Apocalypse*," said Dante, taking another puff of his cigarette. "Max and Mandy are gone, and Skimmer's answering questions."

"Why are you do—wait, my kids," he groaned, straining to sit up. "Where are my children?"

"You need to pay attention, Jack. I said they're gone."

Jack was rubbing the back of his head as he got to his feet. "What?"

"It was the darndest thing I've ever seen. They took your kids and jumped right into the Atlantic. I think they were Atlanteans."

"What? Who?"

Dante recalled a beam of light come out from a humanoid's hand and hit Jack, knocking him out. Jack Williams didn't know what happened to his kids.

He leaned forward and placed his elbows on his thighs. "Listen, Jack. I saw two people take Max and Mandy into the Atlantic. They're gone, and there's nothing you or I can do." He sat back and took another drag on his cigarette. "Although Preston wanted Max, he's thrilled we have the Book."

Jack's mouth dropped open and he began to tremble. He slumped to his knees, cradled his face, and sobbed. "My babies…they were all I had."

Dante threw his lit cigarette at him. "Man-up, Jack! Quit acting like a wimp! You're fighting the most powerful man in the world. Did you honestly expect to win? Come on, Jack, your kids are dead. Deal with it."

Jack scowled at him then lurched forward, ready to charge, when Karim pressed a gun to his temple.

"Easy, tiger," said Karim.

Jack stopped. He was panting to the anger inside him, the writhing hate shown in his tightened gray eyes.

"Preston won't win this," said Jack. "You're on the wrong side."

"And how do you see things panning out?"

"Those entities came for the Book, and now you have it. Do you think your weapons will prevail over those advanced beings?"

The sounds of gunshots and shouting came from the open hatchway. Jack spun around to the commotion. Heavy boots were stomping up the grated metal stairs. Dante pulled out his pistol and wrapped his hand around Jack's throat, while shoving the gun barrel into his cheek. He nodded to Karim who moved out of sight. Skimmer stood in front of the hatchway with a *PX38* pointed at Dante. His face was drenched in blood, but it was his missing left eye that caught Dante's attention.

"Lets him go," said Skimmer.

"I'm surprised you can see us," chuckled Dante. "Right, Karim?"

Two bullets blasted through Skimmer's head. Blood and grey matter burst from the right corner of his forehead, taking out half his face. The front of Jack got sprayed with chunks of brain matter. Skimmer's lifeless body crumpled onto the deck. A puddle of blood formed around his emptied skull.

"No!" said Jack, squirming to release himself.

Dante bashed Jack's head with the butt of his gun, and he hit the deck unconscious. He dragged Jack by the arm and dropped his body in front of Karim.

"Use an Ipon on the fish head, and put Jack in the brig," said Dante. "Preston wants to talk to him."

"Aye, sir." Karim pulled out the black discoid from his pants pocket and tossed it onto Skimmer's body. Pressing his earpiece, he said, "One for the brig…have them come up here." He released the receiver. "We got two problems, sir. They're coming now."

Four soldiers dressed in black ST suits exited the hatchway. Two dragged Jack's limp body away, while the other two stood at attention in front of Dante.

"How did that fish gut get the best of you?" he asked.

"He had a knife, sir," said Wayne, a hefty Californian built like an ape.

A long bloody tear opened the front of Wayne's green camouflage shirt. The other man, Bomani, an ex-poacher from the Congo, had a bleeding gouge on his right cheek.

Dante stood up. "Nothing disappoints me more than failure."

He took his Glock 94 from his holster and shot Wayne between the eyes. The hulking man hit the deck with a boom. Bomani jumped away, terrified. Dante clamped his hand around the back of Bomani's neck and pressed the gun to his forehead.

"Never fail me again!"

"Yes, sir!" stuttered Bomani. "Never again, sir!"

He released him and nodded. "Now set an Ipon on that scum and get out of my face."

Bomani saluted him. "Aye, sir!"

Dante took a seat as he watched the soldier carry out his orders. Skimmer's body had already dissolved, leaving only a small mist of fading gas. He removed a cigarette from his inside pocket and lit it, inhaling as he eased back into his chair, enjoying the victory. Then the realization of what Jack said hit him. He straightened up, alarmed at the thought. Jack had mentioned the monsters wanted the Book. When he and his men had boarded the vessel, the Book was wrapped in aluminum foil. In a panic, he stuffed the Book and its piece inside the steel briefcase, then slammed it shut. He ran to the exit where Karim stood.

"Get us out of here! Full speed!"

"Yes, sir!"

As soon as he entered, Karim pulled the hatch shut, spinning the wheel to seal it. Dante hit the 'CC' button on the elevator panel, and they began their ascent up to the Command Center.

Karim talked into his earpiece. "Full speed to the pickup location!"

Almost immediately, the Magnetohydrodynamic drive sent the

ship into hyperspeed, taking off like a bullet out of a gun, flattening them against the back wall. They would reach the Azores in less than fifteen minutes, and from there a hypersonic jet would fly them to New York.

"What are your orders?" asked Karim.

"This is Priority One. I want to be back in New York in less than two hours."

The elevator doors opened.

"Done," said Karim, and he ran towards the Command Center.

Something inside was gnawing at Dante and he tightened his fingers around the handle of the suitcase. The most evil man on Earth would hold all the secrets to Atlantis, secrets that would allow him to conquer the world. The doors opened and instead of following Karim, he turned right and headed to his office where the fastest copy machine he had ever seen sat beside his desk. He readied his laptop on the desk, then set up the Book on the copy machine. He watched the unit flip the pages as it scanned each one, sending the completions to a folder on his laptop.

This'll be done in no time. His phone vibrated.

The text read: *Alive and kicking. ET*

Way to go, Dex!

CHAPTER 25
Dante, Preston

On Global's seventy-ninth floor, Dante was strutting down the luxurious corridor leading to the main Conference Room, admiring its exceptional design. Preston called it "La Belleza" or The Beauty, and with good reason. Magnificent Calacitta Tiles, valued at over two million dollars for over three-square feet, stretched down the one hundred fifty-foot hallway and up the fifty-foot walls. Over fifteen hundred yellow and red diamonds formed an elegant flower pattern on each tile, which also contained glimmering streaks of pure gold. To walk on such beauty was a sin, so the floor was covered in clear Aluminosilicate glass as a protection, but the pieces on the walls needed no shielding. The shimmering tiles were perfectly cut to surround four, twenty-foot-high by fifteen-foot-wide gilded arched mirrors on both sides of the hallway. And behind each mirror there were full body x-ray machines. Preston's paranoia had already scanned him.

Set between the gleaming tiles around the mirrors were giant brass pilasters rising eighteen feet and ending with angelic crowns. Extending out from the divine creations, two bands of colorful ceramic flora ran the length of the corridor, and inside these were protruding gold figureheads of Isaac Newton, Albert Einstein, Galileo, Da Vinci, Copernicus, Tesla, and many more titans of science. Above this, the barrel-vaulted ceiling contained duplicated Michelangelo murals, hand-painted to match the master.

There's enough money in this hallway to feed a small country.

Dante eyed one of the three lead crystal chandeliers hanging from the fifty-foot ceiling. The traditional style was similar to the Grand Chandelier NIII in the Louvre, except Preston had ordered the curved arms layered with pure gold. Each of the brilliant fixtures carried over two hundred lights and over eight hundred Baccarat crystals embedded with diamonds. Abalone pearls draped between the golden arms, absorbing the luster of the gold and diamonds, making them glittering balls of color ranging from amber to iceberg blue. The illumination from the three light fixtures was tantamount to daylight but in a windowless hallway. It took two weeks to install the fourteen-foot chandeliers weighing over three tons each. La Belleza was valued at over ten billion dollars and considered one of the most spectacular achievements in the twenty-first century.

He stopped and looked back at the other end of the corridor, passed the hidden elevator doors he'd just exited. Brass lion heads and young angels surrounded the twenty-foot gold-plated doors leading into Preston's public office, a secured room where he would meet with corrupt officials. La Belleza was an effective way to flaunt his money and power. Dante's gaze stopped at the carved angels.

Preston has never believed in God, he thought.

The man's belief in a deity was snuffed out long ago. He was five-years-old when his mother deserted him, leaving his abusive father to raise a head-strong child. But as always, Preston eliminated his problems and emerged into a cold, emotionless, hard-hearted individual benign of any humanity.

Did I just describe myself? No, he thought, relieved. *I have Jenna.*

He faced the arcaded mirror to his left and smoothed out the lapels of his black Alexander Price suit, checking out the cloisters of brass flowers and golden angels edging the mirror. He ran his fingers over the twinkling diamonds in the Calacitta Tiles.

"When it comes to opulence," he whispered aloud, "nobody does it better than you, Preston."

He straightened out the collar of the black shirt and slicked back his white hair. His crooked nose had been broken three times by terrorists who don't exist anymore. Thick black eyebrows rested above sunken ebony eyes. Preston had told him his glower could freeze water. His stone-cold glare was something he prized when it came to intimidating people. A slight squint and people would shake. Aside from the three-inch scar on his left cheek, he was pleased with his appearance, and so was Darla.

He noticed a streak of red blood across his black shirt. A rush of satisfaction coursed through him as he remembered Jack Williams lying unconscious in the Dungeon. The beating he had given him was refreshing, and he couldn't wait to finish the job. He pulled on the hem of his suit jacket, sensing the minute bulge inside his left breast pocket. The encrypted phone was still there, and thanks to Dex, it had its own jamming frequency which made it stealth. With a short inaudible vibration, it would alert him to an emergency message from Jenna's doctors. They had strict orders to only text him if her condition worsened and to his relief, it hasn't happened. He called the hospital every other day to check her status. Dr. Roberts said Jenna's emotional condition was degrading. There were only short periods when she wasn't crying. He had Dex create a special laptop for her which worked with the Neural Cognition System or NCS through a pair of glasses. At first, she was happy to receive it and would play games, but now it was failing, and he didn't know what else to do. He sighed.

This is not the time for Jenna, thought Dante, straightening his black tie. *Invert.*

It was a trick Uncle Remi had taught him. "Control your emotions," he said, "don't let them control you."

Remi had used the word 'invert' to turn off all compassion and become the executioner he was so good at, and the reason he was able to murder his own brother. Dante liked the idea and trained himself to do the same thing. One word, one voice in his head, and he became a cut-throat assassin. Remi had told him to never let people know who you are, never let them suspect you. Keep a friendly attitude, be pleasant, convincing, and to never, ever trust anyone.

And you, Preston, are number one.

He grinned, content the killer inside him had returned. His phone rang.

"Speak."

"Are you coming?" asked Preston.

"I'll be there in three seconds."

The entrance to the Conference Room was two twenty-foot copper sliding doors edged with golden vines, exquisite flowers, and carved angels. The doors opened to a dazzling room with all the extravagance of the Hall of Mirrors in the Palace of Versailles, yet this beauty was a facade, a transformable room where piconites constructed anything Preston desired. Even the thirty-foot conference table with its charcoal-tinted glass top was made of the small machines. And everything could be changed in an instant. The entire room was the epitome of what piconites could do in the physical universe.

Dante's heels tapped the artificial Macassar ebony wooden floor, a rare wood coveted by the wealthy worldwide...*if it were real*. The piconite re-creations were spot-on.

Preston was sitting at the table with the two amulet pieces in sealed plastic bags next to the Book. Dante had suggested they not install them in the embossment until all the sections were present, admitting to a slight fear of Atlantean science.

"This find is incredible," said Preston, not taking his stare off the opened Book. His third chin quivered with each word. "It's priceless. The Book says it will alert you as to which section each piece will go, apparently the star in the middle of the carving will glow. We got the **Earth** segment from Jack and now we have only two more to go. I found the coordinates of the **Fire** and **Water** pieces and had them confirmed with the eggheads. The Book says you'll need the **Air** section, the one we stole from Egypt, to get the **Water** piece, whatever that means."

Another good mission is coming on, thought Dante, delighted at the prospect. He took a seat next to him. "Where are they?"

"The **Fire** piece is in a cave on the island of Pantelleria in the Strait of Sicily. **Water** is in the Brazilian Amazon Rainforest. What are your thoughts, my friend?"

It was a no-brainer. "Let me survey the areas and form the teams. Does it mention what the Illum is? Is it some kind of nuclear energy?"

Preston flipped a few pages then stopped. Dante held his breath, shocked at what he was seeing. A three-dimensional rotating ball of light hovered above the paper. The spinning four-inch sphere was mesmerizing. Soft pastel colored beams radiated in all directions. There were no imperfections in the hologram. It was stunning, and he forced himself to regain his composure.

Dante cleared his throat and read. "It says the Illum is pure energy, and an eighth of a teaspoon could keep Atlantis going for over six thousand years. That's amazing! Does it mention the chemical make-up of the Illum?"

Preston flipped the page. "Here," he pointed. "It's gibberish."

"Selaprotean, Proxiude, Aranortean...what are these things? None of them are on our Periodic Table. It says Selaprotean is to be handled with caution because—crap!"

"What?" asked Preston.

"I think Selaprotean is antimatter. It says, "Selaprotean will repeatedly ignite until it depletes every particle.""

"I've heard of antimatter," said Preston, tugging at the black collar around his fleshy neck. "My scientists were looking into using it as a power source for Oveipa but said it would take hundreds of years to create enough to use as energy. Just how powerful is it?"

"When one gram of antimatter clashes with one gram of matter, the force is equivalent to over forty-two tons of TNT, or three times the Hiroshima bomb. That's just one gram. Now one milligram, which is smaller, could send a probe to Pluto and bring it back within a year. How did they do this?" he asked, puzzled at the thought. He got closer to the page and read further. "It says the Selaprotean was capsulized, which means they condensed it. They learned the secret of Selaprotean when—"

From the corner of his eye, Dante saw the Book cover heading for his face, and he jolted back. Preston had slammed the Book shut.

"This is mine!" said Preston, "and you'd better remember that!"

It took every ounce of strength not to grab his Glock and blow Preston's head off. But killing Preston now would only delay his getting Atlantis. The fat slob had a Will stating that if he were murdered, a full-out hunt for the perpetrator was to be initiated, followed by torture and death. It would be years of hiding, and Atlantis would have to wait.

It's not long now, he thought. *The plan to get rid of all his lawyers and their databases is almost ready to go.*

Dante swiveled his chair and faced him. To take Atlantis he had to reassure Preston he was a friend and not a foe.

"I don't know what's going on in that head of yours, but we've been friends for a long time, and you've helped me a lot over the years. Why would I want to take anything from you? You're the best friend I have, and besides, I like what I do. Period. I don't want to be king. I just want to be his hit man."

Preston's expression changed from angry, to nodding his head and smiling.

Dante continued with the ruse. "If the Illum is antimatter, you'll have the most powerful source of energy on the planet. Oveipa would be fixed, and no government could stop you."

Preston frowned as his plump right hand patted the Book. "It's a shame I have to destroy this. I can't let anyone have it."

Little does the idiot know I got a copy.

"You can always keep it in Oveipa," said Dante. "No one would ever find it there." *Except me.*

"That is a good suggestion, my friend. I will have it taken to my ocean kingdom."

"How is Oveipa coming?"

"Not good. We just discovered nineteen submersibles have been sabotaged but we can't figure out who's behind it. It's slowing down progress, and it's got me quite upset. I've had to eliminate three of my best foremen. Nothing came through the security cameras except fish."

Dante stood up and buttoned his black jacket. "If I think of anything to help you with Oveipa, I'll let you know. Right now, I need to create two separate plans. I'll get the *Air* piece from you before I go. And one more thing, have you found out what kind of battery runs Max's wheelchair?"

"It seems our brain child has invented a unique source of energy, but my useless scientists cannot figure it out. Perhaps another head bashing would remind them I am not a patient man."

"Another head bashing would scare the crap out of them and would slow things down. Max is a genius; those guys aren't. Give them more time, then you can threaten them with a head bashing."

"As always, you have come up with a reasonable suggestion."

"You're welcome," said Dante.

He exited the room, happy in knowing Preston's death was only days away.

Fourteen hours later...
Preston

Preston was seated in his private office on Global's eightieth floor, facing the window and contemplating the upcoming events. The Fire Team led by Karim Stone were about to enter the cave on Pantelleria in the Strait of Sicily. The Water Team headed by Dante were on their way to the Amazon Basin in Brazil, one of the most treacherous places on the planet, and because the location was part of a drug cartel's turf, everything had to be stealth.

He laughed remembering how upset Dante got when he told him Armin was his choice to replace Dirkman, thus making Armin his second in command on the Amazon expedition. Dante was defiant saying since he was the one who organized the missions, he would be the one to choose the teams. He had gotten so angry, his pale face reddened and dripped with sweat. Preston was sure he had busted a bulging purple vein in his neck. After ten minutes of straining to hold back his laughter, he suggested Brett Carson as an alternative, and Dante accepted it. His ploy worked.

He swiveled his chair and tapped the glowing red circle on his glass desktop. The window shades lowered and across from him, the forty-six-inch monitor elevated to a vertical position. The Google map displayed a beautiful small isle between Sicily and Tunisia. Pantelleria was a geological "hot spot," complete with an emergent section of a volcano. At over nine miles long, the whole island was thermally active, even the dirt was hot in some locations, able to deform plastic five-gallon buckets sitting on the ground. Steaming fumaroles sprinkled the island which meant a lake of lava lay below it. It was appropriate for the Atlanteans to associate it with *Fire*.

The screen zoomed in on a blinking red dot divulging the exact position of the amulet piece. A drone had discovered a fumarole the size of a Volkswagen Beetle above the treasured relic, blocking any entrance from overhead. Their only option was a cave on the south side of the island.

They called it the "Grotta della Morte" or the "Cave of Death." The entrance was difficult to access, nestled in the center of a five-hundred-foot cliff facing the sea. Since 1910 A.D., fifty-four people had infiltrated the cave and were never seen again, the last six were in 2019. In 2020 the officials of Pantelleria made the area off limits to anyone, imprisoning those who disobeyed. Startled by the ping of the phone, Preston bashed the blue circle with his fist.

"What!" he shouted into the speakerphone, annoyed at the intrusion.

"I'm on the Amazon River and about to brief the men," said Dante. "As far as I can tell, the cartel doesn't know we're here. Mac and Eddie are at the rendezvous point and are finishing up the installation of the Coverters on the helos. Everything is a go."

"Excellent, my friend. I hope this Karim is as good as you say."

"He's better. I'll keep you informed."

Preston heard the click of the phone.

Now if my plan goes right, Dante Kennett will soon be a memory.

CHAPTER 26
Karim Stone

FIRE: Strait of Sicily, Pantelleria Island

Karim Stone was staring at the moonless sky above the calm waters of the Strait of Sicily. A vast strand of the Milky Way soared upwards from the horizon, racing across the sky like glittering diamonds in a hazy cloud. The tranquil sea mirrored the thousands of stars blanketing the heavens. He and his four men, Schooner, Bum, Willie, and Zeek, were dressed in black ST suits and readying themselves to enter the pitch-black "Grotta della Morte."

The raft they used was on a small alcove of beach no larger than the craft itself. They had climbed over two hundred feet up a cragged wall of volcanic rock, setting anchors and ropes at strategic points away from the direct route to the cave. It was decided a clear Escape and Evacuation route was needed. There was a thump on the ground beside him. The last of the dark green nylon ropes lay curled up. He reset his attention on the foreboding passage. The satellite data said they had to descend a half mile into the island to reach the small piece of orichalcum. His on-screen system alerted him daylight was in less than three hours.

"Lights on," said Karim, bracing his rifle against his shoulder.

Instantly, five halogen lamps atop everyone's helmets lit at least twenty yards in front. The science behind the NCS was way beyond his level of intelligence, but he was glad it linked his commands to the other helmets.

It's like something out of Star Warps...or is it Star Wars, he thought to himself.

It was too difficult to analyze, and that's why he enjoyed being a Seal. *Just tell me the mission, how to use the weapons, and I'm good, but this place...just doesn't feel right.*

The floor was loose black dirt, but further in it became solid rock.

Survey, he thought.

On his screen, a grid of blue lines rolled down the cave. It was strange the scan could only penetrate nine inches into the volcanic rock. He tried again and got the same reading. The only thing that could prevent the scanning of the stone was if there was a weird ore the Global satellites couldn't pick up.

Atlanteans, he thought, feeling a shiver run down his spine. *The sooner we're done, the better.*

A soldier came and stood next to him. "Are we good to go, Commander?"

Robert "Schooner" Rendall was a punk kid with an attitude who regularly tested his patience. He stood at five feet, nine inches tall and had two master's degrees in chemistry. Karim's display showed a live picture of him with wild blonde hair, dull brown eyes, rosy-cheeks and an upturned nose that reflected his personality. At only nineteen years old, no one could beat him when it came to bombs. He got the name "Schooner" after blowing up eight sailing yachts of the rich and famous just for fun. At Dante's request, Preston broke him out of prison and gave him a new identity.

"Why didn't Global tell us about the walls?" said Karim.

Schooner rolled his eyes.

Here we go again, thought Karim. *Time for another thrashing.*

"How can I put this in layman's terms?" said Schooner. "Their sucky toys don't always work right. Do you want a drawing, Commander?"

Schooner's smug look told Karim he enjoyed the belittling, so he grabbed his collar and slammed him against the wall.

"You disrespect me again and you won't live another day! You got that, soldier?"

"Yes, sir! Sorry, sir! The Limar units in the—"

Karim bashed him against the wall again. "English!" he shouted, pressing his fists against Schooner's throat.

"…helmets need more power," squealed Schooner, his face reddening to the lack of air.

"Great," said Karim, frustrated.

He let go of Schooner who was heaving his breaths. The inability of the scan to penetrate the stone meant there were booby traps ahead. Their mission just went from highly dangerous to extremely deadly.

"Move out!" he said.

He pressed the skeletal butt of his *PX38* against his shoulder and proceeded forward, balancing himself while stepping over and between scabrous rocks with his size eighteen boot. He frowned at the thought of losing his footing and falling, tearing his ST suit and being poisoned by the noxious gases.

"Warning!" flashed red across his screen. Four feet in front of him a hiss of steam shot out of the stone wall, and he jumped back. Five different chemicals registered, all of them lethal. Their chances of survival dropped five notches.

"If something red appears on your display," said Karim, "get out of its way."

He heard the acknowledgments from his men. They were more like grumbles. These men were combat soldiers and not meant to be underground fighting off massive heat and toxic air in search of some fancy jewelry. Here, the very Earth was their nemesis, ready to devour them.

"Man, it's freakin' hot down here," said Bum, his thick accent revealed his Brooklyn background. "Are you guys seein' this? It's a hundred twenty degrees and it's risin' faster that I can eat a bag of zeppole's."

Bum Zuccarello was an off-the-street thug built like a Mack truck. His big bald head and dark circles surrounding his brown eyes intimidated a lot of people. At five-foot, eight inches he was all muscle but carried a brain that couldn't screw in a light bulb. Bum's endless pranks were infuriating the men to the point they wanted him dead. So, the men called a special meeting without Bum and decided Schooner would be the one to fix him.

And that he did, thought Karim, recalling the night he and Dante watched the event live on a monitor.

When Bum was asleep, Schooner glued a small chunk of C4 with a blasting cap to his underwear over his groin. Upon seeing the explosive attached to his boxers, Bum screamed like a girl, unable to move. Schooner laid out the law concerning the men, and Bum was more than happy to agree. Of course, Schooner took his time removing the bomb, making Bum break out in a drenching sweat. He and Dante had laughed so hard, they almost pissed their pants.

"Stay focused," said Karim, keeping a constant eye on his display. A yellow light blinked on. "Target is sixty-five yards."

Behind Bum was Willie Donnelly, a slender red-haired, blue eyed freckled-faced kid from a small town in Iowa who didn't take crap from anyone, especially Bum who never let up harassing him. The two often got into physical fights but Bum always got him in a headlock. *The man's a bull.* No matter how many times he lost, Willie never backed down.

Last, there was Herman "Zeek" Ziegler, a brainer who was lured over to the team by Preston because of his expertise in petrology and entomology. He was a scrawny man with blanched skin and thick untamed black hair needing a good combing. His dark hazel eyes always had a stare of 'please don't hurt me' through hefty black-rimmed eyeglasses. *Another nerd like Dex.* It was clear Zeek lacked the social abilities to relate to the mercenaries, but Bum took him under his wing, protecting him. Zeek's blaring sneeze squealed through the ear mic.

"Hairball!" said Schooner. "You almost busted my eardrums!"

Bum made a throaty laugh. "Way to go, dude."

"Cut the chatter!" said Karim.

Another argument would ensue if he didn't stop it now. The four soldiers held their weapons firm against their shoulders, shifting their positions from point-to-point, ready to fire. Zeek wasn't allowed to carry a gun because he had shot a scientist in the foot by accident. His nerves always got the best of him. Dante insisted he take Zeek, though Karim argued he was extra baggage. The boss won. Following him was Zeek, then Bum, Schooner, and Willie. On his screen, Zeek's forehead was dripping sweat.

"You okay, Zeek?" asked Karim, raising his leg to step over a jagged boulder with the girth of a basketball.

"I'm fine, sir," he answered with his pinched nasal voice. "I can't believe this place. It was carved out by lava at least nine thousand years ago. This is a geologist's dream."

"Try to stay on point, Zeek," said Karim, which he knew was impossible for the brainer to do. "Or we'll melt from this heat."

"Human skin doesn't melt," said Zeek. "It burns."

"Like meat on a barbecue?" asked Bum.

"Yes."

"I feel so much better now," said Willie. "Thanks, dork."

"Focus!" ordered Karim.

"Aye, sir."

He wasn't sure if Willie's reply was honest or sarcasm. Either way, there was no time to find out. It was his responsibility to get them out alive. After no word from the team in Monte Hacho, it was presumed they were dead. Preston and Dante had decided there would be no rescue. It was obvious the amulet pieces were guarded by death traps, and this cave was no different.

Dante said the heat should have preserved the bones of the last six people who disappeared in 2019, he thought. *Human bones.*

Green scanning lines raced down the tunnel. A moment later, 'Negative' was blinking blue. Karim's brow wrinkled, beads of sweat dotted his forehead.

Where are they? An alarm went off in his head. *Whatever did them in, is waiting for us.*

Fifteen minutes had passed when a beeping sound came from his mask. The temperature reading was now one hundred fifty degrees Fahrenheit and climbing. Lava could rise above two thousand degrees, and although their ST suits absorbed the sweat from the body and cooled their skin, the silk tube cloth maxed out at two hundred fifty degrees. Afterward, the material would break down and melt. His only consolation was someone had to come down here to hide the stupid piece and then return to the surface to record its exact location in the Book.

And then there was the list of gases displayed on his screen. Hydrogen Chloride, Sulfide, Carbon Dioxide, Chlorine, and more. Hydrogen Chloride alone would suppress the lung's ability to absorb oxygen. Suffocation would take less than a minute. He fought back another feeling of dread. The only answer was to complete the mission and get out of there. Karim picked up his speed, leading his men into the bowels of the island. A loud boom shook the cave.

"Take cover!" shouted Karim who pulled Zeek against the wall. Rocks and dirt rained down on them.

"It's a tremor!" yelled Zeek, crossing his arms over his head. "They're expected in this area of the world."

The earth stopped moving. Bum, Schooner and Willie were waving away the cloud of dust.

"This is not what I signed up for," said Bum.

"I agree," said Schooner, coughing. "This is nuts!"

"Sir!" shouted Zeek. "I think I found the piece!"

He was twenty feet away and squatting in front of the cave wall. Karim joined him. The glow of the orichalcum was unmistakable.

"That's it, sir, right?" asked Zeek.

"Yeah, that's it."

"How'd ya see it?" asked Bum. "I woulda' never found it."

"I caught a glimmer."

Zeek was reaching for it when Karim pulled his hand back.

"It might be guarded," he said. "Once I grab this, I want us to haul butt out of this place. Full speed back to the raft. Understood?"

"Yes, sir," they all replied.

"Ready your weapons," said Karim. "On a count of thre—"

A gut-piercing scream came from Willie, and Karim jumped to his feet. Small white insects resembling aphids inundated Willie's whole body. Billions of them were rushing up his legs, swarming his ST suit, looking like an avalanche of snow. Karim's visual screen magnified the tiny bugs. They had at least twelve legs with body spikes protruding from white shells. An open hole at one end was their mouth containing circular rows of sharp teeth. No eyes were visible. Minute tears started appearing throughout Willie's suit enlarging with each moment, becoming ragged holes. The insects were eating the silk tubes like food. Willie's face contorted as he clawed at his mask. Streams of blood gushed from his eyes and nose. Bum and Schooner jumped back horrified.

"What are those things?" yelled Schooner with his rifle aimed at Willie.

"They're—" said Zeek. His body bent forward and jerked.

Karim heard him vomiting.

Zeek continued, "They're extremophiles, insects that can live in extreme conditions. These ones are carnivorous."

"How do we kill those things?" asked Karim.

"I don't know," said Zeek, looking pale. "I've never seen these insects before. They're impervious to the heat and the poisons in the air."

Willie screamed again and then ripped off his helmet.

"No!" yelled Karim, reaching out.

Willie stumbled back. "Don't touch me!"

He teetered on his feet, his bloodshot eyes crawling with insects, then fell backward onto the floor, dead. Karim magnified his screen and saw the tiny creatures moving about in the dark red splotches, their small bodies covered in coagulated blood. They were spreading across Willie's face at bullet speed and within moments, his whole head disappeared. All that was left was his ST suit, and it too was disintegrating. Karim yanked the amulet piece out of its niche.

"Run!" he shouted, stuffing the relic in his velcroed leg pocket.

Karim sped down the tunnel with the men close behind. The passageway rumbled and quaked as fissures burst open the walls, venting hot steam. Schooner was behind him, then Zeek and Bum, who was pushing Zeek to make sure he kept pace. The memory of Willie pushed Karim to run faster. Not he, nor his men would be someone's dinner. The earth shaking worsened, and they struggled to stay on their feet. They held their rifles over their heads for protection. In front, lava was seeping out of cracks in the walls and floor. An agonizing scream came from behind. Karim skidded to a stop. Zeek was sitting on the ground nursing his ankle.

"I think it's broken!" said Zeek.

Without a thought, Bum swung his rifle behind him and tossed Zeek over his shoulder who yelped like a dog.

"Let's go!" said Bum.

"You can't run with the both of us!" said Zeek, his words stuttering with every stomp. "I'm too heavy!"

"I hate to tell you this," said Bum, "but you're a skinny dude with no muscle. Now shut up and lemme' get us outta here."

Schooner waved Bum and Zeek in front of him, and they dashed down the tunnel. Karim noticed the temperature reading was two hundred twenty degrees and rising. The gas readings were off the charts. The on-screen calculations gave them only five minutes to get out, or they were dead.

"Schooner, look out!" shouted Zeek.

A blast of lava jetted out from a sidewall and hit Schooner, engulfing both his legs. He roared and hit the ground thrashing about, trying to loosen the molten rock burning everything it touched. The legs of his ST suit had melted and was adhering to his already burnt skin. Karim rushed to his side, desperate to help him. From what he could see, his legs were charred beyond recognition and the flames were moving up toward his torso.

"Commander," said Schooner, "it's over. Please...."

"Sir?" said Bum.

Karim took a deep breath. *Another young life is lost.* He aimed his *PX38*. "You were the best, my friend, and we will never forget you," then shot him in the forehead.

"You killed him!" said Zeek.

"We saved him from a slow death," said Bum.

Zeek was holding his head moaning and repeating the words, "You killed him...you killed, Schooner."

"Let's go!" said Karim. "Follow me!"

Bum nodded and ran with Zeek on his shoulder. The rumbling sound was deafening, and the dense smoke and dust made it difficult to see in front of them.

"VIT's!" shouted Karim.

A three-dimensional picture of the cave appeared on his mask. Visual Image Technology enabled them to penetrate the vapor; something Global had stolen from the military. The solid earth beneath Karim thrust upwards with such force, he fell and was rammed sideways into the stone ceiling, squeezing him against the rock. There was a crack in his ribcage and the horrific pain stopped his breath. Then the floor dropped. His body bounced on the hard floor and he landed six feet from an open fissure spurting lava. Rolling away he bumped into Zeek who was lying on the dirt unconscious.

"He took a hit to the head," said Bum, flipping Zeek onto his shoulder again. "You all right, Commander?"

He coughed, spitting out blood. "I'm good. Let's go."

Bum held out his hand. Karim braced his left side with his arm, and Bum pulled him up. They bolted down the tunnel again. Karim was stumbling more than running until he spotted the way out straight ahead. Sliding down the ropes was another story. They ground their boots to a stop. Thirty-five feet in front of them the earth had opened, a pond of bubbling lava was spewing over. Beyond that, the exit was only forty feet away.

Zeek woke up. "Where are we?"

"It's at least a six-foot jump," said Bum, putting Zeek down who balanced himself on his one good leg.

"Leave me," said Zeek. "I can't let you die for me."

"We don't leave men behind," said Karim. "Look around, there's got to be something we can use as a catapult."

"You killed Schooner!" yelled Zeek. "Isn't that leaving a man behind?"

"Chill out!" said Bum. "It was either watch 'im die in pain or put 'im out of his misery."

Zeek's gaze lowered to the ground. "I guess you're right. I'm sorry."

"Forget it," said Karim. "We need to jump over the lava."

The ground bounced and rippled, throwing the men back ten feet. Hot steam gushed out of a fissure and burned a path across Bum's left thigh.

"Aaah!" screamed Bum, grabbing his leg.

A gaping tear revealed blackened meat and red blisters.

Second and third-degree burns. "Can you walk, Bum?" asked Karim.

"No," said Zeek, balancing on one leg. "Can you run?" He pointed. "We still have to get over that."

A huge boulder had fallen from the ceiling and into the lava pond, leaving only its top exposed. Belches of lava spurted around the stone, eating away at the rock.

It's sinking!

"We've got to go now!" said Karim, groaning as he pulled Bum to his feet.

Bum threw Zeek over his shoulder. A slew of vulgarities came out of Zeek's mouth.

"You go first!" shouted Karim. "Use your strongest leg and push off as hard as you can!"

"Aye, sir!"

A five-foot section was still above the lava and sinking fast. Bum's right foot hit the solid rock, and he launched into the air. The two roared as they flew over the boiling magma and hit the soft dirt rolling. The stone was glowing red and had sunk more because of Bum's weight. Only a small two-foot section remained. Karim set his sight on the shrinking space, determined not to miss, determined to survive.

He ran with all his might and leapt, slamming his foot on the rock causing the lava to swarm over his black boot. Roaring, he pushed off, stretching his legs as far as they would go. When he hit the dirt, Bum snagged his arms and forced him to the ground. His boot was on fire and he flailed his foot in the air.

"Steady his leg!" said Zeek.

Bum held Karim's calf down. Zeek smothered his boot with loose topsoil, putting out the flames. Karim sat up and Bum slid him to the wall. His black boot had deformed from the heat, the silk tubes had done their best to protect him, but the throbbing pain told him there was burn damage.

"Thanks, Zeek," said Karim, squirming, trying not to reveal his agony. "How's the ankle?"

"I think it's a sprain. We should wrap your foot with the boot on. We still have to climb down out of here."

A deafening explosion jarred the cave, and they huddled, evading the rocks tumbling down from the ceiling.

"We have to go now!" yelled Karim, noting the red "Warning!" sign on his mask. A wall of lava was heading their way. They had twelve seconds. "Bum, the ropes!"

Bum sprang to his feet and grabbed three coiled ropes, tossing one to him and Zeek. Down the passage, magma blowouts were erupting out of the floor and moving towards them at rocket speed.

"Hook in!" shouted Karim, securing his carabiner.

A massive explosion blew the screaming men out of the cave, along with rocks, dirt, and a blazing river of lava.

To be concluded in:

The Key to Atlantis, Vol. II — "Unlocking the Key"

****

EXCERPT FROM "UNLOCKING THE KEY"

…The pyramid before them was unlike anything in Egypt. It had a rounded pinnacle with smooth sides and no visible layers. Burned rootstock and plants once entwining the building now exposed brown steel walls with a matte finish. A portico with thirty-foot wide double doors stood three times the height of Whitey. The readings said the plant life had buried their roots in the metal.

"How could metal be eighty-seven percent cellulose?" asked Dante, noting an additional six rows of "Unknown Element" on his screen.

"This is incredible," said Blake. "The ore absorbs nutrients from the soil and feeds it to the plants. I wonder what these other elements are?"

"Don't know, and don't care," said Dante. "We need to get this done…"

…After ten long hold-your-breath minutes, they reached the dark chamber. Thanks to their digital face masks, they saw an oval room measuring fifty feet high, seventy feet wide, and sixty feet deep. The entire floor was pure white sand except for the small pool of water in its center.

"Sharpy, scatter four more beamers," said Dante. "I want this room lit up like the sun."

"Aye, sir."

The darkness turned into daylight. They stepped onto the sandy ground, their attention still searching for marks. The gleaming lakelet was an oval twenty by thirty feet, but only a foot deep. At the nucleus of the crystal clear blue water, tiny beads of air floated up. No acids, chemicals or parasites registered in the forty-four degrees. It was the purest water he'd ever encountered.

"That is one dark niche up there," said Brett.

A ten-foot high open shelf ran along the whole ceiling.

"The upper ledge has monstrous alcoves," said Blake. "Commander, I do not like this. I suggest we find the piece and leave."

"I agree," said Dante, relieved to see the red blinking words, "Target Acquired."

Next to the bubbles and sticking out of the white sand, the orange-gold glimmer of orichalcum was unmistakable. He was ready to reach into the pond when a reading popped up on his screen.

"A door has opened on the overhead shelf," said Blake. "Water is trickling in."

"Here we go," said Dante. "When I grab this thing, we haul butt out of here. Ready your weapons."

"Yes, sir," were the replies from his men.

"Three-two-now!" shouted Dante.

He snatched the amulet piece out of the pond, and the entrance doors slammed shut with a boom. A rush of water was pouring onto the ledge above.

"Mac," said Dante, stuffing the *Water* piece into his velcroed chest pocket. "Mac, do you read me?" No answer.

"Something is interfering with our signals," said Blake. "We are on our own."

A muffled scream came from behind. The bottom half of Sharpy's body was dangling from the mouth of a fifty-foot black Anaconda. Its massive jaws chomped down on Sharpy who let out a strangled cry. His lower half detached and hit the floor. With a heavy suction sound, the viper retreated to the shelf, out of sight.

"Backs to the pond!" shouted Dante.

They surrounded the small spring, keeping their aim primed.

"I've seen dark green Anaconda's that looked black," said Whitey, "but never one that was solid black. How can this be?"

Dante answered, "The bio-reading said the creature was genetically enhanced. This is bad."

"There are four more of the same kind and size," said Blake. "They are all males but there is a fifth stuck in a bend and is trying to wriggle free. She is the biggest mother I have ever seen."

www.ingramcontent.com/pod-product-compliance
Lightning Source LLC
Chambersburg PA
CBHW050927120626
46552CB00001B/81